To the women in my life I'm lucky to call friends.
Most especially, and for always, to Abby.

# memorabilia

mem·o·ra·bil·ia

1   : things that are remarkable and worthy of remembrance

2   : things that stir recollection or are valued or collected
for their association with a particular field or interest

merriam-webster.com

May 20, 2018

# AFA Announces Recipient of Achievement Award

The American Film Archives has announced Glory Cartwright as the recipient of their annual honorary achievement award, to be presented June 10, in Los Angeles.

The nod to Cartwright, who rose to fame starring alongside her husband, Mitch Beckett, in a string of hit romantic comedies in the seventies, comes nearly thirty years after her tragic suicide at the age of forty-two.

A contract player for MGM when Hollywood's most notorious playboy, Mitch Beckett, convinced his director to cast her as his next leading lady, Miss Cartwright beat out Ali MacGraw and Natalie Wood for the role of plucky moll Bonnie Gold—a role that would not only make her a household name, but win the heart of her leading man. Married within months of the film's release, Miss Cartwright and Mr. Beckett would go on to make six films together, earning their place as one of the most beloved Hollywood couples of the day.

In 1979, at the height of their popularity, when Mr. Beckett announced that he and Miss Cartwright would be taking a yearlong hiatus and set up house in his Cape Cod hometown of Harpswich, Hollywood was stunned. But Miss Cartwright was quick to reassure the industry the move was temporary. "We love our fans and will continue to make movies no matter where we are," she announced.

The promise, however, didn't hold. The famous couple wouldn't grace the screen together again. And despite her attempt to bring the magic of Hollywood to Harpswich by starting the popular Stardust Summer Film Festival, Miss Cartwright never truly warmed to her expat status in the small coastal town, struggling visibly with episodes of depression.

Known for her trademark smoky laugh, she was nominated for Best Actress for her role in *The Lucky Ones* but lost to Ellen Burstyn. At the time of her death, she had just finished filming *A Season of Us,* a supporting role that was to be her long-awaited return to the screen.

Louise Chandler, a family friend and festival cofounder, considers the acknowledgment long overdue: "While fans knew well of Glory's devotion to them, they may not have been aware of her equal devotion to her craft. This award is a testament to her legacy as an actress, wife, mother, and friend; and I have no doubt Glory would be immeasurably grateful for the honor."

# Part One

Of all the gin joints, in all the towns,
in all the world, she walks into mine.

*Casablanca*

# 1

Hollywood

## *The Memory Shop*

The premiere destination for Hollywood collectibles and souvenirs.
Bring home your own piece of movie magic!
Just four blocks south of the famous Mann's Chinese Theatre.
Or visit our store online at: thememoryshop.com.

It always begins with the blush. A feverish flush that starts its creep from the throat to the jaw until finally soaking the entire face. Lips start to quiver before they are rolled inward, caught briefly between teeth and gently bitten. Then breaths, pulled in and exhaled previously in silence, are suddenly audible, and noticeably quicker.

Frankie knows the sequence by heart.

Her mother used to call it The Bolt, the instant when a customer meets the piece of movie memorabilia that's meant to be hers, because it's just like the lightning strike of love at first sight.

The woman currently in a state of infatuation on the other side of the counter is Carol from Cleveland. And Carol, Frankie just learned, has spent all morning on a tour bus, crawling past the gated homes of movie stars, so she only has a few minutes before she and her husband, Joe—he's the doughy, sour-faced man who didn't make it farther than the entryway—have to get back on the bus. But Carol read about The Memory Shop online, and she just had to see for herself. A memorabilia shop where all the collectibles are displayed on mannequins instead of behind glass? Incredible! Joe isn't much for movies, unfortunately, Carol has also explained, but he's allowing her ten minutes to browse, even though Joe doesn't understand why anyone would want to see, let alone buy, a used lipstick—even if it *did* graze Marilyn Monroe's lips.

But Frankie knows Carol isn't interested in lipstick.

Because the minute Carol from Cleveland stepped inside The Memory Shop, her gaze—her heart—belonged to the chocolate-brown leather gloves that Frankie has just peeled off the Barbra Streisand mannequin and set down on the counter for closer inspection.

When the fingers are evenly spread out on the glass, Frankie steps back to allow the rich smell of buttery suede to rise, as warm and fragrant as freshly baked bread.

Because the connection between smell and memory is fierce.

Maeve Simon taught her daughter that, too.

"Beautiful, aren't they?" Frankie whispers in the hush.

"Gorgeous." Carol stares, spellbound, her nostrils expanding with every breath. She bites her lip. "And you're positive these are the ones Katie wore in front of the Plaza when Hubbell came over and she . . . ?" Carol's fingers sweep the air, miming Barbra Streisand's famous farewell at the end of *The Way We Were*, when she lovingly brushes Robert Redford's hair off his forehead, knowing he's never coming back to her.

The gesture is so swift and sure that Frankie suspects it isn't the first time Carol from Cleveland has made it.

"Every item comes with a certificate of authenticity," Frankie says, freeing the sample COA she keeps beside the register and sliding it forward. "But it just so happens these gloves come with extra proof . . ."

When Carol glances up quizzically, Frankie directs her gaze to a streak of peach across the index and middle fingertips.

Leaning in, Carol studies the stain, her eyes growing big, swimming with expectation when she raises them. She swallows hard but still her voice cracks. "Is that . . . ?"

"Robert Redford's grease paint."

"No!" Carol sucks in a sharp breath through the O she's made of her lips and flattens her hands on the counter like a passenger seeking balance on a pitching ship. Her gaze drifts off into the distance. "*The Way We Were* was the first movie I ever saw with a boy," she says, her voice soft with recollection. "Andy Foster." She practically sings the name, and Frankie envisions a young man with neatly combed hair and a smile too wide for his narrow face. "We were at the drive-in in his father's Buick. My sister let me borrow her pink platforms." Carol's lips rise wistfully. "Andy told me I looked like her. Barbra Streisand, I mean. But I was so young then, of course." Somehow her already sunburned cheeks manage to blush deeper. "And thin."

Frankie takes a moment to consider Carol's face—the pale, almond-shaped eyes, the high cheekbones. She can see it.

"Carol!" From the entry, Joe sounds the alarm, shoving his phone screen at them. "It's been ten minutes. Let's go!"

Carol offers a mournful smile before she swivels to scan the room, her fingers still clutching the rounded edge of the counter so tightly Frankie suspects Joe may have to pry her away from these gloves. Maybe even the whole store.

"Where did you get all of it?" Carol asks, partly curious and partly, Frankie suspects, looking to stall.

"My mother started collecting when she first got out here. She worked on film sets and used to bring home what they didn't want. You'd be amazed how much they throw away after a movie wraps. Twenty years in this business and we still are."

We.

Frankie bristles at the pronoun, the ease with which it still slips out. But nearly a year after losing her mother, she still can't seem to use another. Any more than she can call The Memory Shop her store.

Until the day she locks the door for the last time, it will always be their store.

"Wow." Carol's gaze has shifted to the box beside the register that contains her mother's collection of old ticket stubs. "That's a lot of tickets."

Frankie smiles. "My mother and I saw a lot of movies."

"Can I touch them?"

She hesitates, but only for a moment. "Go for it."

Carol drives her hand into the soup of tickets, letting the stubs fall off her fingers like grains of sand. "You're not like the other memorabilia shops."

Frankie lowers her voice to a conspiratorial whisper. "Great, isn't it?"

Accustomed to locked cases and Do Not Touch signs, customers are always surprised, even confused, to see precious artifacts and costume pieces displayed on mannequins, left unguarded, vulnerable to curious fingers. Sellers, of course, are downright horrified. Even the ones who have been visiting The Memory Shop for years still can't hide a little shudder when they step inside and don't see a locked display case in sight. But her mother always insisted the connection between fantasy and reality was found through the senses, not through glass. And that memory was a living thing, and like all living things, it needed air to survive.

And Frankie knows, no matter how badly Carol from Cleveland wants to touch the glove that repeatedly stroked Robert Redford's beautiful, furrowed brow, she won't dream of asking. Because she doesn't think she can.

"Would you like to try one on?"

Carol's head snaps up at the offer, blinking furiously with disbelief. As she shakily slides her right hand into Katie Morosky's glove, they both know her fingers aren't as long and slender as Barbra's, but it doesn't matter. Because when she lifts her hand for another perfect imitation of Barbra Streisand brushing back Robert Redford's sun-kissed hair, she's not middle-aged Carol with the impatient husband waiting in the doorway to shuffle her back to reality. She's teenage Carol, giddy and hopeful in her sister's platform heels, sitting in the front seat with a boy who made her feel special and beautiful and just right. A boy who, maybe, like Hubbell Gardner, was only hers to have for a short time.

And then, after pulling in a deep breath, Carol closes her eyes, and in a voice that is as even and reverential as prayer, she whispers Katie's famous line to Hubbell after seeing his new love waiting across the street: "Your girl is lovely, Hubbell."

"*Carol!* The bus!"

This time Carol doesn't glance back. The glove still on, she tears open her fanny pack, plucks out her credit card, and slides it across the counter, a small but decided smile spreading her chapped lips as she whispers, "Don't bother with a bag."

# 2

Her mother never meant to sell any of it.

In fact, the idea to open the store had come from Maeve's boyfriend at the time, a sound engineer named Chuck, who Frankie thought looked just like Tom Selleck—only with a Brooklyn accent and red hair. A remarkably decent guy, Chuck even cleared out a dresser for Frankie when Maeve moved them into his Echo Park bungalow, a gesture that Frankie deeply appreciated, and she certainly understood why his feelings were hurt when she still hadn't put her clothes in the drawers two months later. She always wanted to, she really did. Especially since she had just watched *The Parent Trap*—the Hayley Mills original; her mother refused to watch remakes—and ever since, Frankie found herself fantasizing about a secret sister of her own somewhere in the world, just waiting to be discovered at summer camp.

Still the drawer remained empty.

Because even at ten, Frankie knew her mother's interest in Chuck would run its course and they'd move on—it was simply a matter of how long it would take.

Her mother's extensive collection of memorabilia, however, would require more than a few drawers, and with Chuck's house and garage already bursting with his recording equipment, it was decided she needed to rent storage to keep it all safe—an idea that withered as soon as she saw how much a climate-controlled unit went for. When

Chuck innocently suggested she think about selling it, her mother looked stricken. He might as well have suggested she sell her child.

"I'm just saying, Maeve. People pay good money for that crap."

"It's not crap," she said fiercely. "It's history, it's heart—and it's not for sale."

And she remained adamant.

Until a week later when one of Chuck's director-friends came over for drinks—a die-hard *Rocky* fan—and, after learning that Maeve owned a pair of Sylvester Stallone's fingerless black gloves, offered her two thousand for them. The man explained that it had been one of his and his father's favorite movies, and that they'd watched it together one more time the night before he moved his father into a memory-care unit. Frankie would never forget the sight of the man afterward, smiling as he sank his fingers into the gloves and stared down at his hands, his face flushing with boyish wonder even as he sniffed back tears.

And that, Frankie has always suspected, was when it occurred to her mother that maybe she'd been unfair, selfish even, by keeping all these memories to just the two of them to pore over in private.

That just because someone could put a price on a collectible, didn't mean they didn't feel a deep attachment to it—and that maybe there was actually something beautiful and pure in the business of movie moments.

The epiphany was startling.

Later that same evening, she and her mother sat on Chuck's living room rug and unpacked the collection.

"The most important thing is that we won't be greedy," her mother said as the familiar smells of unearthed fabrics—nutty suedes and rusty leathers, perfumed satins and grassy silks—began to rise around them. "I'm not saying we'll give it all away—obviously we can't do that—but we'll be reasonable. And if someone really wants a piece and can only offer half, well, we won't inflate things." Considering Audrey Hepburn's black dress from *Breakfast at Tiffany's* had recently sold for over eight hundred thousand, the bar for what constituted inflating was already high.

And so The Memory Shop opened on April 15, 1999.

Their first sale was a pair of Jane Fonda's glasses from *Nine to Five*, bought by a woman who explained that *Nine to Five* was the first movie she saw after her divorce was final—and that it was the first time, in her sixty-two years on this planet, that she'd gone to the movies alone. Frankie had to rub her arms to make the goose bumps go down.

Within the first year, they'd made enough to buy a new car—the eggplant Chevy that her mother would eventually drive through an intersection at the very worst possible moment twenty years later. For the store's fifth anniversary, they held a *Doctor Zhivago* party and served vodka shots and ice-palace cupcakes. Ten years in, they'd been written up in *The LA Times, Auction Magazine,* and *The New Yorker.*

Endearing themselves to other buyers, however, took a while longer, especially the ones who were only interested in the sale and carried no passion in their hearts for the pieces themselves. (Her mother called them "Hoovers"—sometimes to their face—since they might as well have been in the business of selling vacuum cleaners, she said.) But eager to sniff out new competition—or new allies, depending on the day—seasoned dealers began arriving steadily within the year to scan the Simon inventory, or simply offer unsolicited advice, usually to disparage their unorthodox method of display. When a customer with waist-length salt-and-pepper hair, who claimed to have been told in her youth she bore a striking resemblance to Ali MacGraw, asked to see one of Jenny's famous red wool hats from *Love Story,* and her mother insisted the woman try it on, a buyer from Beverly Hills drew them into a huddle at the counter.

"Some advice, ladies: Never let the customer touch the item. Put it all behind glass."

To which her mother's response was: "Then how is it supposed to breathe?"

And yet, despite their growing success, Frankie would sometimes catch her mother blotting her eyes after a giddy customer left with their purchase.

"I promised I would never sell them," she would occasionally whisper.

But when Frankie asked who she made that promise to, her mother would just answer with a sad smile.

There's a generous breeze following her home tonight, rippling the fronds of the gangly palms that line the boulevard, scattering litter and bougainvillea petals across the pink terrazzo stars that compose the Walk of Fame. At last count, there were more than two and a half thousand tributes, and Frankie has memorized their order, a challenge she and her mother took up when Frankie turned five. While most kids her age were learning to read from Dr. Seuss and *Sesame Street,* she learned from daily pilgrimages up and down the famous Hollywood landmark. "Anyone can spell 'cat' or 'ball,'" her mother insisted. "But the girl who can spell Gina Lollobrigida can rule the world."

The new tenant from 2G is on his way out when she reaches the steps, and he holds the gate for her. He and his roommate are having a housewarming party later if Frankie wants to come? She's tempted; he's ridiculously adorable—sandy haired and lanky, a *Bull Durham*–era Kevin Costner, down to the blue eyes and aw-shucks stubble—and if her heart wasn't still bruised from Dennis's recent rejection, she just might.

The courtyard is bathed in shade, the coppery light turning the yellow Spanish-style stucco walls a soothing peach as she walks past the kidney-shaped pool toward the alcove of mailboxes. The High Life is one of the older complexes off Hollywood Boulevard—two floors with everyone's apartments open to the outside so a person would think she might be living in a motel, which is possible, considering the rate of tenant turnover. When she moved in five years ago, the rental agent pulled up pictures on her phone of the building in the forties when it was a chaperoned dormitory for young women looking to get into the movies, and rising stars like Lana Turner and Rita Hayworth crisped poolside. Saul Manheim, who lives in 1E with his Pomeranian, Bogart, has lived at the High Life since '71. He claims Harrison Ford was the building's handyman before he hit it big with *American Graffiti*. Frankie has no idea if it's true, but she likes to imagine Harrison shirtless and sweat slicked on the roof, carefully replacing a stretch of curved Spanish tiles and tossing her down one of his rakish Han Solo grins as she walks by.

Reaching into her mailbox, she pulls out a tangle of flyers, then a padded envelope, the name on the return address causing her heart to swell with affection: Peter Williams, the man her mother had been living with when she died.

She gives the package a gentle squeeze, trying to guess the contents. It shocks her that she could have left something behind, recalling how brutally thorough she and Peter were the day she came over to extract the last pieces of her mother from his apartment; how sure she had been that the hole in her heart couldn't be hollowed out any deeper, only to uncover the sharpest cuts in the most innocuous of places—a near-empty bottle of her mother's rosewater shampoo, a grocery list—and drown all over again. Particularly crushing was finding the still-sealed box of her mother's favorite tea, orange hibiscus, a reminder of a future that was planned and abruptly stolen—but it wasn't the hardest discovery that day. That distinction would always be reserved for the blank birthday card found in her mother's nightstand drawer, bought for Frankie's upcoming thirtieth birthday, forever waiting now for wishes that would never be given.

So what could be in this package?

She hastens her steps up the wrought-iron stairwell to her second-floor apartment, possibility pulsing through her as she pushes inside. Lowering her bag to the couch, she drops beside it, the sweetly stale smell of cold Thai food drifting from the pile of empty take-out containers she left on the kitchen counter with a vow to clean up as soon as she got home, but all that will have to wait now.

Her heart hammers as she tears open the mailer, finding an envelope inside, this one with a Post-it stuck to the top.

*Frankie,*

*I emptied out my file cabinets the other day and this envelope was in the very back. Not sure what's inside but knowing how your mother felt about sealed letters, you should be the one to open it.*

*I'm not sure if you've lost my number, but it's still 555-551-8968. Call me if you ever want to talk.*

*I miss her every day.*

*Peter*

She runs her thumb over the bulk of the envelope, warmed by Peter's words, reminded of how well he'd known her mother—how well her mother had let him know her. Of all the men, there was no question that Peter had held her heart the tightest. But had her mother loved him? She couldn't recall her mother saying so—but then she couldn't remember having heard her mother use the word "love" with any of her boyfriends. Only with Frankie. And then, all the time.

His comment about his number sends a pang of guilt; Frankie's not sure why she's avoided calling him. Far from losing his number, she's kept it on her favorites screen, seeing his name every time she taps into her contacts. She rarely called him in all the years he and her mother lived together, but in the days after Frankie lost her, it felt right to make his number more prominent, as if their mutual grief might bond them in a way they never knew when Maeve was alive. But whenever Frankie thinks to call, fear stops her, fear that their lack of connection will only be amplified now, and that hearing his voice, and knowing her mother's won't be in the background, will only make her mother feel truly gone. And as much as her stomach twists with remorse for not reaching out to Peter, she's just not prepared for that.

Tears prickling, she pulls in several deep breaths, trying to prepare her thundering heart for this second layer of discovery. The crash of hope and fear is dizzying. Hope that whatever is under this sealed flap may be a revelation of some kind, a piece of her mother's past she didn't dare confess until Frankie was older. Things her mother meant for her to know but ran out of time to share. Maybe even, at last, the identity of her father . . .

She studies the sweep of the writing on the front of the envelope. *To Maeve, with love and gratitude. Always.* Was this her father's writing?

When she wedges her fingernail under the seal and rips it free, Frankie can't help feeling like a skydiver pushed out of a plane.

There are two more envelopes inside: notecard-sized with scalloping on the flaps, one to *My Dearest Mitch,* the other to *My Beloved Gabe.* There's also a photograph of a crowd in formal wear on a town dock. In the center of the picture, a man and a woman stand close under a banner that's been stretched across the pier: WELCOME TO THE FOURTH ANNUAL STARDUST FILM FESTIVAL!

Frankie is familiar with the festival—who in Hollywood isn't? Started a few years after Redford's Sundance by Glory Cartwright and Mitch Beckett, a Hollywood power couple before there were Hollywood power couples. Their movies, always pairing them as star-crossed lovers, were some of the biggest films of the seventies.

Having never been farther east than Tucson, Frankie always wanted to attend. Her mother, however, wouldn't hear of it. "We don't need to go all the way across the country to rub elbows with people who live down the block, baby."

She looks between the envelopes, pieces sliding together: the letter for *My Dearest Mitch* must refer to Mitch Beckett—but who is *My Beloved Gabe*? Setting down the letters, Frankie picks up the photo for another look, turning it over to find a single word, in the same handwriting as on the envelopes, *Peace*. Whatever that means?

Glancing back at the man and red-headed woman standing together in the center of the picture, recognition sparks: Mitch Beckett and Glory Cartwright.

A knock on the front door brings her to her feet. Saul Manheim stands in the corridor in a gently wrinkled blue suit and ivory bow tie, holding a huge aluminum pan with both hands. For an eighty-two-year-old, his upper body strength is impressive.

His dog, Bogart, circles his feet, tiny black eyes bulging through a nest of orange fur.

"I thought you might be hungry."

Frankie scans the pan. "Casserole?"

"Lasagna."

She sighs, stepping back to let her neighbor enter. "You really need a bigger fridge, Saul."

"Tell me about it," he says, coming in with Bogart on his heels. "Six years, and they won't take the hint."

*They* are Saul's female friends and neighbors—the Brisket Brigade, as he calls them—who swooped in with their edible charms within days after Saul lost his wife, Ruth—a well-known makeup artist who earned two Academy Award nominations for her work. Pictures of her cover Saul's apartment. Frankie never met her, but she feels as if she knows her.

"You look nice," she tells him as he sets down the pan on her stovetop.

"The community center's showing *An Affair to Remember*. I thought I'd take Maureen from next door."

"I already ate, you know."

"Let me guess: three raisins and a cube of cheese?" Saul snorts. "You Hollywood gals are all meshuggeneh." He looks around her apartment. "Hey, how come I don't see that guy with the great hair anymore?"

She peels back a corner of the foil and leans in for a whiff of garlic and tomato sauce. "Dennis and I broke up."

"Too bad. Good-looking guy. Dead ringer for that Brad Pitt fella."

"Is this the part where you make me feel better, Saul?"

"Sorry, kiddo. What I mean is: Good riddance, the schmuck." He glances over at the envelopes where she's left them on the coffee table. "New acquisitions?"

"They're from Peter," Frankie says, retrieving the letters and handing them to Saul. "My mom was saving them. I'm pretty sure the one for Mitch is Mitch Beckett, but I have no idea who Gabe is."

"One way to find out," Saul says, his thumb dancing toward the flap.

She shoots him a disapproving look. "You know I can't open them."

"'Course not. You'll get more for them sealed."

"I can't sell them either."

He blinks at her. "What are you talking about? You and your mother always had letters in the store. Don't you remember she sold me that one Ann-Margret wrote to Elvis? God, it was spicy."

"Opened letters," she reminds him. "Sealed ones are different."

Saul sniffs. "Yeah, they're worth more."

While there were very few rules that her mother lived by, never being the first to open another person's sealed letter was near the top of Maeve Simon's playbook. Something about opening someone else's confessional love letter when she was young and feeling desperately guilty over it. Frankie's explained this to Saul before. She suspects he's conveniently forgotten.

"This was in the package, too," she says, handing him the photo.

While Saul leans toward the glow of the stove light to study it better, she swipes the side of the pan, extracting a fingertip of melted cheese and frowning as she chews.

"It doesn't make sense. My mother was never a fan of theirs. I don't even think we carried pieces from their movies in the store."

Frankie tries to remember and can only come up with a red bolero jacket worn by Glory Cartwright in one of her early roles, before she and Mitch Beckett made their films together. One item, hardly proof of devotion.

So why had her mother kept these items separate, as if they were precious?

"What doesn't make sense to me," Saul says, "is why she never mentioned knowing a huge star like Beckett."

Bogart lets go a sharp bark, and Frankie lowers a frilly ribbon of pasta into the dog's tiny mouth. "Just because she had this stuff doesn't mean she knew him."

"No, but if she's standing this close, I'm assuming she at least met the man. She's real young here, but that sure looks like Maeve," Saul says, tapping on the woman beside Mitch Beckett, and Frankie is certain all the blood in her face has sunk to her ankles.

She's been so fixated on the letters, she just assumed the copper-haired woman beside Mitch Beckett was his red-headed wife. But now Frankie's chest tightens with recognition.

The woman in the picture is, unquestionably, her mother.

# 3

When her mother would say that Frankie's father was a blank space on her birth certificate, Frankie always thought she was speaking metaphorically.

After all, there were no photographs of her father in their albums, no books on the shelf with his name scribbled inside the cover, so it was entirely believable that he didn't exist. Especially since Frankie had been relentless in her search for him from the time she was old enough to understand that the man whose Malibu beach house she and her mother had been living in for the past two years—Jacob—was a master at pancakes and set construction, but wasn't, in fact, her biological father.

So when her mother asked what she wanted for her eighth birthday, Frankie naturally said: "To see my birth certificate."

Her mother bristled but acquiesced.

"See. Just like I said," she told her when Frankie stared at the empty line where her father's name should have been. And when Frankie continued staring at the space, her mother dropped a kiss on her temple and said tenderly, "It's not written in invisible ink, baby. It won't appear no matter how long you wait."

But she kept waiting, anyway.

Not for a name on a blank line, but for other proof.

She waited for a song to come on the radio and her mother to grow misty-eyed, or a fragrance to spark a sigh or a blush—even for a double take at a stranger on the street. Something damning that would reveal some clue, however tiny, to her father's identity.

In the meantime, her mother moved them in and out of the houses and lives of men she met on film sets: Foley artists and key grips, PAs and set builders. And after several more years, Frankie eventually figured out who her father was. Not a name, nothing that satisfying; rather, she deduced that whoever her father was, he had been the love of her mother's life. Why else would Maeve Simon pathologically—but politely—reject every proposal she received, if not because her heart was forever spoken for? And why else would her mother never allow them a real home if not because she knew there could be no such thing so long as Frankie's father could never join them?

So by the time she neared the end of high school, Frankie may not have had a name or a face for her father, but she had an understanding.

And it became enough.

But sitting here now, working her way through a square of cold lasagna and staring at a photograph of her mother with Mitch Beckett, she's not sure anymore.

She studies the photograph, trying to decide how old her mother was when it was taken. Early twenties? Late twenties? With no date on the back, it's impossible to know for sure.

Or is it?

Her eyes train on the banner: Fourth Annual.

Clicking her laptop awake, she searches the Stardust Film Festival website and learns that the first festival was held in 1985, which means the photo was taken in June of 1988.

She pulls her fingers off the keyboard as if it's a detonated bomb, her heart hammering as possibility flares.

*More,* she thinks. *I need to know more.*

Her hands tremble as she punches in a new search. Mitch Beckett: died of heart failure . . .

She clicks on the link for Glory Cartwright's page, scanning the intro paragraph until she reaches the end: *In 1989, she died on the Outer Banks where she was making the movie that was to be her return to film after a decade away. A note was left by Cartwright's bedside. To protect her privacy, Cartwright's husband declined an autopsy and the death was ruled suicide—*

Frankie sits back, overcome with sadness.

Suicide.

Returning to the screen, she scrolls on.

*She and Beckett had one child, a son, Gabe Beckett—*

To *My Beloved Gabe*.

Possibility sizzles down her arms, flaring like a rash.

Could she have a half-brother?

*—who was adopted by the couple soon after their move to Beckett's hometown of Harpswich, Massachusetts . . .*

As quickly as her skin warmed with hope, it cools again. Did that mean Mitch Beckett couldn't have children?

She clicks back to the actor's Wiki page and skims madly through his bio, finding nothing on the subject. Maybe his wife couldn't conceive? Or maybe they simply wanted to adopt? The possible explanations settle her doubt so quickly that she has to wonder if she hopes Mitch Beckett is her father.

Does she?

She ponders the question as she carries her empty plate back to the kitchen and pours a glass of merlot, adding an extra splash for good measure, then another, then just deciding to bring the whole bottle. Who knows how long she'll be up hunting now?

Back at her screen, she reads Mitch Beckett's page more closely, sure there must be other clues. In the paragraph on his personal life, a link is offered for Gabe Beckett and she clicks it, opening a spare-looking website for Beckett Boat Building and Restoration. So their son still lives in Harpswich?

Clicking back to the previous page, she finds his age—thirty-nine—and then a photograph of a tall man with messy chestnut hair caught stepping out of a store: *Son of Hollywood legends is all smiles running errands in his hometown of Harpswich*. Frankie decides the author of the caption must need glasses, because all she can see is a man scowling at having his picture taken. She's never been much for the rugged type, but she finds herself compelled to look closer, feeling the blush of interest brush her skin as she scans the photo. Or maybe it's just the wine. Reds always make her warm.

Not that it matters if he's attractive or not—she has a connection now, someone she can reach out to for answers.

*And say what?*

She sits back, stymied.

*Hi, there! I think your father and my mother had an affair, so let's share a Lyft to the next family reunion?*

Frankie sighs into her wine.

Obviously she can't get right to it just like that. She needs to build slowly, gently.

She can start by offering him the letters. A brief, flattering email. Nothing aggressive or demanding, just a quick but genuine note to build trust, which will be easily won, since he'll be so grateful for the gift of the letters.

Then, after a few more exchanges, she can dig—gracefully, of course—about Mitch Beckett and how well he knew her mother and let things just sort of . . . unfold.

The bottle drained, and too wired to sleep, Frankie settles in with a bag of microwave popcorn and streams the entire Beckett-Cartwright catalog. Every time Mitch Beckett fills the screen, she taps the PAUSE button to study the still, trying to decide if she sees any resemblance in his features. Three films in, she still isn't sure. Or maybe it's because she soon finds herself far more captivated watching his wife.

While Mitch Beckett is perfectly good at what he does—handsome, charming, athletic, sexy—Glory Cartwright is a wonder.

The nail-biting scene in *Moonlight Magic* when she convinces the car salesman to let her take the Porsche for a test drive while Mitch's cat burglaring magician is hiding in the back seat? Brilliant! And the way she does that thing with her lip when she laughs?

Scrolling through her phone, Frankie finds a clip from a television interview with Glory from 1982 where she talks about how badly she wanted Ellen Burstyn's role in *Alice Doesn't Live Here Anymore*—the one that won Burstyn the Oscar—and the interviewer actually smirks—*smirks!*—and Frankie swears she sees startled hurt flash in Glory's eyes. Because it's an interview, she's got the obligatory glass of water in front of her, and Frankie keeps waiting for her to splash it into the interviewer's face, but Glory Cartwright keeps her hands folded in her lap and her smile polite. Frankie would have soaked the smug creep.

Another search yields page after page of early articles depicting the golden couple at the peak of their shine—movie premieres and award celebrations—but she doesn't have to scroll long before the reports turn sour. Some headlines are subtle—*Trouble in Paradise?*—while others go for the throat: *Beckett's Wild Nights on the Water: Boozing, Brawling and Bedding Beach Bunnies!*

She skims a particularly cruel piece that features a series of unflattering beach photos of a bare-chested and bloated Mitch Beckett and an alarmingly thin Glory Cartwright. The images are grainy, but it's clear the couple is engaged in a heated argument. Mitch's arms are either outstretched or grabbing at his temples while Glory is turned away, hugging herself. And as if the pictures aren't evidence enough, the headline hammers the obvious: *Glory in a Tailspin—Down to 98 Pounds!*

The article, she can't help noticing, is from the same year as the picture of her mother and Mitch Beckett. Frankie knows that 99 percent of what's written in the tabloids is bunk, but the timing can't be completely overlooked. Had her mother shared one of Mitch Beckett's wild nights on the water? One night is all it would take.

Guilt flutters reflexively, but she tamps it down. Glancing over at the counter, she sees the letters where she's left them, and longing swells. The cruelty in losing someone so swiftly—there are infinite cruelties, of course—but one of the very worst, she has learned, is that a person can never be certain of how they might have left you otherwise. If there were things they would have said, pieces of themselves they would have made certain to bestow, confessions they didn't want to take with them. Her mother set the photograph and the letters aside for a reason. If not because they contained some piece of Frankie's own history, then why?

Her rationale for not opening the letters is real—her mother *was* adamant about the sanctity of sealed letters and the nonnegotiable cosmic law that only the receiver should be the first to read—but as she skims through article after article about Mitch Beckett and Glory Cartwright, Frankie must admit there's a part of her that's also relieved she can't permit herself to open them. Because as anxious as she is to know her father's identity, and as hopeful as she is that the mystery of this package might finally reveal him, there's a rumble of fear brewing under the hope, a threat of culpability. Had her mother's affair with Mitch Beckett caused Glory Cartwright such despair that she'd taken her life? As much as she wants answers, she couldn't bear knowing her birth might have been the source of such pain to someone else. The truth could change more than her future—it could change her past, too. Memories may be fluid and unreliable, but they are all people have some days.

And she can't help but wonder: Will Gabe Beckett think so, too?

**From:** Francesca Simon
**To:** Gabe Beckett

Gabe,

I am a memorabilia dealer in Hollywood and recently received some items that I think will be of interest to you: two sealed letters, one to you and another to your father, which I believe were written by your mother. I've attached pictures of both envelopes, front and back, so that you can be assured they are authentic and intact.

As a film lover, I know well of your parents' remarkable legacy in movie history, and I would consider it an honor to deliver these letters to you quickly and safely. I can be reached through email or by phone, (555) 555-6290, and I very much look forward to speaking with you to make that happen.

Frankie Simon

*The Memory Shop*
*thememoryshop.com*

# 4

"If Reggie thinks he's getting four for Mansfield's lipstick brushes, he's higher than his prices."

The gravelly-voiced dealer standing beside Frankie at the preview table is talking to her companion. Their eyes meet briefly, recognizing each other from previous entertainment auctions, and they exchange a nod in agreement to the fact that Reggie Furlani, auctioneer to the stars, has once again inflated the values of his items. Los Angeles may be a city of millions, but the world of memorabilia dealers is small enough that everyone knows one another—if not by name, then definitely by face—which is not to say they're friends, or even friendly. Like any business, there's competition, and it's often fierce. Frankie once watched two dealers come to blows in a parking lot over one of Orson Welles's partially smoked cigars.

Today's crowd, however, seems far better behaved. The fifty or so who are here for the preview shuffle down the rows of display cases like well-dressed cattle. It's an impressive assortment, Frankie decides as she scans the offerings—the collection of a film buff from London who clearly had a thing for blond actresses: Kim Novak's shooting script from *Vertigo*. Michelle Pfeiffer's sunglasses from *Scarface*. Jessica Lange's grass belt from *King Kong*.

"See anything you like?"

She looks over to meet the kohl-lined gaze of Georgia Rosen, one of the first dealers to visit their shop when it opened. Like many women in Hollywood over seventy, Georgia has battled time with the help of a gifted plastic surgeon and facial procedures that could successfully fill the façade of the Parthenon.

"These wigs from *Shampoo* are kind of fun," Frankie says, glancing around for one of the auction assistants to open the case for her so she can get a closer look.

"I've got my eye on the lot of Monroe's liquor and fur receipts for a client of mine in Miami." Georgia deals mostly in costume jewelry but anytime Marilyn Monroe lots come on the block, exceptions are made. "The trouble is he's capped me at two grand and I know with Margot here it'll go to four," she whispers, tipping her head to the right. Frankie leans forward to look down the table and sees Margot Cosper tapping into her phone, her fingernails matching her flawless licorice-black bob. She deals exclusively in Marilyn memorabilia for overseas clients and is notorious for inflating bids; Reggie loves her.

Frankie's phone pings from inside her purse. Normally she wouldn't check the message in the middle of a conversation, but with Gabe Beckett's response still pending, she can't resist a quick peek. She's disappointed to see it's just an email from the property manager of the store, which would usually be spam, but the title, in all caps— RENT INCREASE—sends her pulse racing. The price hike, it explains when she clicks on the note—which will take effect in two months— isn't just a scratch, it's a third-degree burn.

Her face flames. Has Dennis raised the rent on all his tenants—or just the ones who recently stopped dating him?

Georgia's eyes pool with concern. "Everything okay, hon?"

"The rent on the shop," she whispers numbly. "It's going way up."

"Oh damn." Georgia sighs, the thick black wings of her eyeliner crinkling with reproach. "That's why you never date your landlord, sweetie."

It's more than a fair point—but in Frankie's defense, she hadn't planned on dating Dennis Farley. And maybe she never would have fallen for him in the first place if he hadn't confessed to a collection of prop cigarette lighters, including ones from *Dr. No* and *Basic*

*Instinct*—but once he did, how could she resist his invitation to dinner? Especially when she'd lost her mother just three months earlier and believed the distraction of romance would help her move through her grieving (it hadn't) or that Dennis's fondness for big band jazz and Bergman films was proof of his tender heart (it wasn't).

"Maybe it's for the best," Georgia says as she leans in to inspect a signed lobby card from *Vertigo.* "I don't know why anyone keeps the overhead of a storefront these days. Everything's done online now."

Like Georgia's ill-timed dating advice, this isn't news to her either. Long before her mother died, she and Frankie watched competitors close up their shops. They'd discussed the possibility of switching to a solely digital business, too. But her mother had been resolute and Frankie agreed: what made their store unique was that they offered people the chance to immerse themselves in the fantasy—and that required the senses. When a customer called from Paris interested in Kristin Scott Thomas's aviator jacket from *The English Patient,* her mother chastised the poor man for wanting to buy it sight unseen: "Three thousand dollars and you don't even want to know how it *smells*?"

"So how much are you asking for them?"

Georgia's question draws her back. Frankie blinks at her.

"Glory Cartwright's letters," Georgia says. "How much?"

Saul. She feels a prickle of frustration but it's fleeting. Georgia was on the Brisket Brigade for a few weeks before she got wise to Saul's long-term plan to stay single but well fed, and found herself a widower from Beverly Hills who only eats out. They stay in touch on Facebook, which explains how she knows about the letters.

Frankie drops her phone back into her bag. "I'm not selling them."

"Because I'll give you five grand for the pair," Georgia says as if she didn't hear the answer. "I have a client in Tampa who's wild about Glory Cartwright. Laid down ten thousand for the fitted sheet from the bed they found her in."

She winces. "That's disgraceful."

"Hey, look, it wasn't my sale," Georgia says, her palms up. "Personally, I draw the line at postmortem stuff, but not everyone's as classy as you and me." This coming from the woman who bid on the pack of cigarettes they found in James Dean's totaled car. "I'm not sure they'd be very juicy, anyway—what with how much they fought about him dragging her all the way out to the East Coast."

Frankie recalls the endless pages of damning articles she'd stayed up half the night reading.

"Most of what they write isn't true, you know."

"Words lie but pictures don't," Georgia says, jabbing the air with her pen for emphasis. Georgia can believe that; she grew up without Photoshop and the magic of digital foolery. "I know Glory put on a good show for the press and her fans—starting that festival and all that—but if she was so happy, then why did she kill herself? Am I right?" Georgia asks as they follow the stream of buyers into the adjoining gallery, and once again Frankie pushes down a burst of guilt, having to remind herself she has no proof—at least not yet—that her mother, or Frankie herself, had anything to do with Glory's despair. Hadn't most of the articles cited Glory Cartwright's begrudging departure from Hollywood as the real source of her crumbling emotional health? Others mentioning that she'd struggled with bouts of depression even before leaving Hollywood?

Stopped at a case containing Grace Kelly's annotated script from *Rear Window*, Georgia leans over and whispers, "Saul said there was a picture, too. You think you might want to sell that?"

Even as Frankie rolls her eyes, she's smiling. "You're relentless, you know that?"

"Damn straight." Georgia waits a beat, then squints. "So is that a yes?"

# 5

It's three days later, when Frankie is finally drifting off to sleep at 2:00 A.M., that she's woken by the chime of her phone. Reaching out into the dark, she clicks the screen and her excitement swells to see the email she's been waiting days for has finally arrived.

**From:** Gabe Beckett
**To:** Francesca Simon

Yes, this looks like my mother's handwriting.

No, I do not want them.

And definitely not for whatever price you're hoping to scalp me for them.

GB

She scoots upright and braces herself against her headboard, still squinting against the glare of light. She scans the email again, sure she must have misread it, that she's still half-asleep and not understanding clearly, but the words—and the knot of shock in her gut—remain.

*Scalp him?*

She blinks dully into the inky black beyond her screen, then scrolls back to her initial message, wondering how Gabe Beckett might have misconstrued her carefully chosen words, but she can't find a source of confusion.

So she types back quickly:

There's obviously some misunderstanding. I'm not trying to sell you anything. I'm giving you these letters. All I need is an address.

She stares at the screen until another ping signals his reply.

There's no misunderstanding. I know a pitch when I hear one. Everything's for sale for you Hollywood types, so I'm not buying it. Literally.

Forcing herself to take a deep breath, even as her cheeks burn with outrage, she reminds herself that Gabe Beckett doesn't know her, that he can only operate off experience, and apparently his experience with memorabilia dealers, and fans in general, has been unpleasant.

*Okay, fine.*

They've gotten off on the wrong foot, clearly, but it's not too late to straighten things out. Not when, she reminds herself, Gabe may be her only chance of learning if Mitch Beckett is, in fact, her biological father.

So as much as she wants to fire off a scathing reply, she closes her eyes for a calming beat, then opens them before typing her answer:

I should have been clearer from the outset. I didn't buy these letters, any more than I'm trying to sell them. They were in my late mother's things so they obviously had some personal significance to her.

Less than thirty seconds later, another ping sounds.

**Then you should keep them.**

She chews at her lip, trying to decide if his response shows any hint of softening.

Is he being gracious—or curt? She's always thought of emailing like a round of Marco Polo—having no way of knowing the location of your recipient's mood.

She'll choose to believe he's giving her a point of entry and keep digging.

Carefully.

**As much as I appreciate your generosity, I would feel better knowing they were in your hands.**

She slides her finger to the send arrow, then stops to add:

**There was also a photograph, which I would gladly send, too.**

She stares at the screen, waiting for him to ask for more information, but after several minutes of silence, Frankie feels the grip of panic fist in her stomach. Gabe Beckett isn't exactly easy to reach—this may be her only chance to ask.

She types quickly, afraid of losing her nerve.

**The photograph is of your father and my mother embracing during the fourth annual film festival that took place, curiously enough, not long before I was born.**

The response is immediate.

**You don't actually think Mitch Beckett is your father?**

So much for softening.

Before she can type back, another email arrives:

Is this some kind of extortion?

Frankie stares at the word, stunned.
Screw calm.

This is in no way about extortion. I am simply looking for answers.

And to deliver these letters. If you don't want them, or care to give me an address, then I will sell them to someone who does.

YOU CALLOUS, SELF-IMPORTANT SCHMUCK.

She debates the last line for several seconds before she deletes it, hits the SEND button, and slaps her phone, facedown, on her dresser, but her heart still thumps with fury. Too upset to fall back asleep, she pulls on a pair of yoga pants and walks out onto the balcony, hoping there's a soft overnight breeze to cool her rage, never mind her disappointment: Now what is she supposed to do?

The acrid smell of night-moistened pavement tickles her nose. The pastel neon coils of the rooftop bar across the street still sizzle with color as servers clear the café tables of empty wineglasses and tapas plates. The sky is a rich royal blue, nearly teal where it touches the horizon of lights. Margarita blue, her mother would have described it, after their favorite drink, a unique mix of tequila, lime juice, and blue curaçao to give it its trademark color, trimmed with a pair of serrano peppers to give it a spicy kick to balance the sweetness. *Because life is both,* her mother had always said. Frankie needs the reminder more than ever tonight.

Below she hears Bogart's tags shimmering like tiny wind chimes in the night's hush. Walking to the railing and peering over the side, she spies Saul standing with his hands in his bathrobe pockets, inspecting his potted hibiscuses.

"Can't sleep either, huh?" He squints up at her. "How about a little cheesecake? Ruthie used to say it worked better than warm milk."

Frankie can't believe she even bothers to ask. "Where did you get cheesecake?"

"Elaine. A friend of Doris's in 1G." And for once, Saul has the decency to look guilty.

She smiles. "Maybe just a sliver."

While Saul cuts them slices, she wanders around his living room. He still displays a handful of memorabilia from his collection in a glass case by the TV, but it's the gallery of photos that cover the top of the baby grand that Frankie always browses first. Ruth's first headshot from when she was a blond contract player at MGM, a black and white of her and Saul feeding each other wedding cake under the palms. And then, Frankie's very favorite: the family portrait, of Saul and Ruth and a bulging-eyed Bogart, taken against a backdrop of lavender clouds. Frankie can usually get through most of them safely, but the family portrait always makes her tear up.

Saul hands her a paper plate with a wedge of cheesecake that could easily double as a doorstop, and Frankie follows him out to the balcony.

When they're seated, he says flatly, "You think he's your father, don't you?"

She feels heat bloom on her cheeks, startled at the question but a little relieved, too.

"Maybe," she admits quietly, then casts Saul a querying smile. "Is that crazy?"

He shrugs. "This town is crazy, kiddo. You being Mitch Beckett's daughter wouldn't be the wildest thing I'd ever heard."

She leans closer. "And what would that be?"

"None of your business, young lady." Saul slides her a chastising scowl, but his milky eyes are all jest. "That's between me and Liz Taylor."

She laughs through a bite of cheesecake. Bogart sits sentry at their feet, his black eyes shifting hungrily between their rising forks.

"Do you think he could be my father?" she asks.

"Do you want him to be?"

A stray leaf falls on her plate; Frankie brushes it off. "I just want to know, Saul. Whoever my father is, I just want to know."

Saul nods thoughtfully as he lowers a chunk of crust to the ground; Bogart gobbles it up. "Georgia told me the bad news about your lease." His eyes flick up. "She said she offered you five grand for the letters. You're tempted, huh?"

He knows she is. Five thousand dollars could take the sting off the added rent for a year. And now that Gabe Beckett has made his feelings clear . . .

"The son doesn't want them."

"He said that?" Saul shakes his head. "Putz." As soon as the insult is out, Saul shoots her an apologetic look; he rarely uses that one in mixed company, but it's warranted. He drops another scrap for Bogart and offers a sad chuckle. "What can I say, kiddo? Some of us are huge disappointments. And still you bring us casseroles and cheesecake."

She laughs. "That would make a great bumper sticker, Saul."

As they eat, the quiet settles around them, the soft lights of the rooftop bar finally flickering out.

"I could always deliver them myself, finally see the festival," she says, loud enough that Saul can hear but soft enough that she could also just be suggesting it to herself. "I haven't missed it." She saw the dates when she first found the photograph and even then a pang of possibility had fired in her stomach, a comfortable sensation, more relief than excitement—that there existed, if all other roads led her nowhere, one final path to follow. An expensive one, for sure—God only knew how much a plane ticket and hotel would set her back; she hadn't dared consider—but here she is, closer to that last-chance plan than she wants to admit. "One of the women who works for the festival—I think her name's Louise—she actually knew Glory and Mitch well. At least that's what it said on the website." She shrugs. "Maybe she'd want the letters."

When Saul doesn't immediately respond to her idea, Frankie looks over, sure his silence is proof of his reservations, but his milky blue eyes swim with tenderness.

"I could watch the store for you," he offers. "Heck, I wouldn't even take my usual cut."

She smiles. "You're a real mensch."

He shrugs sheepishly. "So they all tell me."

And while Saul disappears inside for another slice, Frankie sits back and scans the sky, reminding herself there are stars somewhere hidden behind all the light pollution, points of light that will be here long after everyone is gone. And in the warm hush, she feels her heart settle into the decision to spend a surely outrageous amount of money—money she knows she could put into the store's lease instead—to travel across the country, to a place her mother pretended to have never been, but eventually wanted someone—maybe even Frankie—to know about.

"Just let me know if you need me to watch the store for you," Saul says as they walk to the door a few minutes later.

In the hallway, she turns to leave, then stops, a flutter of doubt rising briefly over her conviction.

"What if I go all the way there and I don't find out who my father is?"

Saul smiles, the corners of his eyes pleating like tiny fans. "Maybe you're more worried what happens if you *do*."

# Part Two

We aren't here to make things perfect. The snowflakes are perfect. The stars are perfect. Not us. Not us! We are here to ruin ourselves and to break our hearts and love the wrong people and die.

*Moonstruck*

# Film Festival Announces Lineup for 34th Year

June 1

Film lovers, rejoice! This year's Stardust Film Festival has announced the schedule for its upcoming event.

"As every year, we aim to bring the best and brightest of contemporary cinema to our loyal attendees," says media relations manager Louise Chandler, "and we are especially excited for this year's lineup, which includes the most films directed and written by women in the festival's history."

In total, 45 films were selected from 586 submissions—the latter number also a festival record—and buzz has already been building for several of the premiering films, including the new one from Megan Marshall, *Jenny Came Back,* and Amy Cohen's long-awaited sequel to her 2012 hit, *Love on a Lark*.

Started in 1985 by cinema darlings Glory Cartwright and Mitch Beckett, the festival has grown from its early days as a party for Hollywood A-listers looking to escape the LA heat, to a celebration of cutting-edge filmmaking, and is now considered a breeding ground for Oscar-worthy breakouts, where movies from both established directors as well as first-time filmmakers vie for the festival's coveted Gold Heart first-place prize.

In addition to the eagerly anticipated previews of new films, the festival will also feature its traditional screenings of classic films, as well as panels, live music, and memorabilia displays from some of the most famous films of all time.

For more information—and to see exclusive trailers and clips from the scheduled films—visit the festival's website at stardustfilmfest.org.

# 6

## Harpswich, Massachusetts

Destiny is something we've invented because we can't stand
the fact that everything that happens is accidental.

*Sleepless in Seattle*

The harbor is quiet when Louise Chandler pulls into the sprawling
lot—several stretches of parking sit empty—and it's hard not to relish
the relative sanity of the scene, knowing that in just a few weeks,
the wharf—the entire town—will be transformed, its twisting roads
clogged with traffic, its narrow sidewalks swarming with temporary
Hollywood transplants, famous faces hiding behind sunglasses and
eager fans trailing behind for selfies, publicists rushing around on
their phones, actresses and models breaking the heels of their $900
Louboutins on Wharf Street's ancient cobblestones.

The reminder of the scope of the festival sends her pulse racing
again—so many people to make happy on both sides of this event.
Her current role of media director may not be highest on the mast-
head anymore, but she still feels the same nerves and self-doubt as
when she was cochair for all those years.

Of course it had been so much easier when Glory was here—a
star herself, she spoke the language of these people, predicted their
often outrageous requests before they even had to ask. Louise
had always marveled over it. Even during Glory's worst bouts of

depression, when just the simple act of making Gabe a peanut butter and jelly sandwich had caused her debilitating panic, Glory's ability to expertly and confidently handle the fragile egos of the entertainment world never faltered.

Which is not to say that Louise is entirely without people skills. All those years navigating the equally fragile egos of the members on her many civic and philanthropic boards here in Harpswich. She was good at making people feel listened to, comfortable—crucial traits for someone in the hospitality business. "Or a doctor's wife," Russ would always tell her. As if that was the real life purpose she'd always imagined for herself.

The wind kicks up as she descends the walkway, determined to free her wiry gray curls from the clip she's struggled all morning to corral them into. Like the pier, the marina has yet to swell with festival visitors. For the most part, the boats that fill the slips or bob in the harbor on their moorings are modestly sized and locally owned, mostly Whalers and cruisers. Two weeks from now visiting superyachts will dwarf the locals' sailboats and trawlers. Except for Gabe's, of course. The distinctive blue main sail—not to mention her three-legged first mate—make *The Great Escape* a hard vessel to overshadow in any season.

Almost to the stern, Louise hears the whine of music coming from the sailboat's deck, and sees Gabe from the back, sitting on his heels, dragging a paint brush across an inverted bench. She slows, debating how to announce herself without startling him—until Garbo appears and decides for her with a single, gravelly yelp.

Gabe twists, sees her, and rises, his T-shirt streaked with the same robin's egg blue that coats the brush still in his hand. Barely into summer, and already the sun has burnished his dark brown hair to copper. She wants to suggest he might be due a cut, not to mention a shave, but she knows better than to nag.

"This is a nice surprise," he says.

She smiles. "I was in the neighborhood."

"Your timing's great. I was just about to take a break." Gabe motions to Garbo, who has hopped over to the edge of the boat to greet her, the yellow Lab's tail spinning impatiently. "You better hurry up and pet her before she lifts off."

"Oh, we can't have that," she says, delivering several loving strokes to the dog's upturned head. She glances around the boat, trying to see it freshly as Gabe's, an exercise she always works hard at, knowing he's done much to repair the damage left by years of Mitch's neglect. Still, somehow, it will always feel like Mitch's boat to her. Perhaps to Gabe, too, she suspects.

"You're making good progress," she says, determined to compliment him. "Your father would be proud." *Your mother, too*, she wants to add but doesn't, fearful of dimming the appreciative smile he's offering her.

"Hope so." Gabe sets down the brush and wipes his hands roughly with a rag. They consider one another, letting the music and the whir of passing boats fill the silence that follows, the salt-and-diesel-thickened air weighed down with the subject they both want to bring up, but don't dare. Gossip blooms as quickly as lilacs at this time of year, and the flow of foot traffic on the slip is constant—people who know them, people who don't.

Gabe squints at her, but Louise knows it isn't the glare of the sun that's hurting his eyes.

"I made coffee."

Normally she would sooner guzzle a cup of motor oil than a mug of Gabe's coffee—it's only slightly thinner—but today all she can taste is rescue as she climbs aboard and ducks her head through the companionway to follow him belowdecks.

The cabin looks its usual disaster. Bills and tools strewn across every surface. One of those men's magazines—Louise wasn't even aware they still printed them?—sits atop a pizza box; Gabe sweeps both out of sight. She scans a stack of marine catalogs, pretending she hasn't seen.

"I'm not sure how warm it still is," he says from the galley, pulling out used mugs from the sink and giving them each a quick rinse; Louise will pretend she hasn't seen that either.

Beside the stove, a hanging basket of fully browned bananas swings with the harbor's gentle chop, the ripe fragrance making its way toward her, and not entirely unpleasant. There are, after all, far worse smells on a bachelor's boat than overripe fruit.

While he pours, she admires the decades-old father-son carving in a nearby stretch of teak near the dinette, remembering, as she always does when she's below, how Gabe had vowed to replace that board the day he inherited his father's boat. And there it remains.

He joins her on the settee. Above them, Garbo's nails tap out a crisp Morse code across the fiberglass.

She lowers her mug to her lap. "Still planning to go down to the Carolinas?"

Gabe shakes his head. "Not this year."

"So where are you going?"

"Nowhere."

She frowns. His yearly flight during festival week is as much a tradition as the event itself. Even when he was young, and the festival's never-ending trays of crab cake sliders and self-serve popcorn machines held infinite appeal for an always-ravenous boy, Glory and Mitch's son would find any excuse to avoid the crush and chaos of his mother's beloved celebration.

She considers his tipped gaze. "Is something wrong with the boat?"

"The boat's fine." His dark eyes rise to meet hers, and the concern that flashes back at her is answer enough: he's worried about Russ.

She smooths down the wrinkled hem of her tie-dyed tunic and pulls in a fortifying breath, a free diver needing to fill her lungs before a deep descent.

"It's just a small setback, Gabe. He'll be back to his old self in no time."

But she can't bear to meet his gaze this time, certain of the doubt she'll see staring back at her—and terrified her own will reveal the same. In the weeks since her husband's car accident, and then his fall down the stairs, she's given the same confident answer to so many concerned friends and never worried of being seen through. But this is Gabe. The man Russ and she loved like a son—then officially raised as one when Mitch passed away. Gabe knows her, knows Russ, too well.

He sits forward. "And what if he's not?"

She looks down, the heat of dread burning her cheeks—that he should put into words something she has been terrified to admit out loud herself.

Gabe shakes his head. "He's just so depressed."

"Of course he's depressed," she says. "He's spent his whole life strong and secure, and now he can't trust himself to climb a flight of stairs."

"But it's not like him to be so defeated."

Yet another observation she's made to herself in the past few months. "Lots of men struggle with depression after retirement."

Louise knows this because she scours the computer nightly, searching for proof that her husband's condition is temporary, treatable. *Normal*. A search that would, ironically, inflame Russ to no end. His frustration at patients using the internet to diagnose themselves, before he had a chance to, was one of his greatest frustrations in the field. But she finds solace in the activity—is that so wrong? There's comfort in knowing how many others suffer with these same unanswered questions. She won't apologize for doing what she needs to do to get through.

When she looks back at Gabe, he's still studying her expectantly, waiting for more.

What can she give him?

She just shrugs. "He's angry, that's all. He just doesn't understand why he had to quit before he was ready." As if the man who'd been responsible for the health of an entire town for nearly fifty years would ever have been ready to step down?

Gabe stares at her incredulously. "He got so dizzy he drove off the road into a ditch and nearly sent you both to the hospital—he doesn't think that's reason enough to stop?"

"He said it was just an accident." And she told herself the same thing—until a week later, when he'd suffered another dizzy spell climbing their stairs and fallen halfway up, suffering a sprained wrist. That same night, despondent, he confessed to being unable to administer a tetanus shot two weeks earlier because his hand shook, an admission she never shared with Gabe and doesn't plan to. While Russ would accept Gabe knowing of a missed step on the stairs, or even a car accident, having to confess to a failure of duty would break her husband's heart.

Gabe rakes a hand through his hair. "He's seventy-eight. How long was he planning to keep working anyway?"

She smiles. "All the way to the end."

"Yeah, well. It's the end."

She sucks in a sharp breath, feeling the prickle of tears as she sets down her coffee.

Gabe looks up, remorse pooling in his dark eyes. "Shit . . ." He reaches across for her hand and squeezes hard. "I didn't mean it like that."

"I know." She claps her other hand over his, letting the soft slap of the chop against the hull fill the heavy silence.

People had warned her. Friends with recently retired husbands who'd flung open the door to retirement the way one imagines a hibernating bear might throw open the metaphorical door of his cave to let in spring's light, only to find their fierce enthusiasm doused with alarming speed. Just last year, her friend Margaret had confessed over coffee that her husband, Franklin—who would have been hard-pressed to know the names of his children's teachers when he'd been practicing law—was driving her bonkers with his newfound interest in the minutiae of her life. Another friend's husband was emptying their retirement account shopping online and ordering DoorDash. "At least your husband has something to occupy him," had been Margaret's envious response. Louise had sipped in silence, consoling herself with the knowledge that she would never have to endure that. That Russ would never retire. Certainly not with her work on the festival as consuming as ever.

Her naiveté galls her now. Whatever made her think they were immune to life's natural disappointments? She of all people—four miscarriages and countless false starts behind them—shouldn't have been so cocky.

She sighs. "I feel like it's partly my fault."

"Your fault?" Gabe's voice cracks with disbelief—and a faint edge of outrage.

"Here he is, suddenly homebound, and I'm gone for the festival from dawn till dusk . . ."

"So you're supposed to quit doing what you love just because he had to?"

She smiles fondly, grateful for his defense, especially knowing how little love he has for the festival, but she feels a swell of regret, too. Her intention was never to come over here to ask him to take sides, or burden him. God knows Gabe spent plenty of time as a boy cast in the thankless role of referee to a mother and father constantly at odds—even if his allegiance did always fall to Mitch, much to Louise's constant frustration.

Whatever the details of Russ's unraveling, Gabe should be spared them. Just as he should be spared other things. Like the fact that Russ moved into the guest bedroom weeks before he fell down the stairs.

She feels a rash of shame at the memory flush her cheeks. She reaches for her coffee and takes a short sip, determined to steer them to other subjects.

"In case you're wondering," she says, "the schedule for the premiere parties is coming together nicely. Leonardo DiCaprio is planning a midnight cruise after screening his new climate change documentary." She mines his gaze expectantly. His earlier defense of her work on the festival has filled her with a spark of hope. "Are you sure I can't reserve you a seat?"

The offer is reflexive—as is the weary look Gabe gives back to her.

He rises. There's little floor space in the narrow cabin, especially for someone of his height, but he paces it angrily.

So much for her attempt to redirect this conversation.

"It's not your fault, Lou. You've finally found your groove and he's lost his. It's shitty timing for sure, but him sulking about it isn't going to change anything."

Her phone chimes, the burst of sound in the quiet cabin startling them both, and the hard line of Gabe's mouth softens into a grin.

"They found you."

Back on deck, the breeze is soft, the harbor glassy and serene. Gabe shoves his bare feet into sneakers and helps her off the boat, then he and Garbo walk her back up the gangplank.

At the gate, Louise takes the hug from him she didn't get at the outset of their visit.

"Doc mentioned something about some rotted boards on the deck," he says. "I thought I'd come by tonight and check them out."

It's a thin excuse, they both know it, the possible repair being far from urgent, but Louise offers him a grateful smile, even as she reminds him quietly: "This isn't your problem to fix."

The glimmer in his eyes assures her he knows she's not talking about decking. Not even close.

"I know." He shrugs, smiles. "But Garbo always likes a ride in the truck after dinner."

By the time Louise turns into the driveway, it's nearly ten. A few lights still burn on the first floor, but the rest of the house is unlit, and the hush of darkness seems unabashedly hostile as she makes her way up the brick path to the front door of their shingled saltbox.

At first, the lack of lights had filled her with immeasurable disappointment—hurt, really—but recently, within the past few weeks, she's started to experience instead a flicker of hope—God, she even hates to use the word—before she's cleared the curtain of trees. A hope that the house will be completely dark, assuring her that he's asleep, absolving her of having to slow when she nears the guest room door, debating whether or not to wish him good night. Has he been equally relieved for these impossibly late nights, too?

And again, the spiral of despondency swirls: How long can they endure this?

*Lots of older people go through rough patches during retirement.*

Taking the porch steps, she goes through the other set of statistics she's found online, recounting them like a mantra. One out of four older couples sleep in separate rooms. One in four! At first the number had offered her comfort—then a sharp pain that had only deepened as she continued her discouraging research. Most horrifying of all, she learned there was even a term for it: sleep divorce. That was when she broke down, crumpled like a curl of birch bark in a fire. Even now, entering the house, the phrase causes her to shiver. Their enduring intimacy had been a source of quiet pride for her. How after nearly fifty years of marriage, they continued to make love, long after so many couples relinquished that affection, or so the data claimed. Yet another statistic she'd hunted down to soothe her—the relief to know they weren't clichéd in every way. Hadn't been, at least.

And as shameful as it is, she feels this health crisis has granted her an absolution; now there is a reason for their separate spaces.

She pauses a moment in the foyer, setting her purse down softly on the narrow table that has held their mail and keys for forty years, the open space beneath storing muddy boots or closed umbrellas, or, for a time, Gabe's backpack, slid off his rangy teenage shoulders and slung absently against the wall, hard enough that she got the smart idea to take down her mother-in-law's mirror that hung above it, fearful that Gabe's constant walloping of the wall would send it crashing down. And if breaking a mirror was bad luck, God only knew what sort of curse the universe dealt for breaking your mother-in-law's mirror. When Gabe had moved out at nineteen, she'd put it back.

Now she wishes she hadn't. Her reflection startles her: the puffy eyes and the deep lines fanning out beside them, like a collection of arrows; the sagging plumpness of her neck. She presses her hand against the loosened skin, then tips her chin up, disappointed to see it doesn't correct anything. Time and again she's told herself—and others—she doesn't mind aging, feels grateful to be here to experience it, but that's not always the truth. No one is without vanity. And it was easier not to care when Russ wasn't sleeping in a different room. When his fingers—his eyes—swept over hers daily.

She reaches up to unsnap her hair clip, freeing the knot of gray coils and giving them a gentle fluffing. She toes off her Easy Spirits, taking a moment to wiggle blood back into her bare toes before she walks resolutely down the hall to the kitchen, purposefully avoiding the row of framed photos that line the wall, the current irrelevance of them, the brutal reminder of what she and Russ aren't just now. And what if it's not just now, but forever?

Only when she's cleared the gallery does she realize she's held her breath the entire way past, the way she'd done as a little girl passing cemeteries, terrified of breathing in bad luck.

In the kitchen, she's still not safe. There's the refrigerator—the picture of her and Russ taken at Donny Barlow's clambake the summer before. She thinks of the old dieting trick, of putting an unflattering picture of oneself on the fridge to keep from reaching in for a fattening snack. Could having to face a picture of previous bliss sustain a person's marriage to endure troubled waters? Or does the reminder of Russ's more nimble past only deepen his despair?

She listens for the sounds of movement down the hall, but hears only the click of the dishwasher, shifting to the rinse cycle.

The irony, of course, is that when Russ was working, she often came home to a quiet house when he'd be kept at the office with late patients or piles of paperwork. And, busy as she was, she rarely felt his absence. Quickly she understood that if she didn't have the occupation of children, she'd be expected to prove her domestic skills in other ways. That the role of a doctor's wife was to be as much a part of the community as he was, which meant seats on nearly every board in Harpswich—zoning board, Friends of the Library board, the historical society. How swiftly and thoroughly her routine had been carved out for her, after she'd spent so many years thinking that she had control of her future.

The plan had been to wait to marry until after Russ finished his residency and she finished her degree. With both of them in Boston, able to see one another as often as his demanding schedule allowed, there had been no rush. Until, of course, there was. (Marriage wasn't the only activity they'd planned to wait to do.) And when Louise learned she was pregnant, their timetable changed. They were married in her parents' backyard. Her dress had an empire waist and no one had a clue. When she miscarried a month later, she felt sure the universe had played some horrible joke, punishing them for trying to deceive their friends. When Russ brought them back to Boston so he could finish his residency, Louise's relief was gigantic—to be among strangers and finally able to grieve openly. Still she remained determined to start their family. But by the time Russ brought them back to the Cape to join the practice in Harpswich, she'd miscarried again.

*You've finally found your groove.* Gabe's words return to her, and she feels a smile tug at her lips, mostly because he's right. After years of doing work she felt she had to do as a doctor's wife, her only occupation now is something she wants to do, something she loves to do. Surely that was why Glory had put her in charge of the festival from the start. Because her dear friend understood that to be happy, a woman needs a purpose of her own choosing, not one chosen for her by her parents or her husband or her neighbors.

Moving into the pantry, she scans the shelves. She's hungry but too tired to make herself something. What had Russ found for dinner? All those years she made sure to craft a plate for him, wrapped and waiting in the fridge for when he came home. A few times he's offered to save her something, but she always demurs. So why does she feel a pang of disappointment when he hasn't tonight?

These are the things that rattle her most; she seeks proof of his continued devotion in the smallest of places. Leftover food and left-on lamps.

The snap of a switch cuts through the silence, then the spilling of light startles her. She whirls around, her hand at her chest. Russ stands in the doorway; his white hair, always so enviably thick, looks alarmingly thin under the harsh ceiling light. She wishes he wouldn't use it. They must both look like ghosts.

"I thought you were asleep."

"I couldn't remember if I turned off the stove." He tilts his head in the direction of the sink, the cleaned pot turned upside down in the dish drainer. "I made myself some pasta for dinner." He glances at her. "Did you eat?"

"The interns ordered pizza from Rudder's. I had a slice."

She waits for him to begin his tirade about how their pizza isn't as good as it used to be ever since Jerry sold it to that young couple from Philadelphia, but he doesn't add a thing, and she can't believe how disappointed she is at the silence.

"Good day?" she asks, not even sure what that would be for him.

He shrugs. "A day." The dishwasher sighs, finished; Russ looks at it, as if waiting for it to say something else before he continues. "Frank called."

She stares at him, sure her face radiates the hope she feels swelling. "And?"

"They made me the formal offer to take Joe's seat."

She exhales, unaware she had been holding her breath, but it's huge news. The open seat on the hospital ethics board. "You said yes, didn't you?"

"I said I'd think about it." Whatever balloon of possibility had expanded behind her ribs shrinks in an instant. "We both know he's only offering it to me because he's terrified I'm going to try to go back to work."

"That's not true, Russ. They're offering it to you because they can't think of anyone more qualified to take it."

"Yeah, well." He sniffs. "They're wrong."

She frowns at him. He can't honestly feel that way? Her heart hammers, terrified he's ruined this one chance to dig himself out of whatever hole he's fallen into.

He shoves his hands into his pockets; a trademark habit that she never used to think twice about, she now takes personally—an unspoken assurance that there won't be a chance for touch between them.

He chuckles bitterly. "I'm sorry I wasn't more like Mitch. He had the good sense to bow out before they could force him out."

"Don't be sorry." Louise turns for the sink before he can see her face, already feeling the flush of frustration warm her cheeks. "If you'd been anything like Mitch Beckett, I never would have married you."

# 7

1979
Harpswich, Massachusetts

China or Corelle?

Louise raised the two dessert plates and looked between them as the debate raged: Her wedding china—a Blue Willow pattern—was elegant, or maybe too elegant? Would it seem she was trying too hard to impress? The Corelle was serviceable and had a lovely sea-foam green trim, but she didn't want to appear as if she weren't trying at all . . .

She lowered the two with a disgusted sigh. Five-star generals debated over battle strategies in less time than she'd been considering the dishware. But then she'd given the same deliberation—no, more even, it galled her to admit—to which hand towels to hang in the half bath off the hall. It was a wonder she'd managed to get anything on the table to eat, let alone the spread of hors d'oeuvres she'd been baking and slicing and rolling and filling since four that morning. As if she'd been able to sleep last night knowing Glory Cartwright was due to arrive sometime after three.

Glory Cartwright. Coming to her town.

To her kitchen!

Louise slid her hands along the sides of her head, desperate to smooth down the wisps of curls that had come loose. She'd tethered her shoulder-length hair with a tortoiseshell clip at the base of her neck—yet another choice she'd deliberated for far too long.

It didn't help that the earlier breeze had vanished in the last hour, once coming through the screens strong enough that she'd worried the gusts might overturn the flower arrangements that bookended her dishes. Despite it only being the end of May, the temperatures were already rising to midsummer numbers, bringing a blanket of humidity with them. The lavender and white lilac blossoms, soon to be frothy and fragrant on their branches in the front yard, would wilt prematurely at this rate. Heat this early in the season didn't bode well for a cool summer.

She clapped a hand under each armpit, crushed to find the pink polyester damp. Why hadn't she worn the linen instead? Everyone knew linen breathed.

Speaking of breathing—

She glanced back at the stove clock, startled to see it was nearly two thirty. How long did it take to get a bottle of Dubonnet? Unless Gifford's was out and Russ had been forced to travel to Wellfleet, though Louise doubted her husband would take the extra time, not wanting to risk being absent when Mitch and his wife made their grand arrival. Maybe Louise wouldn't have been so insistent if she hadn't found a photograph of Glory Cartwright drinking Dubonnet at an Oscar party. Russ had been dubious, suggesting that someone from the liquor company might have simply stuck it in her hand and snapped a photo, because they did that sometimes, he told her with a ridiculous degree of authority. As if her husband knew anything about Hollywood? As if he was the one who pored over the magazines in the grocery store?

She caught a whiff of fry oil and winced. What happened to the buttery sweetness of the mushroom tartlets she'd just pulled from the oven?

She held her temple, her head spinning. She couldn't remember when she'd been more nervous.

No, that wasn't true.

Her wedding day. She'd been a tangle of nerves then, too. Not over the ceremony itself—no, she'd been sure she wanted to marry Russ Chandler from the moment she watched him gently capture and free a crow that had accidentally flown into their high school's gymnasium in the middle of assembly. No, it had been the threat of exposure that had worried her. Her wedding bouquet of calla lilies had been a serviceable shield, until she'd had to relinquish it during the vows, and she'd been terrified the wind would pick up and press the loose fabric of her empire waist flush against her rounding belly. Looking back on that day always brought with it a twist of regret, that she'd worried so much for nothing . . .

What she really needed was to sit and cool down. She made a valiant attempt, getting as far as the edge of the couch before her attention swerved to a pile of unopened mail on the sideboard she'd forgotten to stuff out of sight. She hid all but the letter on top—a thick electric bill—which she used to fan herself madly as she returned to the kitchen to survey the spread of hors d'oeuvres that looked, not surprisingly, entirely unchanged from the way they had appeared when she'd scanned the table five minutes earlier.

The station wagon charged up the driveway, startling her from her thoughts. She rushed to the window in time to see Russ emerge with a promising-looking brown paper bag under his arm.

She met him at the door as winded as if she'd run in from the backyard. "Did you find it?"

"Two stores later," he said, freeing the bottle from its brown paper sleeve and stepping inside.

So he had gone the extra mile, literally. "My hero." She gave him a grateful kiss on the cheek as she took the popular aperitif from his hand and added it to the collection of liquor bottles on the counter. "Do you suppose they've hit traffic?" she asked as she returned to the table and reached for the tin of Sterno, struggling to pop the top.

"Let me." Russ came beside her and gently eased the tin from her hands.

She offered him a sheepish shrug. "I'm all thumbs today."

The top off, he lit a match, the sizzle of the strike making her jump. Russ glanced at her, his pale eyes tender. "You don't have to be nervous, sweetheart. Just because he's some big star now doesn't mean he isn't the same goofball we grew up with."

She blinked at him as he slid the lit tin back under the fondue pot. Did he really think it was Mitch she was nervous to see?

"Where are the crab balls?"

She wiped her hands briskly on a dish towel. "I didn't bother to make them. What's wrong with hush puppies?"

"Nothing. I just know Mitch always loved your crab balls."

"Then you're welcome to run over to Chowder's and pick up an order if you're so worried about disappointing him," she said, more sharply than she meant. Moving down the counter for a package of cocktail napkins, she could feel her husband's confounded stare burning into her cheek.

He cleared his throat pointedly. "So let me get this straight: I drive all over town for a bottle of Dubonnet for a total stranger but you forget to make our oldest friend's favorite food?"

"Not ours—yours," she corrected coolly. "Your oldest friend who lived in a palace in Hollywood for fifteen years and never once invited us out to see him."

"Because he knew I couldn't leave my practice." How many times over the years had Russ used that rationale to excuse Mitch's neglect? Louise reached back to free the knot of her apron string, plucking the half skirt off her waist and thrusting it into the nearest chair. She'd vowed not to air old grievances, that this was a day for new beginnings. She'd blame the heat.

When she marched into the living room for a final inspection, Russ followed her, joining her by the fireplace while she scanned the mantel for dust.

"Lou, stop. You don't have to make such a fuss."

She turned to face him and sighed, surrendering to the prickles of defeat she'd been feeling all morning. "You're probably right. I'm sure the minute she gets out of the car and sees our simple little house, she's going to want to drive straight back to LA."

Russ leveled her with a stern stare. "That's not what I meant, and you know it."

He pulled her into a reassuring hug, and she lingered there for several beats, taking comfort in the grassy smell of his mint aftershave before stepping back.

"I just can't for the life of me figure out what she's going to do here, Russ."

"I'm sure you can introduce her to people, bring her to things."

She stared at him—he wasn't serious? "Oh, I'm sure Glory Cartwright will be dying to join the garden club. Or maybe the used book sale committee is more her speed?"

He frowned, clearly not appreciating her sarcasm. "All I know is what Mitch told me. He said they needed a break, a little breathing room to reassess their careers."

If they needed breathing room, they'd have little of it in the Connellys' house. Compared to their sprawling estate in the Hollywood Hills—Louise had seen the pictures in magazine spreads of Shadowlands, named after Mitch's first picture—the beach house would seem like a closet.

"It's just a year, Lou," Russ said as they returned to the kitchen. "People can do most anything for a year."

The crackle of arriving tires sailed through the screens; her breath caught in her chest.

Russ glanced at the window above the sink. "They're here."

She was smaller in person than she was on the screen. That was Louise's first thought when Glory Cartwright stepped out of the ivory Cadillac that had just pulled into their driveway. Or maybe anyone would be dwarfed under that gigantic-brimmed hat and those enormous sunglasses—though there was no mistaking the lithe form that her shiny emerald jumpsuit revealed, tight as a second skin all the way down to her waist, where the pant legs flared out like two sails. Louise looked down reflexively at her long corduroy skirt, the one she'd felt so stylish in five minutes earlier, and flushed with regret.

In the next second, Mitch burst out of the driver's seat with a loud hoot. The matching denim jeans and shirt may have been a strange style for the son of a fisherman who had once preferred bare feet to cowboy boots, but the slow grin that spread under his moustache when he saw them was entirely familiar.

Louise slowed at the edge of the steps, her heart thundering behind her ribs. "I'll wait here. I'm so nervous I'm liable to trip down the stairs."

Russ smiled, taking her hand and tugging her forward. "So I'll catch you."

Mitch closed the distance between them in a handful of long strides, lunging first for Russ like a boxer looking to land a punch. Louise hung back while they embraced with several hard shoulder slaps, grateful for the gift of distance while the old friends beamed at one another. Her time in the welcoming line would come soon enough.

"Lou . . ." When Mitch's eyes slid to find hers, she'd already secured a polite smile. "Man, you're a sight."

"Hello, Mitch," she said tightly.

His arms spread wide and Louise stepped into them, allowing him a brief hug—and nearly choking on a smoky breath of his woodsy cologne—before he stepped back to call to Glory, who was still scanning the yard from the car.

"Glow, come on!"

"Coming!" she cried as she pranced across the driveway, slivers of cork platform heels peeking from beneath her pant legs. Louise felt a bolt of panic—she just prayed the woman didn't break her neck on the uneven surface of crushed shell.

"Glow, I want you to meet my oldest friends," Mitch said, swinging one tanned hand in their direction while he pulled Glory against him with the other. "This is Russ and Louise Chandler. Russ, Lou, meet the woman who finally made an honest man out of me."

"Don't you believe it," Glory said with a coquettish grin as she dove forward to offer her hand, a stack of turquoise bracelets colliding at her thin wrist. She swung off her sunglasses and appraised the house, her heavily shadowed eyes blinking approvingly. "Oh God, Mitch, it's adorable! And there's even those little shell wind chimes you promised," she cried, pointing her folded sunglasses at the clattering collection of stringed sand dollars hanging from the rafters. Adorable? Louise savored the compliment, feeling a flush of relief, then another of doubt—would Glory Cartwright still think so when they came inside?

Russ took Glory's outstretched hand and covered it with both of his. "We're honored, Ms. Cartwright."

"Does this mean I have to call you Dr. Chandler?"

"Only when he's sticking a needle in your arm," Mitch teased.

Russ smiled, flushing slightly. "Of course not."

While her voice may have been different, Glory Cartwright was certainly every bit as beautiful as she appeared on-screen. Did Russ agree? Louise stole a glance at her husband, but his smile remained even, his gaze moving between Mitch and Glory with equal interest.

"You know, I was bracing for a crowd," Glory said, searching the lawn.

"No crowds, baby. Not yet." Mitch tugged her against him. "I made Lou and Russ promise not to tell anyone when we were coming in," he said with a quick wink in Russ's direction. "I wanted our landing to be private."

Still caught in Mitch's clutch, Glory turned to catch Louise's gaze. "Private?" Glory laughed. "Where's the fun in that?"

They spilled into the kitchen.

Glory Cartwright swung off her hat and revealed her trademark auburn mane, the sides feathered back in two perfect wings. Louise had always marveled at those fashionable waves in the magazines and on TV, always convincing herself they were some sort of trick of the camera, that they could never look that perfect in real life. She felt a flutter of envy. So much for her theory.

"Drink orders?" Russ asked.

"G and T for me," said Mitch, already circling the table of food.

"I'd love a splash of Dubonnet, if you have it," said Glory.

Louise flashed Russ a small smile of satisfaction.

"Please help yourselves," she said, sweeping her hands like a game show hostess to display the spread of hors d'oeuvres.

Mitch stepped forward. "Lou, you can go ahead and put away that celery and those carrot sticks," he said, casting Glory a teasing smile. "I told Glow as long as we're here, she's not allowed to eat anything that hasn't been brought up in a net or fried within an inch of its damn life."

"And I reminded him that he's not the one who has to worry about fitting into a pink cat suit for our new film next summer," Glory said, lunging for a whiff of the centerpiece of bright blooms of wildflowers and dried grasses that Louise had assembled that morning. "These are beautiful. You'll have to be sure to give me the number of your florist."

Louise smiled, feeling a flicker of pride. She reached back nervously to test her hair clip. "I did the arrangement myself."

"Really?" Glory Cartwright blinked at her as if Louise had claimed to have built the Pyramids. Was she honestly so impressed?

"Lou's quite the gardener," Russ said, returning with their drinks.

"And what about these?" Glory asked, her attention pulled to a stack of sand dollar coasters, picking one up and studying it with wonder. Louise leaned closer and drew in a whiff of jasmine. Just a few minutes inside and already Glory Cartwright's sugary perfume had overtaken the greasy smell of fried batter.

"I found those at one of my favorite boutiques," she said. "But they sell them all over town."

Mitch dragged a chip through the bowl of clam dip and pointed it at Glory. "Lou and you should go shopping this week. She can give you decorating tips—can't you, Lou?"

Louise shot him a wary look. As if she would presume to advise someone with Glory Cartwright's expensive taste how to decorate her house?

She smiled politely. "I'm sure you won't need my help . . ."

"Oh no, I'm counting on it," Glory said. "The house comes furnished but I want to add a few touches of my own." She glanced between Russ and Louise. "They filmed *Jaws* near here, didn't they?"

"I think that was on the Vineyard," said Louise.

"You know, I was actually up for the part of Brody's wife," Glory said, peeking into the living room. "But Lorraine was just so perfect. She and Roy had the most fantastic chemistry."

"Glow, sit," said Mitch, plunging a wedge of bread into the fondue pot.

"Lou loves movies," Russ said. "We don't get to the movies nearly as often as she'd like."

"You're not missing anything these days, trust me." Mitch tipped the skewer into his mouth and pulled off his cheese-soaked catch. "It's still all this cinema verité crap."

Glory cast him a disapproving stare over her shoulder. "Just because you refuse to try something different doesn't make it crap."

"If by 'something different,' you mean I don't feel the need to starve myself or not sleep for a week to get into character, you're right, I don't."

Glory rolled her eyes. "It's called method acting."

"I know what it's called, Glow. Who the hell do you think had to wait in his trailer to film a thirty-second scene because De Niro wanted to do sprints up and down the lot for three hours?"

"He won an Oscar, didn't he?"

Mitch swatted the air as if to close the subject and turned to Russ. "Did I tell you I'm getting *Essie* back on the water? I called Curtis before we left LA to make sure she'd be ready. Can you believe he kept her stored for me all these years?"

"Do you like to sail, Ms.—" Louise stopped herself. "Glory."

"Not yet—but she's going to love it," Mitch said, glancing over his shoulder to find Glory peering down the hallway. "Glow, if you want a tour, all you have to do is ask, you know."

Russ stood. "Gladly."

"You two start without me," Glory said. "I'll catch up." She looked at Louise and smiled. Louise had never seen such white teeth in her whole life. "Which way to your restroom?"

When fifteen minutes had passed and Glory still hadn't returned to the kitchen, Louise assumed Mitch's wife had joined the house tour—until she passed the slider and saw Glory outside, skirting the flower gardens and puffing madly on a cigarette. A part of Louise wanted to remain inside, let the woman wander and smoke in peace, but another part, the hostess part, felt compelled to make sure she was okay.

Hearing the slider whirl down the track, Glory turned, her face lighting immediately into a sheepish smile. "I promised myself I wouldn't start again and look at me," she said, waving her cigarette as Louise approached. "Not exactly the best first impression to make on a doctor, huh?" She glanced at Louise's empty hand. "Where's yours?"

"Oh, I don't smoke."

Glory laughed. "Well of course you don't. I meant your drink."

She raised her glass and sipped. "I'm always grateful to find another Dubonnet lover. Mitch can't stand the stuff. He refuses to keep it in his bar."

His bar. The pronoun wasn't lost on Louise. Still she felt a short flush of pride at the unexpected compliment; it never occurred to her that Glory would think she kept a bottle in the house normally. Maybe Louise would pour herself some when they found themselves back inside later. Maybe just a pinch. It was a celebration, wasn't it?

They circled the perimeter of the gardens.

"I still don't understand why you two never came out to LA to see us."

"I suppose because Mitch never asked," Louise said flatly. Why lie?

"Good God." Glory groaned and rolled her eyes. "I love that man but he is such a Neanderthal. He thinks people will just show up, like stray cats. Consider this your official invitation to come visit." Glory flicked her cigarette; Louise marveled at the perfect crescent of fuchsia gloss left on the crisp white filter. "I'm sorry if I rambled in there. Mitch really doesn't want us talking about movie business. He said the whole point of coming here was to get away."

"It's understandable you'd want a break. It must be exhausting work."

"You're just being kind—we're not exactly brain surgeons." She tapped off another coil of ash. "I think people who need a break from being paid ridiculous amounts of money to play make-believe should be rounded up and fed to wild boars."

Louise chuckled. Glory's glossy lips rose into a smile.

"Do you want to know the real reason we're here?" Glory's voice lowered conspiratorially; Louise leaned in. "John Cassavetes wants to cast us in his next picture and Mitch doesn't want to do it, so he thinks if he pulls us out of Hollywood for a few months, I'll lose interest. As if I could. The man's a genius." She took several quick puffs, like someone drawing oxygen from a mask. "But Mitch says, why do I want to make a movie where all we do is scream at each other? And I keep telling him: That's not the whole of it. The beauty of Cassavetes's work is in the range." She pushed out a sigh with her ribbon of smoke. "Range. Now there's a word never associated with a Beckett-Cartwright movie."

Louise nodded thoughtfully, but not with too much conviction, unsure if she was meant to agree or not.

A flock of sparrows swept across the lawn; Glory watched them land and rise over the gardens for several seconds before she turned back to Louise, whatever indignation that had flashed there seconds earlier now cooled.

"So how much do you charge?"

Louise blinked at her. "Charge?"

"For your flower arrangements."

"Oh, I don't sell them."

"You should. People in LA would pay a fortune. Where did you learn to make them?"

Did she really care to know? Louise eyed Glory quickly, searching her flashing green eyes for proof before she answered. "I worked at a flower shop all through high school, and then for a few years while Russ and I were in Boston for his residency. When we moved back here, I even considered opening a shop of my own."

"Why didn't you?" Glory asked, as if opening a business were as easy as opening a jar of peanut butter. Louise felt a prickle of shame.

"Life stepped in, I suppose," she said. "I had no idea that being a doctor's wife would be a job in itself. Expected seats on boards, fund-raising . . ."

"It's never too late."

*If only that were true,* Louise thought as she gazed wistfully at her beds, recalling the cool, herby smell of freshly cut stems she couldn't wait to breathe in every morning, the narrow corridor of their work area, the counter always splashed with blossoms, like the canvas of one of the abstract artists she so enjoyed viewing at the MFA. How much peace and distraction it had provided her in those impossible days after she'd miscarried.

She glanced up to find Glory studying her intently as she drew on her cigarette. "You know, I tried to contact you years ago."

Louise blinked, startled by the confession, sure she'd misheard.

"When Mitch and I were making *One Summer in San Clemente*," Glory said as they circled a patch of violets. "I played a doctor's wife."

Louise recalled the film well, how Russ had spent the drive home from the theater critiquing Mitch's performance, wondering why they never asked real medical professionals to review scripts, how her own envy had swayed between Glory's glamorous wardrobe and her take-charge persona, the snappy comeback lines she fired off with such confidence.

"I wanted to shadow a real doctor's wife for the role," Glory continued, "so I asked Mitch for your number . . ." Louise stared expectantly while Glory sipped her drink, the wait excruciating until Glory finally swallowed. "He could never find it."

That she should be disappointed over something years past was absurd, still Louise felt a short pang of remorse. "That's too bad. I would have enjoyed that very much."

"And I'm sure you would have been far more helpful than the plastic surgeon's wife I ended up shadowing for a week. All she did was take two-hour lunches at the Beverly and train with her tennis instructor, Julian." Glory rolled her eyes. "But it looks like we'll get our chance to team up after all."

Louise tilted her head. "How do you mean?"

Glory smiled. "You can show me how to play a proper Cape Cod wife, of course."

Louise wasn't sure which part of the sentence—"proper Cape Cod wife" or "play"—unsettled her more, when the whoosh of the slider sailed across the lawn, pulling her attention to the house before she could decide.

Russ and Mitch stepped out. Mitch waved.

"We've been spotted," Glory whispered playfully, waving back.

Mitch raised his bare wrist and tapped it pointedly.

"I'm sure you're anxious to get settled," Louise said, steering them back up the lawn toward the deck.

"Do you know the house he leased?" Glory asked.

"I do. I used to know the owners."

"I told Mitch I didn't want anything too fancy. That if he wanted us to live here for a year, I wanted to experience a real rustic beach house. No frills."

Louise smiled agreeably. She'd get her wish, all right.

"You gals making plans already?" Mitch asked as they climbed the steps to the deck to join them.

"How's Monday for our shopping date?" Glory cast Louise a wishful look. "Ten o'clock?"

Mitch came behind Glory and crossed his arms around her. "And while you're at it, Lou, take her by Wards and get her some proper shoes, will you?"

"What's wrong with my shoes?" Glory cried, swatting playfully at his hands as he squeezed harder.

Ten minutes later, Louise and Russ waved them out of the driveway.

"Looks like you two were getting along famously." Russ waited a beat before grinning at his own pun as he followed Louise back into the house. "And you were worried she'd hate it here." He chuckled. "I've never seen anyone gush over coasters before."

"She talks about moving here like she's come to film a movie, Russ. Like it's a role she's set to play."

He shrugged. "Is that so strange?"

"I suppose not."

Louise surveyed the remainder of the hors d'oeuvres. "I made too much food. She barely touched any of it."

"Mitch enjoyed himself enough for both of them," Russ said. "Hopefully she'll actually eat when you have your lunch date on Monday."

"Don't be silly, she was just being polite," Louise said, picking up a stuffed mushroom and popping it into Russ's open mouth. "I'm hardly going to put it on the calendar."

And she didn't.

Which was why, when Mitch's cream Cadillac charged up the driveway on Monday morning at 9:52, Louise was elbow-deep in a bowl of bread dough at the kitchen counter. She gave her hands a brisk rinse, still digging out leftover dough from the webs of her fingers as she hurried down the front hall and opened the front door to find Glory Cartwright in skintight black jeans and a garnet velour blazer.

"Don't tell me you forgot?" Glory swept off her sunglasses and looked her up and down, her eyes pooling with dread when she finally settled them on Louise's face.

Louise blinked. "Of course not—I've been looking forward to it all weekend," she lied quickly, reaching for her purse where it sat—thank God—on the entry table. "I'm all ready to go."

Glory bit back a smile and gestured to her waist. "Are you sure about that?"

Louise looked down, seeing her apron still tethered, and flushed.

The house was fine, Glory explained as she spun them out into the street, fast enough that Louise reached for the door handle to keep from tipping into the center of the seat. She thought at once of their movie *Moonlight Magic,* the heart-pounding car chase as Mitch tries to outrun the bounty hunter hired to find them.

Coming around a curve, they encountered a slow-moving sedan. She glanced to Glory's feet, silently willing her white pumps to hit the brakes as they drew dangerously close to the upcoming car's bumper.

"What's Mitch up to this morning?" Louise asked, gripping her purse like a flotation device.

"He mentioned something about surprising Russ at the office and taking him to lunch," Glory said, nearly kissing the bumper before she swung them around the car without so much as a glance in her rearview mirror.

Louise closed her eyes and pulled in a steeling breath, grateful when they entered town a few minutes later and Glory had to bring them to a crawl at the first intersection.

"Is it always this busy on a Monday morning?" she asked.

"This is nothing," said Louise. "It's still early in the season. After Memorial Day, the traffic will be impossible."

They were barely into one boutique before a trio of young women rushed Glory at a display of sundresses and asked for autographs, which Glory graciously granted while Louise slipped off to browse a shelf of sandals. But even from the other side of the store, she could still make out their conversation, the girls' high-pitched praises and Glory's warm replies as she signed a napkin, then a restaurant receipt, then finally the back of a picture of one's boyfriend. "Oh, he won't mind, don't worry," the girl had assured Glory when she'd hesitated. When the flushed fans had dashed off with their prizes, Louise made her way back to Glory's side, only to find more adoration when they reached the cash register.

After a second store—and another succession of requests—they agreed it was time for lunch.

"Where should we go?" Glory asked as they started down the sidewalk.

"I'm sure Mitch has recommended plenty of places to you." Louise could already imagine them. Grease-soaked fish shacks, with picnic tables that would surely give you splinters.

Glory's smile was downright mischievous. "He has, but I want to go somewhere you'd go. That special place you and your girlfriends meet when you want to have pie for lunch and tell secrets about your husbands."

"I don't really have that."

"Pie for lunch?" Glory grinned. "Or secrets about your husband?"

Louise flushed with apprehension. She might have admitted to having none of the three things, but confessed to only one: "A group of girlfriends."

"Well"—Glory threaded her arm through Louise's and tugged her close—"you do now."

Still an hour before the lunch rush, Petite's was barely a quarter full when Louise and Glory stepped inside. Unlike so many of the Cape's quintessential restaurants, Petite's bore a decidedly European flavor—more Parisian café than fish shack. Where most local eateries hung netting and faded buoys from their ceilings and walls, Petite's strung white Christmas lights and covered their tables with ivory tablecloths edged in lace.

"If you want someplace more traditionally coastal, we can always try—"

"Oh no," said Glory, already settled into her side of the window booth. "It's darling. Very *American in Paris*."

Louise wondered if there had ever been a time in Glory Cartwright's life when a setting didn't have a film comparison.

She recognized all three of the waitresses behind the counter—local girls who in a few weeks would find themselves having to share their tips and their beaches with college students who came for summer work. The tallest of the group hurried over to their table, already wearing the flush of excitement as she greeted them, her hands shaking visibly as she set down their settings then freed her order pad from her pocket, holding it out to Glory. "Could I have your autograph, Ms. Cartwright?" Glory obliged her with a warm smile. But even after the waitress had returned to her group with her prize and their lunch order, the girls' gazes continued to flick in Glory's direction, their cupped hands concealing whispers.

Louise took a small sip of ice water. "It must be so strange."

"What's that?"

"Everywhere you go. Being recognized. Being stared at. Don't you ever get tired of it?"

"Never."

Louise studied Glory, unconvinced. "But surely some days it must wear on you? Always having to act happy to sign an autograph, or pose for a picture?"

"I'm not acting happy—I genuinely love it," Glory said, taking up her glass. "The truth is signing autographs is one of the few times I don't have to act happy."

Louise sat back, considering the claim as Glory swirled her straw. Surely she didn't mean she was just acting happy for all other times in her life?

"Well, I couldn't do it," Louise said. "But then, I'm not an actress."

"Don't be so sure." Glory slid her a teasing look. "All women are actresses at some point. We have to be."

"Do you really think so?"

She pressed her hands on either side of her setting and leaned in, her voice dropping conspiratorially. "You can't think of one time that you pretended to feel a certain way to make someone happy?"

The memory arrived in an instant. "There was this very unflattering sweater that Russ bought me for Christmas two years ago . . . ," Louise admitted quietly, looking up to find Glory smiling sympathetically.

"And you didn't want to hurt his feelings, right?"

"Of course not."

"See? We've all earned Oscars at one point or another."

Louise laughed.

"I know I was acting long before I got to Hollywood at fifteen," Glory said.

Louise blinked at her. "They hired you at fifteen?"

"I told them I was eighteen. But trust me, if I'd waited three more years to get out of my stepfather's house, one of us wouldn't have made it out alive."

Despite Glory's attempt at humor, Louise felt a chill at the confession.

She shook open her napkin and laid it across her lap. "I read that you were discovered at a modeling agency."

"That was just for the magazines," said Glory. "Every new girl gets a story spun. It's all make-believe. Even the part that's not supposed to be." She made a small sound, something between a laugh and a sigh. "*Especially* the part that's not supposed to be."

Their waitress returned with their food. Louise held her breath while the girl set down her bowl of minestrone, the surface shuddering.

"Speaking of acting . . . ," Glory said as she freed the toothpick from her turkey club and carefully inspected the contents. "As of this morning, Operation Betty Crocker is officially underway. I promised Mitch I'd make him these crab ball things he loves so much and I haven't the foggiest idea how to even begin. Any advice?"

Louise sank her spoon into her soup. "I have some frozen I could give you," she said, feeling a short flutter of chagrin recalling how quickly she'd dismissed making some fresh for Mitch just a few days earlier. Yet now the offer seemed natural—urgent, even. "They thaw quite nicely. He'd never have to know you didn't make them."

Glory leaned forward, her eyes flashing. "You'll be like my stunt double."

"I thought they only hired those for dangerous action scenes."

"My point exactly—I nearly burned the house down yesterday roasting a chicken!"

They laughed, loud enough that the waitresses glanced over.

Glory loosened a tomato slice from her sandwich and cut it into quarters with her fork and knife. "You should know, I don't have them either."

Louise looked up, confused.

"Girlfriends," she said. "I never really had the chance to—and it wasn't as if I dared to tell anyone about what went on in my house, with my stepfather's drinking and my mother letting him take everything out on her and me."

Louise swept her spoon through her soup, letting Glory's confession sit a moment in silence.

"I'm sure it's hard to make real friends in Hollywood. To know who to trust."

"I think it's hard anywhere," said Glory, removing the top slice of bread and picking delicately at the stack of turkey slices with her fork. "Especially if you're a successful person." She hitched her chin at Louise. "You know all about that, I'm sure."

Louise shrugged. "Russ doesn't have many close friends here."

Glory lowered her fork. "I was talking about you."

"Me?"

"Well, of course you. Look at how quickly those girls behind the counter stopped their conversation when they saw you come in."

Louise waved her hand. "Don't be ridiculous—they did that because they saw *you*."

But Glory continued to study Louise's face, clearly refusing to give up her point, even as she abandoned her sandwich entirely and moved the plate to the side, still considering her as she sipped her ice water.

"You have confidence, Louise. It's quiet but it's clear. I sensed it in you from the minute I met you."

Louise felt the warmth of the compliment heat her cheeks, hiding the color as she leaned over for a spoonful of soup.

"A toast." Glory raised her glass. "To girlfriends," she said. "And a place of our own to tell secrets."

Later that night, when she and Russ had both shut off their reading lamps, plunging their bedroom into inky blue, Louise asked him: "Did you know Glory ran away from home at fifteen?"

Russ reached back to shift his pillow. "Mitch had said something about a tough childhood. That she's been through quite a lot. She's had several episodes of severe depression over the years."

"Do you suppose she takes medication?"

"It's possible. I didn't want to pry. I just said I could recommend some therapists if she ever needed to see someone."

Louise nodded, letting the room fall into a warm hush.

She stared up at the ribbons of moonlight shuddering across the ceiling, a second confession desperate to spill out.

She smiled. "Glory Cartwright thinks I'm confident."

In the dark, the bed shifted and groaned as Russ rolled over to face her. Louise could feel his gaze traveling over her profile.

"And why shouldn't she?" he asked.

Louise felt the warmth of his hand graze her thigh, and she closed her fingers over his.

Why, indeed.

# 8

## Saturday

Oh, I see, young people in love are never hungry.

*It Happened One Night*

Frankie hoists her backpack higher up on her shoulder and tents a hand above her eyes, scanning the line of ferries at the end of the pier until she finds *The Stardust Express,* its telltale teal and terracotta flags snapping furiously in the salt air.

The ship is only called *The Stardust Express* during festival week, the woman at the ticket booth told her when Frankie let slip that this was her first visit to the Cape, prompting the woman to offer other scraps of advice while they waited for Frankie's credit card to ring up. Such as, to get in line at the bar for one of the festival's signature margaritas before the boat sails because the line builds quick, and to find a strong ponytail holder against the wind if Frankie doesn't want to be untangling her hair for the next week.

By the time the men in yellow vests swing open the gate to let passengers on, Frankie has already twisted her long waves into a sturdy knot. She can't imagine not being up on deck when they sail into Harpswich harbor, not seeing her destination appear on the horizon, having thought of little else in the past four weeks after making her reservations. She touches the front pocket of her pack—a comforting stroke, as if to reassure the envelopes stored inside of their safety, like nervous pets she's brought to the vet.

Passing through the cabin on her way to the stairs, she sees the onboard bar and slows at the sign's impressive menu. As promised, the Stardust Margarita tops the list. Ten dollars with a commemorative cup, five dollars without. But as much a fan as she is of memorabilia, she can no more afford the extra five dollars than she can the space in her bag for the bulky plastic trinket.

"Can't decide, huh?"

The man behind the bar is bald with a gray beard. His polo shirt is the same teal as the ferry's flags, but the swirling sleeves of tattoos that run up both meaty arms are shades of midnight blue as he wipes shot glasses with a bar towel.

"I was told to get in line early," she confesses. Already several passengers have arrived behind her.

He slaps the towel over his shoulder. "Ah. First timer."

She smiles. "If I don't order a Stardust Margarita, do I get kicked off the boat?"

"Nah." He winks and leans in. "We just make you ride in the engine room."

He turns to make her drink—the crash of ice cubes dumped into a cocktail shaker. She thinks she sees him reach for a bottle of blue curaçao but isn't sure.

"You picked a good year," he says, slamming the top on the shaker and giving it a rough shake as he swivels back to her. "I heard Leonardo DiCaprio's making an appearance. Something about a huge party on his yacht."

"I can't imagine there's been a year that wasn't good," says Frankie.

"Now, sure. But it wasn't always that way. I remember when the festival first started. We'd be lucky to get a couple hundred, maybe a thousand people here for it."

Piqued, she leans forward. "And you've been here for all of them?"

"I've missed a few, but, yeah, I've worked most of them."

When he empties the shaker into her cup and tops it off with a splash of ginger ale, she's startled to see the glittering teal nearly identical to the color of his shirt, and remarkably close to the color she's always trying to get the bartenders at Pepper's to replicate of her and her mother's margarita.

When he reaches for a pair of speared serranos, her breath catches. She blinks as he drops them into the glass.

"Never seen hot peppers in a margarita before, right?" He chuckles as he sets the finished drink in front of her, frothy and fluorescent and fragrant with orange and spice. "Most people take 'em out. Don't like the heat."

Frankie wants to tell him that she has seen peppers in a margarita before, in fact, and that's why she's tongue-tied—but the line shuffles impatiently behind her, forcing her to leave before she can.

Up on deck, having managed to climb the metal stairs without losing a drop, she stows her backpack under one of the benches and carries her drink to the railing, watching the growing lather where the engines are churning to life, wonder growing with every sip.

*Lots of drinks are teal, right?*

But the taste—sweet, with a hint of ginger . . .

And a pepper garnish isn't exactly common, is it?

Resolve washes over her, rinsing away whatever doubt may have traveled with her on the plane ride from LA. Not even ashore yet, and already she's found proof of her mother's connection to this place.

An hour later, the ferry's thundering engine finally slows to a shudder as they near the harbor, the clear salt smell of the open ocean thicker now, heavy with the tang of tidal mud and diesel fumes. Taking her place with the rest of the debarking passengers, Frankie waits until the metal gates yawn apart and the line lunges, sending everyone clattering down the gangplank and spilling out on the wide expanse of the pier, signaling that she has, fourteen hours after leaving Los Angeles, finally landed in Harpswich, Massachusetts.

Or has she left LA?

Looking around at the crush of activity, Frankie's not so sure.

White VIP tents line the edge of the wharf, paths of red carpet and velvet ropes stretch up from boat slips, some empty, others boasting huge yachts. Several stars—many of whom she recognizes—snake through a crush of crowds, their assistants trying to clear a path to the collection of drivers who wait at the curb with their signs. Names are yelled out and cell phones dart up from the sea of heads, straining for a photo. One actress—Annie Something, Frankie can't recall her last name—slows to sign autographs and even pose for backward-running paparazzi who butter her with compliments as they click away, their calls muted by the clomping of wheeled bags trampling over the wooden pier like Clydesdales. She was expecting a grizzled cast of sunbaked sea captains and fishermen—extras from the set of *Jaws* or *The Perfect Storm*—but if not for the lack of palm trees, she could still be in Hollywood.

Surely there were locals here who didn't look as if they just came from lunch at the Chateau—or do they all leave town for the festival?

She pulls out her phone and taps in a search. According to the GPS, she's within walking distance of her hotel, but her stomach grinds with hunger, the fuel of her airport breakfast sandwich finally depleted. She scans the area and decides she could easily starve just trying to get through the crush of people lining the curb to find their car services and cabs. In the other direction, the sidewalk winds its way down a short hill toward a squat, shingled building—the words on the side hand painted: Marina Store. Surely they sell snacks?

She hoists her backpack higher and follows the narrowing pavement through the parking lot of pickups and trailers. A chain-link fence runs the length of the perimeter, dividing the lot from another stretch of slips occupied with far more modest boats than the yachts moored at the main pier. A yellow Lab sniffs along the base of the fence, his muzzle drawn back into what Frankie decides amounts to a dog smile as he—she?—digs along the ground, but he holds one of his front legs up when he trots. He's clearly hurt his paw, or maybe even sprained the whole leg. Whatever the reason, he clearly can't put weight on it and alarm fists in her stomach. Slowing to look closer, she spots a few tags hanging from a navy collar. The wounded animal has an owner. Surely someone inside the marina store must know who?

Pulling open the glass door, she slows in the entryway, grateful for the bracing splash of air-conditioning as she takes a quick survey of the crowded interior. Men—and a few women—dressed in similar uniforms of loose shorts and looser T-shirts wander around displays of nautical supplies and racks of sportswear. Some wear rubber boots, others flip-flops. The cool air smells of plastic, especially when she cuts down an aisle of inflatable rafts. A trio of boys in baggy board shorts—she guesses their age to be nine or ten—tease each other over the bikini-clad model on the front of one box. Seeing Frankie approach, the middle one elbows his partners, silencing them immediately. One more turn down an aisle of marine paint, and she emerges to find the counter, manned by an older woman with close-cropped white hair and glittery red readers whose T-shirt reads: 'WICH WAY TO HARPSWICH? The woman laughs with three sunburned men—all sporting beards and white rubber boots—buying huge coils of rigging.

Frankie smiles. So this is where they hide the locals.

Or maybe just where the locals hide? She can't envision any of the men at the counter waiting behind velvet ropes to get selfies with Nicole Kidman.

She snakes around them to a cooler and gives the sliding glass top a shove.

"Are you looking to feed some fish or yourself?" The white-haired cashier, having finished her sale, has arrived and blinks expectantly at Frankie over her reading glasses.

Frankie looks down and sees the label she was too hungry to notice on her charge over. BAIT.

She lowers the top and steps back, grinning sheepishly. "So much for looking like I know what I'm doing."

"Easy mistake." The woman offers her an absolving wink. "But if you're hungry, my neighbor makes delicious muffins," she says, pointing to a box on the other side of the register. Frankie walks over to inspect them, catching a tangy whiff of warm cranberries. "They're not as fancy as the ones they sell at the festival booths"— she arches one penciled-on eyebrow—"but then you won't have to sell a kidney to pay for one either."

Frankie laughs. "I'm fine with that." While the woman extracts two from the box, she remembers her other mission. "Would you happen to know who owns that yellow Lab in the parking lot? I think he's hurt his paw."

The woman peeks up over her reading glasses again and smiles widely, sending a web of laugh lines traveling from her eyes to her chin.

"You mean Garbo."

Frankie frowns, genuinely confused. "Is that the owner, or the dog?"

"The dog," she says, still smiling as she tilts her head to the left. "Gabe over there is the owner."

And in the blissful and impossible instant while Frankie turns to look, she convinces herself that there must be other Gabes in tiny Harpswich, Massachusetts, that her timing couldn't be so terrible that she would find herself, entirely unprepared and not even here ten minutes, thrust in front of Gabe Beckett.

But here he comes, stepping around a display of oil filters, his hair slightly shaggier and wilder than in the picture she found, but the same shade of burnished brown. His sneakers, dingy white Converse Chucks, are laceless. White paint slashes the thighs of his canvas pants, and the hem of his beige T-shirt looks as if it has doubled as a hand towel for a very long time—neither of which stops an entirely unwelcomed prickle of interest from blooming somewhere deep in her stomach.

"I heard my name."

He sets a stack of small boxes on the counter and lands his heavy gaze on her, making her glad for the cloak of her sunglasses. Her throat feels as sticky as fly paper.

She swallows. "I think there's something wrong with your dog's paw."

Gabe Beckett stares at her coolly for a long moment, and Frankie reminds herself that he has no idea who she is, that he couldn't possibly recognize her. And that even if he did, she's not the one here who should be mortified.

So why won't her heart stop pounding?

"There's nothing wrong with it," Gabe says finally, and far too calmly. "She just doesn't have a paw on that leg." He nods toward the door. "See for yourself."

Frankie steps forward and finds the dog now sitting just outside the store, scanning the parking lot, the leg held up and bent as if she's a waiter ready to have a napkin draped across it. Frankie can see where the leg tapers to a rounded stump, but her tail swings merrily as a group of men approach and stop to pat her head on their way.

She has to admit the dog does look pretty carefree.

"So what happened to her paw?" she asks.

Gabe Beckett leans back on the heels of his sneakers and shakes his head slowly. "It was a tough winter on the boat this year." His voice deepens, rough and scratchy, like he's just woken up. "Ran out of food in March. We were starving so we drew straws . . ." He chucks his chin toward the door. "Garbo lost."

Frankie blinks at him, incredulous, but he holds his grave expression.

The cashier sighs. "Oh, Gabe, for heaven's sake. The poor girl was just trying to help." She sends Frankie an apologetic smile as she bags the muffins. "This all for you, hon?"

"Yes, please." Frankie swears she can feel Gabe Beckett staring at her as she waits for the cashier to ring up her card, but she refuses to look over, especially since her face continues to flare. She can remember plenty of days when money was so tight that her mother would toss a bowl of ramen noodles with saved-up ketchup packets and call it dinner. That a man who probably has the means to buy out this whole store should joke about going hungry offends her almost as much as his belief that cooking up his dog's paw passes as humor.

Thinking she might just tell him so, she turns back after thanking the cashier, but finds the three boys in his place instead, then the sudden heat of fresh air as the front door swings open, Gabe Beckett strolling through, his three-pawed dog quickly galloping after him down the steps.

# 9

"I'm sorry, but there's no reservation under Simon."

Apparently the universe isn't done having its fun.

Fifteen minutes later, after having squeezed through several blocks of packed sidewalks, Frankie has found her quaint and charming inn—complete with grass rugs and blue gingham loveseats—waited in line for half an hour drawing in deep whiffs of lavender essential oils, and reached the front desk only to be told her reservation wasn't, and has never been, in the system.

"But I got a confirmation email . . . ," she says, ransacking her purse until she finds the folded sheet—she never travels without hard copies—and slides it toward the clerk. The young woman leans over just enough to give the page a brief scan, then offers a polite but unaffected smile.

"You were confirmed for the waiting list," she says, enunciating the last two words as if she's teaching a foreign language. "You would have received another email if a room had opened up. That's why I always tell people to steer clear of third-party reservation sites—they're straight-up thieves."

Frankie leans in. "But if a room was to open up—"

"It won't," the clerk says sharply. "They never do." She looks past Frankie. "Next in line, please."

Numb, she slips back from the counter and turns to scan the room for an empty seat, but all the clusters of overstuffed sectionals are occupied with guests. Smiling, relaxed guests.

Guests who aren't on waiting lists.

Checking her phone, she feels a fleeting tremor of relief to see it's not yet five. Her plan had been to give herself the evening to get settled and unwind, then find Louise Chandler tomorrow. But since she may not be here tomorrow, she'll move her schedule up.

The building that houses the Stardust Film Festival offices is hard to miss, its wood and steel façade sleek and startlingly modern, or maybe just appears so nestled between two classically rambling Victorians. Frankie pushes through the heavy glass doors and enters an unapologetically industrial space, high ceilinged with exposed pipes and polished concrete floors. Oversized black-and-white portraits of movie stars hang from the whitewashed brick walls, the most prominent of which is a giant print of a Glory Cartwright movie still that floats above a curved, copper-topped reception desk. Behind it, people dash in and out of glass-walled offices.

A display case rises up from the middle of the busy floor like a fountain in the center of a park. Frankie slows as she passes, heartened to find a collection of memorabilia from past festivals inside: a signed photo of Sandra Bullock introducing a screening of *While You Were Sleeping*—"Beautiful festival! Beautiful town!" swirls just above her autograph; one of the prop pennies from *Ghost* with a lobby card signed by Demi Moore; one of Holly Hunter's bonnets from *The Piano*, given after a screening at the '93 festival.

Only a few people are gathered around the reception desk, all young with the exception of a white-haired man who stands stiffly at the end with a padded folder under his arm, one of his wrists wrapped in a support brace. While the others appear to be in conversation, the man frowns impatiently. Slowing as she nears the queue, Frankie tries to catch his attention to make sure he isn't next in line.

When their eyes finally connect, a simple gesture is enough to garner a response.

"Go ahead," he says, in a voice not nearly as gruff as his expression. "I'm just waiting to drop something off."

When a woman with a pixie cut and hammered silver hoops waves her over, Frankie asks to see Louise Chandler.

"Is she expecting you?"

"I don't have an appointment," Frankie says, dread sinking in her stomach. "I was just hoping to ask her a few questions about the festival."

She steels herself for the same frosty response she got from the hotel clerk a few minutes earlier, but this young woman's face softens kindly. She reaches for her phone. "Give me a minute—let me see if I can get her assistant on the line."

She turns back to find the man with the wrist brace smiling at her. "If it makes you feel any better, they put me through the same thing, and I'm her husband."

Prickles of hope continue to rise.

"Russ Chandler." He starts to extend his wrapped hand and stops, smiling sheepishly as he offers his other instead. "Three weeks with this stupid thing and you'd think I'd remember by now."

"Frankie Simon," she says, shaking with her opposite hand to accommodate him. She gestures to the brace. "Carpal tunnel?"

He chuckles. "Nothing that impressive. Just good, old-fashioned clumsiness. You're press, I assume?"

She hesitates, the urge to lie rising, knowing it might grant her entry, but she tamps it down. What happens when they ask to see her credentials?

"No," she says. "I'm—I just had a few questions about the history of the festival. For personal reasons."

She worries her vague answer will unsettle him, but his smile remains intact.

"I'm not nearly as informed as my wife but I might be able to answer them for you," he offers. "Considering I've seen every one of these circuses come to town from the very beginning." He gestures across the lobby to the clusters of red velvet armchairs that cover a black-and-white block-print rug. "Since we're both waiting, we might as well make use of the waiting room."

Following him across the lobby, Frankie's grateful for the few moments to collect her thoughts. In the excitement of the past few weeks since she's made her plan, she's neglected to prepare an explanation of why she's here. Not that she doesn't have reasons—several, really—but the thought of putting them together in some coherent way that doesn't make her sound like a loon is something she hasn't prepared.

But when she takes a seat across from Russ Chandler and meets his crinkled blue eyes, there's a warmth in them that makes her think it's okay if she doesn't.

"It all started with a picture my mother had—"

A group of young men and women spill into the lobby, loud enough that she has to wait for them to pass before resuming. When they've settled into the chairs on the other side of the rug, a sea of dark denim, distressed leather, and smocked tops, Russ appraises them warily for several seconds before he shakes his head and sighs.

"I don't know how my wife does it," he says. "Around all these young people, all day long. It would make me feel so old." He cuts her a quick look. "No offense to present young people intended."

Frankie smiles. "None taken." She glances back to the reception desk and the wall of windowed offices beyond it, spotting a few people in their late forties, but not many. "Or maybe it has the opposite effect," she says.

"How's that?"

"On your wife. Maybe it helps her feel younger."

Russ cocks his head in a way that makes Frankie think he has never considered the possibility, studying his shoes for several seconds.

When he looks up again, he squints. "You said something about a picture?"

Frankie reaches down to her bag and withdraws the photo where she's stashed it safely in the pages of her notebook, handing it to him in its plastic sleeve. "The woman in Mitch Beckett's arms there," she says as he scans the photo. "That's my mother. And I know it sounds crazy but I never knew who my father was, and I've done the math and there's a very good chance that she met my father here, so I thought I'd . . ."

When he lifts his eyes to find hers, the rest of her explanation withers in her throat. His gaze is so exacting that she feels a flutter of worry, but his voice crackles with wonder.

"You're Maeve's daughter."

Her breath catches. "You knew my mother?"

"I—Lou and I—yes. We knew her well." He considers her a moment. "She never mentioned us?"

There's enough disappointment in his voice that Frankie almost hates to answer.

"No," she says. "And I would never have known if she didn't leave this photo."

Russ's gaze locks on her again, pooling with understanding. "She passed away?" His voice lifts at the end, but Frankie suspects it's more with surprise than question.

"She was killed in a car accident. Last year."

"Oh no." The strain that passes across his weathered face startles her—the genuineness. It reverberates in his voice, too. "I'm so sorry."

She smiles weakly. "Thank you."

"And she never told you she was here?" When Frankie shakes her head, he says, "That's . . . Well, that's surprising. I mean, working for a famous movie star seems like the kind of thing you might mention at some point."

Frankie blinks at him, feeling her face flame with surprise. "My mother worked for Mitch Beckett?"

"For Glory," he says. "His wife, Glory Cartwright. Your mother was her assistant for over a year. She lived with them in the beach house. Glory, Mitch, and Gabe."

"She—she *lived* with them?" Frankie can barely get the words out.

Russ Chandler smiles tenderly as he scans her face. "I think it's a good thing we decided to sit down. You look like you might just fall over."

Louise pulls out the rice bowl Lana has delivered to her desk and mines the empty bag. One day—twenty-three hours, to be exact—from opening night, she's not kidding herself that she'll have time to run home for dinner.

"Wasn't this supposed to come with a side of chips?"

Lana brushes her long hair over her shoulders. "Oh, I told them to skip the chips. I figured with the press event first thing tomorrow you wouldn't want to risk looking puffy on camera. All that salt."

She levels her willowy twenty-three-year-old intern with a disapproving stare. "I happen to like salt, Lana."

But the young woman's disinterested gaze is already trained on her phone screen. "By the way, I ran into Anna and she says she should have those ferry shots you wanted for the video retrospective in the next few days."

Louise sighs as she pries off the top of the container. "She does realize the event will be over in the next few days, yes?"

"Should I tell her not to bother?"

"It's fine—I'll still use them. You haven't seen those signed stills from the new Emma Thompson film, have you?"

"Not since they came in yesterday. Did you get my text that your husband is waiting out there?"

She looks up. "Russ?"

Lana pulls her lips into a smirk. "You have another?" She leans out the door and waves in the direction of the lobby.

Louise stands, feeling her pulse hasten as she waits for Russ to appear, worried the trip will have sapped him, but when he arrives, his color is remarkably bright.

"How did you get here?" she asks.

"I walked." He hands her a padded envelope. "This was on the table. I thought you might have left it by accident."

She peers in and sighs with relief. The stills.

"You didn't have to bring them. It could have waited until tomorrow."

"I'm glad I did," he says. "You won't believe who I ran into out there." He scans her face expectantly—is he smiling? "You remember Maeve? The woman who worked for Glory and Mitch?"

She stares at him. "Of course I remember her." That she would forget the woman who abandoned Glory—who abandoned them all—when she needed her most? Even now, almost thirty years later, the reminder still makes her bristle. "Why in the world are you bringing her up?"

"Her daughter is here," he says. "Her name's Frankie. She's right outside."

Her daughter? Louise comes around the desk and walks quickly to the wall of glass that looks out onto the lobby, prickles of alarm skittering across her scalp as she scans the crowd. "Where?" she asks, even though she doesn't need direction. There's no question in her mind the woman sitting in the waiting area with the thick, messy twist of auburn hair is Maeve's daughter.

She turns back to Russ. "Don't tell me Maeve sent her here to get some kind of . . ."

The thinning of his smile stops her.

"Maeve's dead, Lou. She was killed in a car accident."

The burn of shame scalds the back of her neck. An image of Maeve running barefoot up the stairs from the dunes flashes, sympathy and remorse briefly burying Louise's frustration. She couldn't have been more than fifty-five.

The edge of suspicion in her voice softens. "Did her daughter come here to tell us?"

He shakes his head. "That's just it. Maeve never mentioned us to her."

There's a flutter of disappointment in the news, but it cools quickly. Really, how can Louise be surprised?

"Of course she wouldn't mention us," she says, hearing the edge return to her voice. "I'm sure she never forgave herself for leaving Glory like that. After everything Glory had done for her." She considers the woman again. "So why *is* she here?"

"Because Maeve left a picture of her and Mitch and . . . Well, Frankie thinks Mitch could be her father."

"She what?"

He shrugs. "Apparently Maeve never told her who her father was."

"And I assume you explained to her that wasn't possible."

"There wasn't really time but . . ." He scratches his temple. "I did tell her she could stay with us."

Louise leans back, the shock of his offer as sharp as a sting. Has he forgotten that he currently inhabits their guest room?

"There was some kind of mix-up with her reservation, Lou. She wasn't fishing, if that's what you're thinking; I offered and she flatly refused, but we both know she won't find a room between here and Boston this week. I figure she can have Gabe's old room."

"You mean my office."

"But there's the pullout in there," he says. "And it's not like you'll need to use it during the festival."

It's true, of course. She'll be lucky to see the inside of her own bedroom in daylight for the next week. But it chafes her that he's made all these decisions, extended invitations without even asking her.

But how can she say no? He's right—the woman won't have any luck finding a room free now.

She studies Maeve's daughter another moment through the glass. "Do I at least get to meet her?"

"Of course. I told her I'd check in with you first. I didn't want to spring her on you, in case you were busy."

"Of course I'm busy, Russ. The festival starts tomorrow."

He waves his hands, warding off her complaint. "You know what I mean."

Did she? Lately she isn't sure.

"I thought I'd get her settled at the house," he says as he starts for the door. "Maybe pick us all up something for dinner. Unless . . ." His voice trails off as his gaze catches on her desk and the rice bowl.

Louise drifts back to the glass, finding the woman—Frankie—again.

"She's really very lovely, Lou."

They'd certainly thought the same of Maeve, hadn't they?

She rolls her lips together, not sure what he wants her to say in the strained silence.

Her husband may no longer feel the sting of betrayal, or remember that fraught time after Maeve settled into their lives, burrowed in deep, only to steal away in the middle of the night when Glory needed her most, but Louise certainly does.

Just as she remembers a time earlier, years before Maeve blew into their world and their hearts, when it was just the four of them.

And then some days, just two.

# 10

1980
April

"We could still turn around, Lou," Russ said when they were less than a mile from Mitch and Glory's cottage. "Go home and call. Tell them something's come up and we can't make it tonight."

"It's okay." Louise turned from the open window, where she'd been using the air to keep her tearing eyes dry and offered him a stoic smile. "I want to go. It will be good to be around friends." And with only a few months left before Glory and Mitch were due to return to Hollywood, she didn't want to squander a chance to spend time with Glory. They'd grown close. Louise was going to miss her terribly.

Russ reached for her hand where she was worrying the pleats of her plaid skirt and pressed his palm over her fingers to still them. She knew why he worried. The week before, celebrating Mitch's birthday at a restaurant in Truro, the discussion had turned to children, then been cut short. Even in the low light of the restaurant, Louise had seen the wash of frustration pass over Mitch's face, dimming his festive smile. Driving home, Russ had explained that Mitch had confided in him that he wasn't able to get Glory pregnant and that they'd been discussing adoption. The reminder briefly softened the sharp edges of her grief, that there was comfort in their shared struggles. Louise was just grateful they hadn't shared the news of her pregnancy. After four miscarriages, she had learned to keep secrets.

Parked, Russ opened the trunk and watched Louise lift out the covered Bundt cake. He cast a look at the pan, then raised his eyes to meet hers, his lips wrinkling with a smile that was both chastising and amused. "They've been here almost a year. You're going to have to stop this charade and let her cook for herself eventually, you know."

"Says who?" But mounting the sand-dusted steps to the house, she glanced over to find her husband studying her, one side of his lips rising with intrigue. "What?"

"Nothing," he said. "It's just that I never thought I'd see the day when you'd be doing something to make life good for Mitch Beckett."

She sniffed. "Who says I'm doing this for him?"

Glory met them at the door in a creamy ruffled blouse and purple satin pants, her teased hair pulled up on one side with a gold comb, looking more like she was leaving for a night at the disco than hosting friends for fried clams and beer.

"Lou must have forgotten to tell me this was a black-tie affair," Russ teased as he stepped into the foyer. Louise slowed, glancing around, afraid of being seen by Mitch walking in with dessert.

"Don't worry—he's out on the deck," Glory whispered conspiratorially, her eyes big as she took the covered pan from Louise's hands and carefully peeled back a corner of foil. "Mmm . . . So what amazing dessert did I bake today?"

"Apple swirl cake."

Glory giggled. "God, I've gotten good, haven't I?"

"Let's hope it tastes as good as it looks."

"Speaking of good taste"—Glory steered them forward—"I need your opinion on something . . ."

The home's first floor was an open floor plan, combining kitchen and living space. At the far end, a wall of glass offered a view of a high deck that overlooked the private beach. It was by far the home's most striking feature. The rest of the house possessed all the trademark trimmings of a modest Cape beach cottage—whitewashed wood walls; grass rugs under simple, rustic furnishings accented with shell motifs. If it caused Glory Cartwright deep pain to live in such a spare and rustic décor after the sprawling, high-gloss luxury of her Hollywood Hills estate, she cloaked it well.

"Perfect timing!" Mitch flung open the deck slider and stepped inside, balancing a tray of clam strips and barefoot despite it still being a crisp spring day. While Glory's physical transformation from Hollywood starlet to pragmatic New Englander was slow-going after almost a year here, Mitch's return to beach-bum casual was nearly complete. His dark hair, no longer combed back and gleaming, swirled wildly around his scalp; the chiseled jawline that had graced hundreds of magazine covers was shrouded beneath a curtain of stubble. A slight paunch already strained the waist of his T-shirt, no doubt thanks in part to her secret dessert donations. If not for the memory of his rant on his disdain for method acting, Louise might have accused her husband's oldest friend of throwing himself into this new role.

"Just finished a batch," Mitch said, holding up a pair of tongs and clacking them for dramatic effect. He set the plate down on the breakfast bar. "Careful, they're hot."

Louise leaned in, the thick breaded forms so fresh she could still hear the fry oil crackling when she bit carefully into the tender meat. Despite Mitch's many faults, there was no question he cooked a perfect clam strip.

Russ nodded approvingly as he bit down. "Your dad would be proud."

"Fifteen years gone and I can still remember how to make a Beckett batter by heart," Mitch said, shooting a wink in Glory's direction as he set down the plate. "Told you all you health food nuts out there couldn't turn a fisherman's kid soft . . ." He patted his rounding stomach as he tugged Glory against him and buried his whiskered face into her neck. "At least, not where it counts, right, baby?"

Glory gave him a shove. "Stop, you'll get grease all over my shirt."

"Who told you to wear something so fancy? What happened to that jumper I bought you?"

Russ extended the plate of strips to Glory, but she waved them away.

"Thank you, but I already had one," she said.

"She had *one*," Mitch repeated, shooting a disapproving smirk in Russ's direction as he crossed to the fridge. "Get you a beer?"

"Please."

"I'm trying to love them," Glory insisted. "I really am."

Louise toured the edge of the room, slowing at a porthole mirror in the dining alcove. "That's new."

"A housewarming gift from that man at the marina," Glory said, joining her.

"His name's Curtis, Glow," Mitch called over. *"Curtis."*

Louise smiled as she scanned the curved, gilded edges of the enormous mirror. That certainly looked like something the harbor master would pick out.

"He also tried to gift us a wagon-wheel coffee table that was absolutely covered in barnacles," Glory said. "Now I'm all for atmosphere and setting a scene, but that's just creepy. I mean, what if something crawled out of one of those things in the middle of a party?"

"Crawled out—like what? A dancing girl?" Mitch plucked off a pair of cans from their plastic rings and handed one to Russ. "They're dead, Glow."

"I don't care," she said hotly. "It still gives me the creeps."

The mirror wasn't the only new addition to the room. "Where did that come from?" Louise asked, pointing at the mantel, where a black magician's hat sat proudly in the center.

"Isn't it fabulous?" Glory joined Louise at the fireplace and lovingly stroked the curve of the hat's velvet rim. "I wore it in our film *Moonlight Magic*. My agent, Dotty, saw it at a memorabilia auction and knew I'd get a kick out of it."

"Really goes with the décor, don't you think?" Mitch said, casting an arched brow at Russ.

Glory made a face. "It's just one little piece, Grumpy."

Mitch snorted. "I'd sooner take my chances with the barnacles."

"It smells just like the wardrobe building at MGM." Glory leaned close. "When I get homesick, I just close my eyes and take a great big whiff."

Russ came over and leaned in. "Smells just like our old locker room at Harpswich High."

Mitch cackled, snapping open his beer.

"Men," chided Glory. "Not an ounce of heart in the lot of you. No wonder we live longer."

Louise laughed into her iced tea.

"Apparently they were selling my old cowboy hat from *Shadowlands,* too," Mitch added, sauntering over to his plate of strips, his beer held against his chest.

"How do you know that?" Glory asked.

"Dotty told me when she called."

"Dotty called?" Glory spun around, her hands falling from the mantel. "When?"

Mitch bent a clam strip into his mouth and chased it with a swig of beer. "Yesterday."

"Why didn't you tell me? What did she say?"

"Something about wanting us for that new space picture. I told her I don't look good in moon boots."

"Very funny." Glory bit her lip, looking genuinely concerned. "If we put her off much longer, she'll stop calling."

"Promise?" Mitch's sunburned face broke into a huge grin, but Glory's lips remained a tight line.

Louise exchanged a quick look with Russ over the top of her glass.

"Hey"—Mitch pointed his beer at the wall—"I thought you were going to ask Lou's opinion on the colors."

A not-so-subtle change in subject, but it seemed to do the trick. Glory whirled back to Louise. "Oh, right! So what do you think?"

Louise scanned the half-dozen streaks of soft blues and creams, confused. "I thought you said they wouldn't let you paint."

"Not for a year lease they wouldn't," Glory said. "But now that we're staying on one more . . ."

Louise blinked, first at Glory, then over at Russ, who looked equally surprised. Excitement stirred. They were staying?

"Wait!" Glory pointed to Russ's beer. "Before you open that." She looked at Mitch, who clapped a hand over his forehead.

"Oh, shit, right," he said, returning to the fridge to pull out a bottle of champagne.

Glory hurried to the kitchen to help. "I can stomach that awful beer well enough most days, but this calls for a proper toast." She set out four flutes and stood back while Mitch freed the cork with a startling pop, sending up a chimney of champagne smoke. "Thank God he hasn't forgotten everything," she said.

Louise watched Mitch tip the bottle, the sizzle of the bubbles filling the expectant quiet.

"Now you both know we've been wanting to start a family," Mitch said, handing Russ and Louise a glass. Louise took hers, alarm tracing her spine. "We didn't just come here for a break. Glow and I thought it might be easier . . . all the way over here, you know. Out of the spotlight . . ." He stopped to glance at Glory. "Then yesterday, we get this call . . ."

"A baby boy outside of Boston." Glory was practically breathless. "Not quite a year old."

Louise looked over to find Russ watching her, concern pooling in his eyes.

"It's sudden, I know," Mitch said. "But honestly, it just makes sense. What better time than now, right? Glow can focus on being a mother—"

"Because I know as soon as we get back to LA, I'll be pulled in a thousand directions," Glory said, nodding effusively.

"So we'll stay another year, give him a little more time in the place he was born . . ."

He. Louise took a generous sip of champagne, grateful at how quickly the bubbles drowned her envy. This was news to be celebrated, after all. Even if the timing seemed particularly cruel. But how was Glory to know the loss she and Russ had suffered the day before?

Russ lowered his glass. "Then it's confirmed?"

"As much as it can be." Glory looked over at her husband. "Mitch says we shouldn't get our hopes up. That it's better not to be disappointed in case it doesn't work out."

"That's good advice," Louise said softly, feeling Russ's worried gaze seeking hers across the room as she sipped her champagne, hiding her fading smile behind her glass.

She managed to get through dinner, through coffee, and even through most of the ride home, until they'd left the rutted dirt turns of side roads for the pavement of the main road, before she let herself cry.

Russ searched across the seat for her hand. "Lou . . ."

She took a tissue from her purse and dabbed her nose, her eyes. "Did you know?"

"Of course not," he said. "I never would have let him make such a big deal like that."

"Oh, Russ, why shouldn't they celebrate? They have every reason to be happy."

"That's not what I meant."

He glanced over at her, his strained expression blank for only a moment, then understanding washed his features smooth.

Louise sat back, staring at the sweep of the headlights across the road. She spread her fingers out in her lap, her palms suddenly sticky with sweat.

Her voice was damp, thinned from tears. "I want the X-ray, Russ."

She watched his grip on the steering wheel tighten, his knuckles whitening.

She'd learned of the procedure in a magazine and pressed Russ for more information—he'd balked.

She turned to the window and rolled it all the way down, wishing she hadn't agreed to that second glass of champagne. A dull ache was growing at her temples. The night air was tinged with frost; she closed her eyes and let it needle her damp skin, strangely grateful for the sting. Her mother, one of seven children. Louise, one of five. The only one still to bear grandchildren.

"I can't keep doing this," she whispered. "I want to know. I need to know."

He reached across the seat and pressed his palm over her thigh, the heat of his hand like a switch, sending another wave of tears, faster this time, spilling too fast to be smeared with fingertips. Louise didn't even try. She just laid her fingers over his and kneaded them hungrily.

"All right," he said.

But his voice was strained, and she couldn't decide if it was with resolve or regret.

# 11

"If you need more blankets, Lou keeps some extras in the hall closet," Russ tells Frankie as he sets the stack of linens on the desk and moves to the couch. "Here, let me help you get this open."

He's already breathing heavily with the exertion of drawing down the linens from the closet; too heavily, Frankie thinks fearfully—never mind he has that brace on his wrist—and she gently steps in front of him before he can continue.

"I can make it myself later."

"Are you sure? It gets stuck halfway sometimes."

"I slept on a pullout for years when I was a kid. It was a total beast, with these big fat springs that sounded like a garbage truck compressing trash whenever I rolled over. But it was the only place we had to sit during the day so I got really good at putting it together. My mom used to time me. It was our little game."

He smiles at the last part, and she feels a swell of affection, and surprise. That she should be here, a place she's never been, talking about her mother to someone she doesn't know, but who knew her mother. And at a time before Frankie ever did. The symmetry of it is dizzying.

There's a small dresser near the desk; Russ points to it. "Lou uses that for papers and such but she always keeps the bottom drawer empty. You're welcome to put your things in it."

Frankie smiles reflexively, reminded of all the offers of drawers she's been given over the years. "Thank you," she says, even though she worries she could no more fill this one than any of the others before it. Just a few days. It's not nearly enough time.

*But it is a lovely house,* she thought as she followed Russ Chandler through it on their tour. It even smells the way she imagined a house here might smell. Warm and woodsy, pleasantly musty, and that constant tang of sea salt on every breeze, different than the ocean air in LA. Heavier, somehow—riper. And Russ Chandler, who himself is what she imagined a local man here might look like. Despite his cautious gait, there's still a ruggedness to him—and those sky-blue eyes that remind her of an older Paul Newman.

Glancing around the warmly lit room, seeing the tidy piles of papers, the computer screen, the printer, she feels a pang of guilt.

"Are you sure it's okay for me to stay here? I don't want to put anyone out . . ."

"You're not. Don't worry." Russ smiles. "Lou won't need the room this week. I'll be lucky to see her at all." Frankie watches his smile dim briefly before he resurrects it. He rubs at the back of his neck, and it occurs to her for the first time that he's wearing a collared shirt, the kind men wear to work, with ties. His belted khakis and shoes are businesslike, too. Not exactly the uniform of the leisurely retired man.

Outside in the hallway, she slows at a row of framed photographs.

"Is this you and your wife?"

He smiles wistfully. "On our wedding day."

"You look happy."

"We were," he says, then blinks. "We *are*." There's a force to the latter statement, as if she's misunderstood something.

The next picture is of Russ and Louise with Mitch Beckett and Glory Cartwright, posed on the porch.

"That was taken right after they moved here in '79," he explains.

"She looks like she's going to some big awards gala."

"Glory always looked that way. Ten years here and she never dressed the part," he says, though there's nothing harsh in the comment, or in his wistful smile as he digs in his pockets. "I never complained. Only so long a person can look at bleached-out grays and bone whites his whole life."

Frankie moves to the last picture—another group photo, this one on a beach—and her gaze trains on Mitch Beckett, trying as she did when she'd watched his films to find hints of herself in his features. "The picture I have—he doesn't look quite so . . ."

"Fit?" Russ chuckles. "He got heavy living back here. The magazines weren't nice. The irony is that after Glory died, he lost it all in a matter of months. But what did it matter then? All the tabloids could say was he was wasting away with grief. Which, of course, he was." The digging in his pockets slows. He glances up at her, squinting as if he's seen a streak of lightning and now waits for the inevitable clap of thunder. "You should know . . . Mitch couldn't have children."

Disappointment lands like a stone; Frankie's startled by the weight of it. And yet, just as quickly, resignation falls on top of it.

She looks back at the photograph, studying Mitch Beckett freshly.

"In my heart, I think I already knew that," she says quietly. "When I found out their son was adopted. A part of me wondered."

"But it's understandable you might still hope."

Hope. That word again. But this time the flutter of possibility turns to a dull ache.

If not Mitch Beckett, then who? The math remains unchanged; there is still a good chance her mother met her father here.

"I'll let you get settled then." Russ claps his hands together. "If you get hungry, there's food in the fridge. Wine, too, if you like." He moves to go, then hesitates a moment, appraising her with what seems oddly like wonder. "You know I almost didn't bring those pictures in to Lou today. Funny how the universe works, isn't it?"

If he only knew, Frankie thinks, recalling her earlier encounter with Gabe Beckett. Is it always like this living in a small town, running into neighbors everywhere you go? That could be convenient or exhausting—depending on the neighbor, she supposes.

His smile thins, his blue eyes softening. "I really am sorry about your mother, Frankie. Maeve was a great help to Glory when she was here. We were all very fond of her."

Her eyes fill with gratitude, the need to thank him again pressing, but he's already turned away and headed down the hallway.

# 12

## Sunday

I have a house, and family, and things like that . . . not like
I'm complaining or anything, because I have a cat, I have an
apartment, sole possession of the remote control. That's very
important. It's just, I never met anyone I could laugh with.

*While You Were Sleeping*

In Frankie's dreams, her mother is always waiting for her at the store.
She is running desperately late, missing buses or slowed in some horrendous pedestrian traffic on Hollywood Boulevard, or stuck waiting
for a scene to finish filming before she can cross the street. She'll
burst through the door, usually in tears, certain she's missed her, and
there Maeve will be, her thick red hair in a loose nest on top of her
head, barely tethered with a pair of chopsticks or pencils, calmly selling something to a rapt customer, or maybe just admiring a mannequin she's recently dressed. And Frankie won't remember that she's
gone until the very end, until she wakes, confused for a terrible instant. Then she loses her all over again.

Awake now, she squints against the blast of light. Too enamored
with the fresh air coming through the screens the night before, she
left the blinds up. Now daybreak, white and hot and speckled with
dust, fills the bedroom, illuminating the morning's new truths
with it.

Her entire life, it was just the two of them. Men had come in and out, sure, but at their core, they were a family of two, never landing anywhere too long, never belonging to anyone but each other.

And now Frankie understands there was a community here who cared for her mother, who sheltered her, considered her a friend, a sister. Family. And with this knowledge come more questions, equally baffling: Why had her mother never shared this remarkable season of her past, if not because she wanted to protect the identity of Frankie's father?

She sits up and lets the covers drop to her waist, her bared skin prickling. Her phone says seven fifteen—four fifteen, West Coast time. Outside, a fine mist hovers over everything, causing the breeze that billows the sheers to be startlingly cool and thick with the tang of tidal mud and wet grass. There's a noise, a rhythmic knocking. Pulling the sheets around herself again, she leans over to the window and looks down into the sloping backyard to see tools strewn around the dew-soaked lawn, the sound of hammering coming from somewhere on the deck, but the edge of the roof hides the source.

Hopeful that the morning chill won't linger, she tugs on a pair of cutoff jean shorts and a gauzy poet's shirt, slips into her sandals, and emerges to find the house quiet. Like her room, the downstairs is bright with morning and a little raw. She holds herself as she tours the first floor in search of company, rubbing her arms as she scans the rooms. Nearing the kitchen, she hears the faint purr of running water and finds Louise Chandler at the sink, her back turned. She's dressed sharply in a long silk skirt and matching tunic, her gray hair pulled back with a silver clasp.

Not wanting to startle her, Frankie knocks lightly on the doorjamb.

Louise glances over her shoulder, her expression strained for a moment before the tight line of her mouth softens into a small smile, and Frankie feels a prickle of regret. Was it a mistake to disturb her? Their introduction the night before had been brief, Russ's wife seeming somewhat distracted throughout it, which Frankie had understood, considering the late hour of her return. But now, despite Russ's assurances that Frankie's staying here isn't a problem, worry flickers. After a night's sleep, does Louise regret their generosity?

Or maybe the morning's light has brought with it other misgivings; maybe Frankie's reason for coming, thinking Mitch Beckett could have been her father, has made Louise suspicious . . .

"Good morning." Louise wipes her hands briskly on a dish towel. "I thought you'd be tired after all your travel yesterday—I didn't want to wake you." As if on cue, the hammering resumes, closer now. Louise's gaze narrows pointedly on the sliders. "I suppose I shouldn't have worried."

Frankie smiles as she eyes a short breakfast table, wanting to take one of the two chairs that flank it but not sure if she should. A stack of papers sits on the counter under a purse. Louise appears to be getting ready to leave.

"I can't thank you enough for letting me stay here, Mrs. Chandler."

"Louise. Please." She tips a bag of coffee beans into a grinder, and Frankie decides the commitment of making coffee is permission enough to sit.

While the scream of the grinder fills the quiet, she scans the view of the backyard, admiring the flower beds she can see through the ribbons of fog.

"The mist usually burns off before noon," Louise says. "In case you're wondering." She knocks the fresh grounds into the basket, the rich, nutty smell drifting close. "There're some blueberry scones if you're hungry."

"I thought I'd walk into town, maybe find a café or something for breakfast."

"Chowder's is good if you want just basic diner food. Buttercup's makes the most decadent crab Benedict but you might be a good two hours waiting for a table now . . ."

As Louise continues to give her recommendations, Frankie's

trepidation thins. She seems looser now, warmer. Frankie had simply startled her. She scolds herself silently; she's being too sensitive.

"Russ tells me you've never been to the Cape before," Louise says, rinsing out the carafe.

"Maybe he also told you I had this wild idea that Mitch Beckett was my father."

Louise nods. "He mentioned that, yes." Her lips thin, as if she's holding something back.

"I can't help thinking that there's still a good chance my mother met my father here in Harpswich."

"Of course it's possible."

"I want to try to find him . . . and I was hoping you could help me?"

Louise glances over, alarm straining her features. "Me?"

"Russ said you spent a great deal of time with her. Maybe you remember a boyfriend, or even someone she may have gone out with?"

Louise walks the filled carafe back down the counter, hesitating a moment before she tips it into the coffee maker.

"There was someone," she says. "But your mother broke things off." Frankie realizes she must be staring at Louise with such expectant intensity, because when she meets her gaze, Louise adds quickly, "I never met him. I just remember Glory talking about it. Something about him being older, I think . . ." She glances over at Frankie again. "It was a long time ago. I could be mistaken."

"I'm grateful for anything you or your husband can remember." She glances around the kitchen. "Speaking of Russ, is he up yet?"

Louise settles the carafe on the warmer and clicks the brew to begin. "He's probably outside with Gabe, supervising. As if Gabe needs it."

Frankie blinks. "Did you say . . . ?"

The whoosh of the slider swallows the rest of her question—a gust of cool air, and then he's stepping through the open glass, a dented to-go mug in one hand.

"Speak of the devil." Louise gestures to his mug. "It's nearly done."

Barely inside, Gabe Beckett stops, his gaze locking on Frankie, his dark eyes narrowing with recognition.

"I know you."

Heat soaks her throat.

Louise looks quizzically between them. "You've met?"

"Not . . . officially," Frankie says.

"Gabe." He reaches over, his hand extended—Frankie stares at the smears of paint that cross his palm. "Don't worry, it's dry."

As if getting stained with wet paint is what worries her about this exchange?

"Frankie Simon." She slides her hand into his and scans his face expectantly while the hard heat of his fingers sizzles up her arm, sure that he'll remember her name from their unfortunate email exchange, but there's no spark of recognition.

She tugs her hand free quickly, like pulling out a plug in a lightning storm to avoid a power surge.

"Gabe, you might remember Frankie's mother, Maeve," Louise says, drawing down a travel mug from the cabinet. "She lived with you all for a year. You were eight, maybe nine . . . ?"

A flicker of something charges across his face, but his eyes remain even on hers.

"Doesn't ring a bell."

Disappointment sinks like a stone; Frankie dips her gaze to the slider.

Gabe drags his arm across his forehead, brushing sweat into his hair. "So you must be here to take selfies with the stars." There's a not-so-faint edge of challenge to his voice. Or maybe judgment. She scans his hard gaze, trying to decide which, but Louise answers for her.

"Frankie's from Hollywood, Gabe. I'm sure she doesn't need to come all the way out here to see movie stars." She turns to Frankie. "But I can set aside a pass for you if you want to come by the office this morning. It will get you into some of the exclusive premieres and after-parties."

"And don't forget the all-you-can-stomach schmooze bars," Gabe says sourly as he throws open the slider and steps through, tipping his head toward the counter. "I'll come back for the coffee."

Louise casts a weary look at the deck door after he's closed it. "You'll have to forgive Gabe. He always gets a little grouchy this time of year. The festival isn't exactly his favorite thing."

Recalling his unfortunate attempt at a joke at the marina, Frankie doesn't even want to imagine what is.

As Louise promised, the mist has already started to thin when Frankie steps out onto the porch an hour later. She scans the driveway, seeing Gabe Beckett standing at the back of his truck, using his lowered tailgate as a work surface. The question of whether she can possibly avoid him runs through her thoughts as she scans the stretch of lawn and driveway that separates her from the road to town. There's a tidy stone path, clearly the recommended choice, but it snakes dangerously close to the truck. She exits off the far side of the porch instead, narrowly avoiding a row of marigolds to allow herself the widest possible berth past him.

She's nearly home free when she hears: "You could have just mailed them, you know. Would have been a hell of a lot cheaper."

She slows her march, feeling the burn of discovery flare across her scalp.

So he had made the connection, the rat.

She swings around to face him, her heart hammering with indignation as she waits for him to look up from his work.

"If you knew who I was that whole time, why didn't you say something?"

"I could ask you the same thing about the marina yesterday." He stretches a measuring tape down the length of the wood, then lets it snap back into its case.

"I guess your poor taste in jokes left me speechless." She folds her arms. "So was that just to spite me back there?"

Gabe frowns at her. "Was what?"

"You don't remember my mother—or were you just saying that?"

He resumes his measuring and shrugs. "I might, I don't know. I'd have to think about it."

"Like you thought about my offer for the letters?"

He glances up at her, his eyes flashing contritely. "Look, I get a lot of people trying to contact me and claiming all kinds of crazy shit—especially this time of year."

"So you just uniformly insult every stranger who reaches out to you?"

"Trust me. I've dealt with plenty of you Hollywood types and I know how you—"

"You don't know anything about me."

He leans back. "I know you wear sunglasses inside."

She squints at him, dumbfounded by his reasoning. "So you automatically assume I'm a Hollywood type?"

"You were savvy enough to secure yourself some nice rock star housing, that's for sure," he says, gesturing to the second floor with his tape measure. "Not to mention scoring an all-access pass."

Her cheeks flame. Is he honestly accusing her of working some kind of scam?

"For your information," she says tightly, "I had a reservation at a hotel in town"—which is true, dammit. So what if the reservation was a farce? He didn't have to know, the smug creep—"but Russ insisted I stay here. And as for the pass, you were standing right there when Louise offered it to me out of the blue."

Gabe shoves the length of wood back into the bed. "Out of the blue. Sure."

She spots the tape measure beside him, thinking how good it would feel to chuck it at his head. Hard.

"What the hell is your problem?" she says.

"Just looking out for people I care about."

"Are you suggesting I came here to upset something?"

"I already know why you came here."

"No, you don't." The sun shifts, clearing the top of the roofline and blinding her; she steps to the side, finding shade again. "I didn't come here to bring you the letters. I have other reasons for being here."

"Oh, right . . ." Gabe flicks his gaze up at her again. "You thought we might be related."

He's smirking; she's sure of it.

"You could have just told me your father couldn't have kids."

His eyes narrow. "I didn't see how it was any of your business."

Frankie feels a tremor of remorse and lowers her gaze, unable to argue his point.

A cavalry of cyclists in colorful jerseys sail by, the collective buzzing of wheels piercing their heated silence.

Gabe throws up the tailgate and claps his hands clean. "So you think my jokes are in bad taste, huh?"

"I think someone with your resources shouldn't make light of people going hungry."

He cocks his head, one eyebrow rising. "Now who's making assumptions?"

*Whatever that means,* Frankie thinks sourly, feeling a tickle on her big toe. She frees one foot from her sandal and rubs off damp blades of cut grass.

"I've done the math," she says. "There's a very good chance my mother met my father here. Which means there's a chance he's still here."

"Doubt it." Gabe slides on a pair of sunglasses that look very much like the cheap ones they give out after LASIK surgery. There are fingerprints of white paint on the frames. "Tourist towns are like carnivals. People come and go with the seasons. Chances are any guy your mother met didn't stick around past the summer."

She pushes out an exasperated breath. "Are you this pessimistic about everything?"

"I prefer the term 'realist.'" He tosses his tape measure through the driver-side window. "I'm just telling you how it is around here."

"I'm aware of how tourist towns work. It's not a complicated concept."

He throws open the driver-side door—easily five shades darker blue than the rest of the pickup—climbs in, and turns on the ignition, the engine grinding loudly to life. The front bumper rattles violently. Frankie takes several steps back, genuinely afraid the truck might explode.

As he sends the pickup lurching forward, Gabe leans out the window. "Good luck with it all."

Frankie glares at the back of the truck as it swings out of the driveway.

Schmuck.

She doesn't need luck.

And certainly not from him.

# 13

Louise is drawing down a travel mug from the cabinet when Russ enters through the slider.

"I thought I missed you."

"Just on my way now," she says.

"Gabe's going to have to come back with some longer pieces." He glances toward the stairs. "Is Frankie up?"

"She just left. You didn't see her?"

"She must have gone out the front." He scans the empty counter. "She didn't want breakfast?"

"She wanted to get something in town." Louise can hear the edge of impatience in her voice even before she sees Russ's gaze slant with curiosity, and she feels a pang of regret. She knows she should be grateful to find him so upbeat this morning—hasn't she spent the last three months wishing for one cheerful morning?—but all she feels is hurt: that she's been trying to stir him out of his sullen moods for weeks, and Frankie's put a smile on his face after just one day.

She moves to the carafe and pours coffee into her mug.

Russ comes beside her at the counter, his voice deepens purposefully. "There's really quite a bit we have to tell her, Lou."

She slides him a dubious look as she reaches into the fridge for the cream. Isn't he being a bit dramatic?

"I'm not sure there's so much," she says, her hand inexplicably shaky as she tips cream into her coffee, then presses the top on her mug harder than necessary. "But if you think so, then share away."

She feels him studying her as she gathers her purse and keys, knowing he's regarding her in that detached way he used to study his patients, trying to diagnose them before they could reveal their symptoms. She feels like something in a jar and it vexes her.

"Lou, what's the matter?"

She sets down her mug and faces him with her arms folded. "Exactly what should we tell this young woman, Russ? That her mother threaded herself into our lives, made us trust her, and then disappeared when Glory needed her most?"

His lips straighten into a pale line.

"Or maybe," she continues, "that even after Glory died and it was all over the news, Maeve still didn't reach out to all of us to offer her sympathies? *Or*"—her heart thumps hard behind her crossed arms—"we could tell her the curious timing that Glory's memorabilia collection disappeared around the same time her mother did?"

"Maeve wasn't a thief, Lou." His eyes pleat, his features tightening with hurt. "She was good to that family—to all of us. And now that we know why she left, I think we can be a little more forgiving, don't you?"

She straightens. "You think she left because she was pregnant?"

"It certainly seems more likely than she just abandoned us all to be deliberately cruel. If anything, I would think you'd be relieved."

She shoves her keys into her purse. "Stop talking like you weren't there, too, Russ." But, he had been equally judicious on the subject even then in the wake of Maeve's disappearance, careful to never blame Maeve, to never speak ill of her. He even refused to entertain the possibility that she had stolen some of Glory's memorabilia collection.

"Lou, I know you blame her, but it's not as if things weren't hard in that house before Maeve left it—or before she got there, for that matter."

She swings her purse higher on her shoulder and picks up her mug. "I'm terribly late."

He follows her out onto the porch. "Maybe tonight we could have dinner, the three of us. Maybe even ask Gabe—"

"I can't possibly tonight," she says. "It's opening ceremonies."

Disappointment washes over his features. The unflappable smile finally sinks. "Of course," he says. "Maybe tomorrow night, then."

But even after she's pulled onto the road, Louise still feels the prickles of vexation, unsure if it's being behind schedule, or because she knows Russ's point is a fair one. That long before Maeve Simon ever arrived in Harpswich, there were dark days for Glory.

# 14

1984
September

The familiar patchwork of vehicles already filled the cottage's gravel circle when Russ pulled the station wagon in, many of which had likely been on the beach since morning. Clambakes were serious commitments. An hour to dig the pit in the sand and collect fresh rockweed to lay over the food, two to three to get the fire strong enough to heat the rocks, then another hour or two to cook. Nearly five years back in Harpswich, and Mitch Beckett was now, without question, the reigning clambake king.

"I can't believe he's squeezing one more out of the season," Russ said.

Louise arched a brow. "I can't believe you think this is the last."

The breeze was warm for late September and carried with it the briny scent of baking clams. With Labor Day weeks behind them, and the crispness of fall in full view, everyone who'd come to celebrate had brought layers to fend against temperatures that didn't drop but rather plunged this late in the season. Louise knew the beach would grow cold when the sun went down, despite the crackle and pop of the pit fire that steamed in the sand. Eventually someone would start a bonfire, the flames growing robust just in time for the last streaks of daylight to fade completely, allowing Mitch and his guests to languish well until midnight if they wanted—which they always did, growing unbearably sunbaked and sloppy, and always making a willing audience for Glory. Despite her enduring distaste for seafood, she never missed a bake.

Mitch appeared before Louise had a chance to take out her contribution from the trunk—a pan of still-warm brownies—but she unpacked it anyway. After five years of being Glory's stand-in baker, she didn't bother to hide her deliveries anymore.

He gripped a beer in one hand. Louise wondered how many had come before it.

"Kenny's back from his charter," Mitch said, slinging an arm over Russ's shoulder. "Come see the tuna he caught."

Louise turned toward to the house. "I'll take these up—they need to be cut."

"Tell Glow to come down, will you?" Mitch said, already steering Russ down to the dunes.

Louise frowned in the direction of the cottage. Glory was still up at the house? It wasn't like her to miss an audience of fans.

The blur of Gabe dashed past them.

"It's the Flash!" Mitch cried, lunging playfully for his barefoot, five-year-old son but too out of shape to catch him. Louise would never forget the day Glory's agent, Dotty, passing through on her way to New York their first year here, had told Mitch he was starting to remind her of Richard Burton—and though the clarification was never made, everyone knew the comparison wasn't based on his acting chops, but his appearance. Mitch had sulked over it for days.

"I need a hat for our sand serpent!" Gabe yelled over his shoulder.

"Wait for your Aunt Lou!" Mitch called after him.

Louise smiled. "I'll make sure he gets in."

Balancing the brownies, she followed Gabe up the sand-dusted stairs, marveling at the way the boy took the steps two at a time, how long and lean he'd become when they weren't looking. By the time she caught up to him, he'd already managed to tug the slider down the tracks and dashed into the house, leaving the glass door open in his wake. *Men.* Louise chuckled to herself as she crossed to the kitchen, snaking around a collection of boxes that had been stacked haphazardly around the edges of the living room, labels addressed to Glory, with California or New York origins. Apparently Glory's mercurial interest in acquiring Hollywood memorabilia had grown serious.

"Is it safe to come down?"

Glory appeared at the top of the stairs, swimming in a chunky peach sweater with pink leggings, her hair wound up in a soft bun, a small box tucked under her arm. "I could have sworn a herd of elephants just ran through."

"No herd," said Louise. "Just your son."

Down, Glory crossed to the island to deliver Louise a hug, smelling heavily of her signature jasmine perfume.

Leaning back, Louise eyed her carefully. "Are you okay?"

"I'm fine—I just got a little chilled."

But Louise knew it was something more. After five winters here, Glory's seasonal decline at the onset of autumn had become as predictable as the tides. Usually the collective energy of company buoyed her. Not today, apparently. Louise felt flickers of concern trace her spine. She reached for Glory's hand, wanting to know more.

The whoosh of the slider cut the quiet, too hard to be Gabe.

Louise spun to see Mitch staggering in.

"We're out of beer."

She scanned the space behind him, hoping to see Russ following, but Mitch slung the glass door closed. Passing her in the kitchen, he slowed to take a brownie from the stack she was building and tore off a bite, casting a drowsy look in Glory's direction as he chewed.

"Lou brought brownies."

"And they smell amazing," Glory said, unmoving from her side of the counter.

Mitch plucked another from the plate. "Have one."

"Maybe later."

"Have a damn brownie, Glow," he said again, shoving it at her.

Glory glared at him, flushing with embarrassment. "I said I don't want one."

Louise stiffened, the air suddenly charged with alarm while Mitch stared hotly across the island at his wife. Outside, the watery light of dusk had dulled the harsh crimson of his complexion. Now under the fluorescents, Louise could see how fierce a red his cheeks had turned. Whether the color was a result of a day on the beach or a building discontent borne of too much alcohol, she didn't dare guess.

"I keep telling her we can both get fat now, Lou," he said, his gaze still trained on Glory, "but she just keeps getting skinnier."

When Glory wouldn't grant him a response, he stuffed the last of his brownie into his mouth and wiped his hands roughly on the sides of his shorts. Once he'd moved past her for the fridge, Louise shot Glory a tender look, seeing the blush of distress briefly color her thin cheeks, then Louise's attention was drawn to the fireplace, where Gabe had just wrenched Glory's prized magician's hat off its stand. Startled, she blinked, enough that Glory turned to look.

"Gabe!" Her voice was high with panic as she dashed into the living room. "Where are you going with that?"

Nearly to the door, Gabe spun around, winded from his race down the stairs, his shaggy bangs flopping over one eye—the visible eye radiating impatience. "It's for our sand sculpture. The serpent needs a hat."

"Oh no, baby, that's too special." Glory gently eased it from his sandy hands. "Why don't you put one of your baseball caps on him instead? I bet he'd look so handsome."

Mitch snapped the tab on his beer, the sizzle of released air like a slap. "Jesus, Glow, it's just a damn hat."

"You know it's more than that," she said, settling the hat back safely on the mantel.

"And what about the rest of this crap?" Mitch demanded, swinging his beer at the stacks of boxes.

"It's not crap. They're pieces of Hollywood history and they're important."

"If they're so important then why the hell are they sitting in the middle of the goddamn floor?"

Glory's lips trembled with exasperation. Her voice grew shrill. "Because this house is too small and I can't find a good place for them!"

"I know a great place . . ." Mitch's mouth curved into a bitter smile. "We're about to start the bonfire."

Glory flinched as if he'd pinched her.

Louise glared at him. "That's not funny, Mitch."

"Yeah, well, neither is a broken toe." He took a hard swig.

"Gabe, wait." Glory rushed to the slider just as Gabe swung it open and dropped down beside him. "Baby, I have something for you."

"Mom, I gotta go. Pete's waiting for me!" He shifted impatiently on his bare feet while she dashed back to retrieve the small box she'd left on the counter.

"Here," she said, handing it to him. "I was going to save it for your birthday but . . ."

Gabe tore at the tape and dug inside, filling the room with the crackle of tissue paper until he extracted a wooden stick, six inches long and beveled to resemble a crystal.

He considered it, his small brows furrowing.

"Don't you recognize it?" Glory asked breathlessly. "It's from *Superman*! It's a crystal from his ice palace."

Gabe eyed her warily. "But it's wood."

Mitch snickered. "Now see, that really *is* kindling."

Louise shot him another chastising look, but he just slugged his beer, his expression flat, unrepentant as he swallowed.

"It's wood because it's a mock-up, baby," Glory said, her attention still fixed fully on her son. "A tester. But it's from the *Superman* set. See?" She leaned in and helped him turn the stake to where a few pen marks rode up the side. "That's the name of the special effects director. And the date. Isn't that fabulous?"

Gabe chewed skeptically at his lip. "But you can't see through it."

"I know, sweetie, but it's still something from his ice palace."

He turned the rough piece of wood in his fingers and looked back at Glory, his dark eyes wary. "It's called the Fortress of Solitude, Mom."

"Oh. Right. Sorry." Her smile fell briefly before she resurrected it; Louise's breath hitched. "So . . . do you love it?"

Gabe's thin shoulders rose and fell; his smile not nearly as convincing as hers. "It's pretty neat, I guess. Thanks." He set it down on the table and fixed a freshly expectant look on her, the gift, Louise suspected, already forgotten. "So are you gonna come down and see our serpent before the tide takes it away?"

"Sorry, kiddo." Mitch arrived and gave Gabe's shaggy hair a hard ruffling. "Your mom's got to stay up here and sulk."

Louise bristled. Gabe pulled free and spun out through the open slider.

Glory leapt to her feet, hurt swirling in her eyes. "Why do you have to say things like that?"

He picked up the wood model and gave it a dismissive scan. "What did you expect him to say, Glow? It's just some junky piece of wood."

"It's a collectible." She took it from him and settled the stake carefully back into the box.

"What does he care about that? He's a kid. He wants something normal he can show his friends."

"I thought he could show that," she defended. "You act like I'm trying to make him some kind of freak."

"Because you are. Just let him be normal."

"Are you saying I'm not?"

"I'm saying we don't live with all that shit anymore. We live here."

Her wide eyes filled. "Is it so wrong that I miss our life?"

"This *is* our life." Mitch jabbed his finger toward the beach. "Those are the people who care about me. Who care about *us*."

"They care, all right," Glory said, her trembling voice steadying, hardening bitterly. "They care that you invite them over for bottomless buckets of clams and crabs and endless kegs of beer. You honestly think they'd care if you stopped showering them with gifts?"

"Everything okay up here?" Russ stepped through the slider, closing it behind him. "I could hear you from the dunes."

Mitch retreated, burying his scowl into his beer. Glory sank into the couch.

Russ looked at Louise, his eyes radiating concern, and Louise flushed with gratitude at his rescue.

"We ran out of plates," he said simply.

Louise stepped forward. "I'll get more."

When she'd returned from the pantry, Russ gave her hand a gentle squeeze as he took the stack of plates. He crossed to Mitch and clapped a hand on his shoulder. "People are asking for you, pal."

Mitch muttered something as Russ steered him toward the slider, guiding him outside.

Louise tugged the glass door closed behind them, relief falling over her like a chill.

She turned back to find Glory with her face buried in her hands.

"Don't listen to him," Louise said, sliding beside her on the couch. "He's had too much to drink."

Glory lowered her hands to her lap and stared out at the slider. "He's right." The thinness of her voice was unsettling. "I don't know how to be a mother. Not to a boy like that."

"That's absurd," Louise said, leaning in. "Of course you do."

But Glory's gaze remained fixed on the glass doors—a woman walking calmly toward the edge of a cliff, resigned to the fall. "I try to show him I love him and he looks at me like I'm just a fool." She sniffed, using the edge of her index finger to gingerly wipe the bottom of her lids. "I only want to share something of myself with him. Mitch does it a thousand times a day. He doesn't even have to try . . ." Her voice sank with defeat. "If I can't make him happy at five, what hope is there for me when he's fifteen? Or thirty?"

Louise touched her arm carefully, as if any kind of contact might spook her. "Don't get ahead of yourself," she said, disliking the sound of her advice as soon as it was out of her mouth. As if she had any business being so confident about what it took to be a good mother. As if she ever would know.

"I never thought it would be this hard. That I wouldn't know how to be this person—this wife, this mother. Someone who could do this . . ." Glory's arms swept the room, as if to suggest it was just the room she couldn't manage, when Louise knew *this* was a state far larger than this house.

"It's understandable. You thought it would just be a year."

*He lied to you.* Louise stopped short of saying the words, though when she met Glory's misty eyes and saw the pain flashing back at her, she knew she didn't have to.

The room hushed, swelling with strain, and Louise's own need to soothe it.

"You could still go back," she said gently.

Glory searched Louise's face. "Mitch didn't tell you?"

Louise shook her head.

"Dotty dropped me. She called this morning. Mitch practically kicked up his heels." Glory sniffed. "I'm surprised he didn't rent a plane to write it across the goddamn sky."

"Oh Glory . . ." Louise reached for her hand and squeezed it, her chest tightening with disappointment. No wonder she'd refused to join the party. And Mitch had accused her of sulking? Louise glared in the direction of the water, as if her angry stare might pierce the glass and travel down to the beach to find its target. How cruel could one man be?

Glory buried her face in her hands and crumpled forward again, her thin frame shaking with muffled sobs. Louise crossed back to the kitchen in search of a tissue but had to resort to a hot-pink cocktail napkin.

"Thanks." Glory took the napkin and wiped roughly at her nose. "I don't know what I would do without you, Louise."

"Probably find something softer," Louise said, wanting to lighten the heavy air but failing miserably. They both knew this wasn't about a tissue.

They leaned into one another, the cries of activity from the beach floating through the screens, the sharp, fresh smell of bonfire smoke filtering in with it.

"You must think I'm a horrible person," Glory whispered.

"Why in the world would I think that?"

"How fortunate I am, all that I have, my beautiful son, and I still feel lost . . ." Glory's gaze drifted toward the slider, glassy with numbness. "It's not that I'm not grateful. I need something that's just mine. I had that once and I need it back . . ." Her voice was thin and faraway. "Mitch doesn't understand, Louise. That I need something that's still mine. That I still need *me* in all this." She looked over, her eyes welling. "Please don't hate me."

"Never," said Louise, shaking her head. Not out of kindness, or out of charity, but with understanding.

Because she agreed. Because she knew.

"Then you have to find something that's just yours again," she whispered firmly. As if she had any idea. As if she hadn't herself been searching for the same thing her whole life.

"The Stardust Film Festival."

Glory made the announcement as soon as she and Louise had slid into their favorite booth at Petite's. A week after the disastrous clambake, Louise had allowed herself to forget the painful scene, including her impassioned plea to Glory to find her own purpose again.

Glory, clearly, had not.

Louise frowned at her, confused. "Is that an event?"

"Not yet—but it will be." Glory set her palms down on either side of her coffee, her newly manicured nails nearly the same shade of scarlet as the checkered tablecloth beneath her fingers. "If I can't go back to Hollywood, then I'll simply bring Hollywood here," she said firmly. "We'll screen all of our movies, auction off memorabilia, host parties. It'll be named after our first movie together." Glory blinked at her expectantly. "What do you think?"

Louise sat back, still taking it all in. What wasn't to like?

"I think it's a wonderful idea," she said. "I'm sure the town would be thrilled for the revenue."

Glory's face, frozen for a moment with anticipation, broke into a relieved smile. "Oh, I'm so glad you think so. Because I don't know the first thing about running a huge event like that, I wouldn't even know where to begin."

Their waitress arrived with their coffees.

Louise sugared her coffee and sank her spoon into her cup. "I'm sure there are plenty of people you can call on to help you."

"I know there are." Glory leaned in, her eyes sparkling with resolve. "I'm looking at one right now."

Louise stopped stirring. "Me?"

"Who better?" Glory said, adding a splash of cream to her coffee and stirring it briskly. "You've been spearheading boards and committees for years here."

"Sure, for garden tours," Louise said, already feeling prickles of panic skitter up her spine. "For library auctions. I don't know a thing about running a film festival!"

"You love movies, don't you?" Glory raised her cup, her lips curling into one of her irresistible smiles behind the rim. "And you love me, right?"

Louise sank back with a defeated laugh. "Yes—and yes."

"Then it's settled." Glory took a quick sip and set down her cup. "Now I'm not thinking anything too grand to start. A daylong event, maybe two. If we get enough sponsors, we can keep prices low, maybe some things can even be free. Down the road, of course, we can expand. Maybe more like a week—"

"A week?" Louise's voice hitched. She took a quick sip of her coffee and swallowed hard, growing dizzy. "And Mitch is on board with this?"

The inspiration that had been twinkling in Glory's green eyes dimmed in an instant. She looked down at her coffee.

"He's fine with it," she said with a loose shrug and a smile that was far too quick.

The same man who couldn't even bear to keep props from their old films in plain sight?

Louise leaned forward, dubious. "Glory . . . ?"

"All right, maybe I haven't mentioned it." Glory looked up, her eyes flashing defensively. "Louise, we both know he won't want me doing it."

"You don't know that."

But she did. They both did.

But did it matter?

This would be about Glory, something of hers alone. And maybe, just maybe, it could be something of Louise's, too.

She looked up to find Glory smiling at her.

"I told you we'd make a good team, Louise Chandler."

And so she had. That muggy spring day when Glory Cartwright had first landed in Harpswich, trotting across their driveway in those ridiculous cork-heeled wedges. And Louise had been such a foolish combination of starstruck and wary, sure she could never find something to talk about with someone like Glory Cartwright for five minutes, let alone a whole lunch. And now, friends.

More than friends. Partners.

Louise sipped her coffee, letting the possibility continue to float through her thoughts as their waitress arrived to take their order, a flutter of pride rising like steam.

# 15

The only thing Frankie has ever known about her father is that he preferred gin martinis to vodka ones. A tidbit her mother let slip after draining a pitcher of sangria on a friend's rooftop deck when Frankie was a teenager. Not exactly the sort of distinguishing feature you can recognize someone on the street for, or suspect you've inherited when you study yourself in the mirror. But then, she's often wondered, would it be better to know if her father had, say, wavy blond hair or a cleft chin, and be cursed to stare at every man she crossed paths with who bore either of those features, wondering if he was the one? Despite being smart enough to know how unlikely, how impossible, that would be?

Yet, that's exactly what she finds herself doing. From the time she marched away from Gabe Beckett's truck and followed the road's sandy shoulder to the crowded sidewalks of downtown Harpswich, she's been looking at men of a certain age in passing cars, in storefront windows, walking by, and asking: Does she see herself in any of them? Inside a café, waiting for coffee and a wedge of spinach quiche, she spots a man with slicked-back salt-and-pepper hair reading a newspaper, and finds herself staring, wondering.

By the time she reaches the festival offices a half hour later, curiosity has become compulsion. Will she spend the entire visit here doing this, she wonders as she steps inside the high-ceilinged space and reflexively surveys the sea of faces for possible candidates.

The same woman who greeted her yesterday arrives to help her again.

"I'm here to pick up a pass Louise Chandler left for me. My name's Frankie Simon."

"Right"—she reaches for the phone—"Louise said she wanted me to ring her when you came by."

While she waits, Frankie checks her emails—most of which can hold until she gets back, with the exception of one from a collector in Anaheim who's interested in anything Hitchcock, and she thinks immediately of their pair of Jimmy Stewart's baby-blue pajamas from *Rear Window*. Typing her response, she wonders if this is her future, coordinating sales with faceless, voiceless customers, then she logs in to the store's various social media accounts to make sure no one's posted anything urgent. Wandering the edge of the lobby, she spots another display case filled with film memorabilia. An annotated shooting script from *Doctor Zhivago*, a prop gavel from *Inherit the Wind*, a string of pearls from *Some Like It Hot*.

"Sorry to keep you waiting."

She looks up to find Louise crossing the lobby, a pamphlet in her hand. In the few seconds before she arrives, Frankie scans the woman's face for clues to her mood, still worried that Frankie's occupancy in their guest room remains a source of distress, but her smile remains as even as her strides.

Louise reaches into her tunic pocket and pulls out a laminated pass hanging from a teal lanyard. "As promised."

Frankie swings the badge over her head and settles it on her front. "Thank you for this."

"You're very welcome." Louise hands her the booklet. "I wasn't sure if you had a copy of the schedule for the week."

Frankie flips through, amazed at the daily offerings. Screenings and panels, parties and premieres. Even daily champagne tastings! "There's so much," she marvels. "How does anyone ever do it all?"

"They don't," Louise says matter-of-factly. "And we don't want them to. Otherwise they wouldn't have a reason to come back." She nods at the display case. "Fun, aren't they? We have a few others around the lobby from Glory's collection."

"Glory Cartwright was a collector?"

"I'm not sure she set out to be," Louise says, her expression turning wistful. "In the beginning, I think it was just a way to stay connected to Hollywood from afar, but over time it became more of a mission for her. To preserve that world." Her gaze flicks to Frankie, then settles back on the case, her softened brow knotting. "There was much more than what you see here. She had the most incredible collection of costumes. Hats and gloves and shoes . . ."

"What happened to them?"

Louise runs a fingertip under her collar, drawing it away from her throat as if she's trying to cool herself down. "No one knows. I'd finally convinced Glory to build climate-controlled storage in their basement. She was just letting it pile up all over the house and Mitch was having a fit . . ." She stops and rolls back her shoulders. "The point is it was kept very safe."

"That was smart. All that salt air would have been murder on fabrics—not to mention the moisture."

Louise looks over at her quizzically.

"We have—I have—a store," Frankie explains. "Movie memorabilia, costumes, props. My mother opened it when I was a kid. She worked on film sets, so she was always coming home with things. Eventually she wanted to get bigger pieces from older movies—the classics—so we started going to auctions." She smiles. "Glory obviously inspired her."

Louise nods slowly, but Frankie still has the impression of something unsatisfied in her study.

"And you make a living doing this?" she asks.

"Not a particularly luxurious one," Frankie says, with a little laugh, "but enough. Although it may not be going forward. They raised the lease. I don't think I can keep it open much longer."

A chime rings out. Louise extracts her phone from her tunic pocket, giving the screen a quick scan. "I really should get back to work."

"Of course." Frankie steps back, giving the badge a flutter. "Thank you again for the pass."

"Enjoy it," Louise says, her voice just sharp enough that Frankie worries she's said something to offend her, but the older woman turns on her heel before Frankie can search her expression for proof, swallowed quickly into a teal sea of T-shirt-clad festival volunteers.

# 16

"*Evergreen* was so much better," the flawless blonde in front of Frankie says to her equally flawless boyfriend as the lights in the theater come up and they all rise from their seats. "He's pandering to the masses now. So disappointing."

The reviews continue as they all file down the theater's tight and muggy hallway, excited voices rumbling like a hungry stomach, until they spill out into the damp, salty night air of the sidewalk, where the wind off the water is almost warm, and then it's on to celebrating. Both sides of the narrow street offer options, pubs and restaurants with their doors opened to let out enticing sounds and scents. But it's the doors that are closed—and manned by marble-faced bodybuilders (did they import them from LA, too, Frankie wonders?) and red velvet ropes—that will draw the most attention. She spots the lead actor of one of the most-buzzed-about films on the schedule darting into a loud bar across the street, having snaked successfully around a group of women taking selfies and oblivious to his proximity. With her pass, she could get in any of the after-parties, but knowing that she's got a whole week of them ahead, and still not entirely rested from the trip, she decides a glass of wine in her room sounds more appealing as she steps into a spirits shop and searches the aisles. She could sit by the window, pull apart the sheers, and watch the other kind of stars.

It's a short walk back to the Chandlers' house, but she takes it slowly, not just to savor the way the harbor sparkles at night, but to keep from twisting her ankle. Her choice in footwear for the evening had been an important one—strappy sequined heels worn by her mother's very favorite actress, Meryl Streep, in *Death Becomes Her* had been the perfect way to honor Maeve tonight, but they made for dangerous walking on the town's uneven sidewalks. She admires the stretches of squat, shingled cottages, the teeming pots of geraniums swinging from their porches. The fever of celebration has bled out from downtown. The sidewalks are busy with festival guests, bunched and loud, groups large enough that she has to step off to avoid being stampeded every few blocks. She thinks about her mother's fondness for movies set in small coastal towns—*Mystic Pizza, In the Bedroom, Summer of '42*—surely this place had inspired her affection? Nearing the house, questions continue to bloom. If her mother had gotten pregnant here, why hadn't she stayed? She had a place to live, a good—a great—job, people who clearly cared about her. Had Frankie's father made her leave? Or had he simply broken things off and her mother had fled, heartbroken?

At the top of the Chandlers' driveway, she slows, seeing the pickup with the mismatched door parked beside Louise and Russ's Subaru.

Gabe Beckett is still working at this hour?

Memories of their earlier confrontation flit through her thoughts as she follows the glow of floodlights around to the back of the house where she finds him on his knees, wrestling a deck board loose with the pointed end of his hammer. She approaches slowly, worried she might startle him, but his dog appears—Garbo, was it?—giving her away with a deep bark.

Gabe glances over his shoulder. "You're back early."

"It's after midnight," she says.

"I thought that's when things started to get interesting for you people."

She shoots him a narrowed look as he continues to battle with the rotted plank. "You're as much those people as I am."

"I doubt that." He lets go of the board and sits back on his heels, appraising her. "Must have been quite a party."

"What makes you think I was at a party?"

He wipes his forehead with the back of his hand. "Those ridiculous shoes, for one."

Her face flames. "These shoes happen to be very special to me."

"I like the dress, though." He takes her in again, slowly enough to send a flicker of chill down her arms. "But it's no wonder you're cold," he says.

"What makes you think I'm cold?"

"I can see your goose bumps from here."

She reaches with her free hand and grabs her upper arm, startled to find he's right. "It was warmer in the theater," she says, trying to rub down the traitorous bumps.

"I'll bet. All that hot air." He frees the board and tosses it to the side, grabbing another—this one smooth and flawless—and drops it into the gap in the decking. "Push those nails over to me, will you?" he says, gesturing to a small box on the step.

Frankie gives the container a shove, sending it sliding across the deck.

He reaches for it, his forearms shiny with sweat. When he bends back around, she sees a Rorschachesque inkblot of perspiration spreading out along the spine of his T-shirt and follows it down to a generous sliver of slick skin between where his shirt ends and the waist of his pants starts.

She rubs her arms harder. "So, have you remembered anything about my mother?"

He digs through the box and pulls out a pair of nails. "Nope."

Liar. The word flashes at her, blares like one of those road signs, alerting drivers to a narrowing lane. "She was here a whole year. I find it hard to believe you don't remember anything."

"I was nine," he says. "How much do you remember from when you were nine?"

"A lot, actually."

"Lucky you." He twists back to the boards, one of the nails

wedged between his teeth. Garbo hops past with a long branch that scrapes the deck. Gabe plucks the nail free, centers it at the end of the board, and lands his hammer with several hard whacks.

She winces at the sound, looking around for signs of disgruntled neighbors flocking to their windows. "Aren't you worried about waking people up?"

He circles the yard with the hammer. "Do you see anyone around here sleeping?"

As if on cue, a mirthful crowd of retiring festival celebrants tumbles past, laughing loudly.

Gabe moves down to the other end of the board. "Doc told me you sell that collectible crap."

She bristles at the last word, sure it's Gabe's description and not Russ's. "I told you that in my email." She shifts her feet, careful not to let her heels sink into the grass. "You really do have a lousy memory, don't you?"

He drives in a second nail, then a third.

"Louise said your mother was a collector, too."

He sniffs. "You know it. Props. Costumes. Adoring fans. Hell, she even added a kid to her collection." His strokes intensify. Frankie suspects the head of the nail he's trying to sink is long buried.

"So is that why you don't want those letters?"

The hammering stops. He sits back again and drags his sleeve across his forehead, waiting a beat before he reaches for the can of beer beside the stack of planks. Frankie watches him take a long pull, then tip the can toward a small Igloo on the edge of the deck. "I'd offer you a cold one but I see you've brought your own." He gestures to the bottle in her hand. "Expecting company?"

"Just a few dozen friends," she says. "I find nothing says 'thank you for your hospitality' like bringing a horde of strangers into someone else's home."

One side of his mouth dances up, flirting with a grin. "So you're saying you plan to drink that whole bottle by yourself?"

"Maybe. Do you plan to empty that whole cooler by yourself?"

Both ends of his lips rise now, fully committed to a smile, and she gives in to a small one, too, feeling oddly victorious. Maybe the grouch has a sense of humor after all.

A beat of silence falls between them, the earlier clatter of passersby momentarily absent, allowing the sizzle of night insects in the nearby bushes to fill the air.

He points his beer toward the house. "I hear you're sleeping in my old room."

She blinks at him.

"They didn't tell you? I used to live here. Doc and Lou adopted me after my dad died." He finds her gaze and holds it. "Adopted twice—crazy, right? Seems like I should get some kind of award."

Frankie knows he hopes for her smile to grow, but there's such an edge of longing in his words that whatever rise her lips enjoyed falls immediately. The grown man he is now can joke—but the boy he was must have been devastated.

"So if you come across the pack of Marlboro Reds I stashed and could never remember where, feel free to help yourself," he says.

"Thanks, but I don't smoke."

"Oh, right. I forgot. Your bodies are temples out there. No smoking. No fried foods . . ." He climbs to his feet, dusting his hands on the sides of his jeans. "Sounds like a real party."

Another group strolls past, another tumble of laughter and shrieks. Frankie glances at the slider, feeling suddenly conspicuous. She moves for the stairs. "I should get inside."

"Watch your step," Gabe says over his shoulder. "Especially in those shoes. Some of those gaps are pretty wide where I haven't nailed the boards in yet."

She rolls her eyes. "I walked all the way from town in them, I think I can make it across a—"

Her right heel sinks and holds.

"Shit," she whispers.

She tugs sharply, desperate to free herself before Gabe knows she's stuck.

"Hang on."

Before she can contest, he's beside her, dropped down to his heels and grabbing her shoe in both of his hands as he tries to work it loose. He's so close that his head is brushing her calf, his hair tickling her bare skin. The smell of him rises, coppery and damp, like a penny pried out of warm dirt.

The breeze sends the hem of her dress fluttering up—she tries to force it still.

"You don't have to do that. I can just undo the strap and—"

The heel gives and she's free. Gabe climbs to his feet and she steps back, too fast, and teeters for balance.

"Careful." His hand shoots out to catch her elbow, steadying her. She meets his gaze and wonders for a crazy moment if she asked him in for a glass of wine—into the house he used to live in—if he'd say yes. Or if it's just the two champagne cocktails she had at the opening talking and not the fact that she can still feel the heat of his grip around her ankle.

She brushes back a few loose tendrils. "Thanks."

He nods, a slow, patronizing smirk starting to slide across his mouth, and she bristles with understanding, piercing him with a hard stare.

"You know," she says, "I was really looking forward to drinking this, but if you say, 'I told you so,' I swear I'll break this bottle over your head."

He puts up his hands in surrender and steps back to let her pass. "I would hate to have you waste the wine."

She slides the door closed while he's still watching her, and she manages to keep from smiling until she's out of his sight.

A few small pours later—too eager to get upstairs, and not wanting to rummage through her hosts' cabinets, she opted to use the bathroom's water glass in lieu of a proper goblet—Frankie shrugs into a T-shirt and savors the velvety cool of the sheets on her bare legs when she climbs into bed and snaps off the bedside lamp, letting her thoughts wander in the blue black. Was Gabe telling the truth when he said he didn't remember anything from the year her mother lived with them? Nine is young but not so young. Unless he'd willed his memories away. Had they been painful? Surely they weren't good ones if he didn't want his mother's letters.

But did he think she was lying when she said she recalled memories of her life at nine? She wasn't. It was the year she fell in love for the first time. The Galaxy Cinema was having an Arthur Hiller retrospective and her mother woke her up for the midnight showing of *Love Story,* tucking them both into a taxi that quickly grew fragrant with the sweet, buttery smell of the popcorn she made to smuggle into the theater. Frankie would never forget sinking back into those spongy velvet seats as the lights dimmed, her mother leaning over to whisper, "Your first movie is like your first kiss. You never forget it. Even if it's horrible. *Especially* if it's horrible."

Even now, lying in the dark, Frankie can recall the papery scent of the stiff napkin her mother pulled out of her coat when they'd run out of tissues, the movie not even finished, Oliver yet to walk fragile Jenny through snowy Central Park one last time. To this day, she won't leave her seat until all the credits have rolled. Even if she doesn't need the extra time for her tear-soaked cheeks to dry. Some tributes are small.

A tangy sea breeze dances through the screens beside her bed, fluttering the sheers and bringing with it the faint, oily smell of wood stain and the rustlings of Gabe Beckett, still working below, audible in the night's hush. She tries to imagine how the room might have looked when he lived in it, where his gaze might have fixed in the dark as hers is doing, which part of the ceiling he'd traced with his eyes when he couldn't find sleep . . .

*Adopted twice—crazy, right?*

She rolls toward the window and slips her fingers between the sheers, just enough to offer a sliver of the backyard, and Gabe still at work, his stretched back illuminated in the cone of the deck lights, heat stirring as she watches him. When he moves farther down the deck, she opens the seam for a wider view, sure he won't detect her study. But when Garbo appears behind him, he turns to pat the dog, and his gaze—possibly drawn to the flicker of the sheers—catches hers, holding briefly. Frankie drops the sheers and darts back, so fast she nearly slips off the bed.

# 17

## Monday

When you realize you want to spend the rest of your life with somebody, you want the rest of your life to start as soon as possible.

*When Harry Met Sally*

As long as Russ has been staying in the downstairs bedroom, Louise still can't get used to the empty space in their bed. For the first few weeks, she understood her body's obedience to habit, how she would always wake on her side, never finding her legs and arms cast out to fill the mattress. But after two months, she assumed she might begin, even slowly, to absorb the whole bed. Still she keeps to her side, as if her body is determined to reassure her: *It's only temporary—don't get used to all this space.*

Still she feels the knot of worry cinch every time her fingers search the cool emptiness, reminded of the one time—as if she needed the humiliation repeated?—she suggested moving downstairs to be with him, only to have him tell her that his sleeping patterns had become impossible, that he's up and down so much she'd never get a full night's rest. And indeed, she does often wake in the night to hear muffled steps and the click of closing doors through the dark hush in the middle of the night. But lately, not so much. Still . . . To ask again and risk rejection. She's not quite up to it.

When he first moved downstairs, she wondered if there was—and it causes her breath to catch even now to think about it—someone else. What wife wouldn't have considered the possibility? Russ had always been handsome, kind, and tender—he was a healer, after all—so what woman wouldn't have enjoyed his company, or maybe lingered too long at an appointment?

Over the years, there were a few notably admiring patients, mostly summer visitors, women her own age whose husbands had returned to Boston for the work week. They'd come to Russ for something small, easily diagnosed and treated at the pharmacy in town. One woman, a lawyer's wife, would drop by the office with thank-you gifts—smoked fish and wine, always addressing the cards to Russ alone, and always with offers to visit their compound if he ever found himself on the Vineyard. Louise wasn't proud to say she found herself wondering.

Even Maeve caused her suspicion that one year. When Louise learned that Russ and Maeve went out to lunch, her thoughts festered with doubt, which crushed him when she finally confessed.

Her trust never wavered again.

And anyway, would that infidelity were the problem. Louise only wished she could diagnose her marriage with such a straightforward affliction.

But it's another sort of shuffling she hears as she comes down the stairs this morning. The shuffling of pots and pans, drawers sliding open and closed. And something else—humming?

She steps into the kitchen and finds Russ rummaging through the cabinets. "You haven't seen the slow cooker, have you?" he asks.

"I—I think we put it up in the high cabinet." She blinks at him. "Why?"

"I thought I'd make my chicken chili for us tonight." Us? "I'm sure Frankie would enjoy a nice meal at home. We could invite Gabe. He's coming by in a bit to finish the deck."

She scans the counter, confused at the assortment of cans and pots that weren't there when she went to bed the night before, feeling suddenly like a stranger in her own home.

A stack of photographs sits on the table.

"What are these?" she asks, reaching for the pile.

"I went through the old albums last night and found a few pictures of Maeve. I thought Frankie might get a kick out of them— Ah, there you are, you rascal."

Louise glances up to see him at the top of the step stool, and panic fires. "Russ, be careful!"

"I think I can manage to take down a slow cooker," he says, setting it down on the counter and fixing his fists on his hips. "Now let me see if I can remember what I need without hunting up the recipe." He squints in thought. "White beans, Parmesan, chicken, beet greens . . ."

"Russ"—she releases a defeated sigh—"I don't have time to go to the store."

"I know you don't—I'm going."

He walks past her and out into the hallway. She hurries after him. "To Diamond's?"

"Diamond's doesn't carry beet greens, I'll have to go to Shop-n-Save," he says in a matter-of-fact tone meant to calm her, she suspects, but which somehow does just the opposite. All the way into Provincetown? She can't remember the last time he drove that far by himself since the accident.

"Traffic will be awful," she tries.

"Not this early—everyone's still sleeping off last night's party."

She watches him dig the car keys out of the basket on the foyer table, flushing with ambivalence. A part of her is thrilled to see him charging out of the house, purposeful and confident—another part is fearful that he's foolishly emboldened by his desire to impress Maeve's daughter—which, of course, also gnaws at her.

But, despite her annoyance, it could be the right angle to sway him to stay put.

"Maybe you should wait until Frankie wakes up. Maybe she could go with you?"

He swats the air impatiently. "She didn't come all this way to keep an old man company at the grocery store, Lou. And anyway, it needs a full six hours to cook." He tilts his chin toward the kitchen. "I left her a note."

Louise feels a swell of longing. They used to leave notes for each other all the time. In the days before Post-its, on the back of receipts or index cards. One from when they first bought the house and he'd had to rush out for wood screws, she used as a bookmark forever. She recalls seeing it recently, stuck somewhere. She wants suddenly to hunt for it, to make sure it's safe.

Then she remembers her news.

She drops her voice to a whisper. "I was right. Maeve took it all."

He squints at her. "What are you talking about?"

"She and Frankie had a store. They sold memorabilia."

She scans her husband's eyes, waiting for the flash of outrage to spark, but all she can detect in the silvery pools is something closer to exhaustion.

"You have to admit it's an awfully big coincidence, Russ."

"Lou." His voice is tinged with reprimand, enough that she feels herself flush. "What would it even matter now? Maeve's gone."

She watches him tug his windbreaker off the coat stand, feeling a flicker of shame. Only when he's out the door and she's watched him pull out onto the street—with her heart nearly sitting under her tongue—does Louise realize she's still holding the stack of pictures.

She sifts through them, a rush of memories washing over her, lost now found, slowly smoothing out the sharp edges of her frustration, not even aware of the small smile that has started to bloom until she glances up at her reflection in the foyer mirror.

# 18

1988

It was May, and the warm tease of high season tickled the air, as playful as a whisper; Louise felt its flutter against her cheek as she and Glory crossed the street for Petite's. Harpswich was about to enter into Glory's favorite time of year—summer, when the tourists would roll off the ferries and into town like a tipped jar of marbles, bringing their fresh eyes and gushing admiration—and making up for too long a stretch of unimpressed locals who, after nearly a decade of sharing sidewalks and shorelines with Glory Cartwright, had long stopped being starstruck by Mitch Beckett's glamorous wife. There would be blushing requests for autographs and pictures again. And those who loved Glory would release a collective sigh of relief that she'd survived another dark and lonely Harpswich winter, her already-tiny frame thinned further by poor sleep and a lack of appetite.

Summer also meant festival season. Four years after Glory had first suggested the event as a modest one-day gathering, the Stardust Film Festival had blossomed into a three-day celebration, casting Glory back into celebrity once again every June with film screenings and parties, newspaper articles and the occasional television interview. This year's event promised to be their biggest yet. Cher, fresh off her Best Actress win for *Moonstruck,* had tentatively agreed to give the opening night toast, the biggest name they'd been able to feature.

Glory should have been beaming, but all morning while they'd worked, spread out on the cottage's living room rug—their make-shift office for the past four years—Louise had observed her friend's attention pulled repeatedly to the view of the water, Glory's gaze strangely vacant when Louise had finally drawn her back to the conversation. When she'd blamed low blood sugar for her lack of focus, Louise had clapped their notebooks closed and decided on an early lunch.

But now as they took their seats in their usual window booth, the buttery smell of toasted bread fragrant, Louise worried it wasn't just hunger that had distracted her dear friend. While Louise had slipped free of her twinset cardigan, Glory kept her denim blazer on. Despite the bright sun, the air was still crisp with spring frost. Louise could feel chilly breaths off the glass.

"Are you cold? Because we could take a table in the back today," she offered. "It's always colder by the window."

"I'm fine." But Glory's smile was uncharacteristically tight. "I just need some coffee to warm me up." She turned to scan the empty counter that divided the bistro's kitchen from the rest of the narrow room. "I don't see the girls."

Louise twisted in her seat, not seeing either of the two waitresses who typically worked Monday's lunch. After nine years of weekly lunch dates at Petite's, she and Glory knew the waitstaff by name.

A heavy thud sounded, and a young woman with a leaning pile of auburn curls pushed through the swinging kitchen door, a pot of coffee in each hand.

"She must be new," said Louise.

The woman scanned the restaurant floor, saw them, slowed a moment, then approached. She set down her coffee pots to pluck an order pad from the waistband of her cutoff shorts. Her silver hoop earrings were so large they skimmed her shoulders. But despite her harried entrance, her smile was big and warm, and a peppering of freckles soaked her creamy skin. Louise sat back to allow a requisite beat for the young woman to realize she was serving the famous Glory Cartwright, but when her hazel eyes flashed expectantly between them, recognition didn't register, an oversight that was becoming more and more common with each passing year. Louise only hoped Glory didn't take the slight too hard.

"Sorry for the wait, ladies. Donny had to run out for more eggs so I'm doing double duty until he gets back." There was a lilt to her words, a faint accent Louise couldn't place. She raised her pot. "Coffee?"

"Please." Glory pushed her mug closer. Louise nodded for the same.

"What's your soup of the day?" asked Louise.

"Cream of mushroom."

"I'll take a bowl of that."

Glory offered a tight smile. "Just coffee for me."

"You said you were starving," Louise reminded her when their waitress had left.

"No, I said my blood sugar was low." Glory tore open a pack of Sweet'N Low and sent a shower of crystals into her coffee.

Louise raised her cup and squared a hard look at Glory over the top, not wanting to push.

"All I know is that when we move into the office next month, I'm buying us a proper coffee pot. Maybe even an espresso machine. Those fancy commercial ones with the steamers that foam the milk." After four years of operating from the living room floor of Glory's beach house, the festival would finally be moving operations into an office space downtown where Louise had secured them the top floor of the old glass factory.

"Louise, about the office . . ." There was an edge of wariness in Glory's voice; Louise set down her coffee carefully. "I think we should wait another year before moving operations."

"But we've been over this, Glory. The beach house is too small. You barely have enough space to store your memorabilia collection.

And what about Mitch? You said yourself you were tired of him constantly grumbling about the clutter and the intrusion."

Glory let out a defeated sigh. "My husband grumbles about everything to do with our festival. Moving to an office building won't change that."

There were, however, other concerns—the least of which was the constant threat of Gabe getting tangled in the snakes of telephone cord as he bounded across the carpet on his way to the water. Now nine, he didn't walk, he raced, moving from task to task as if he were being timed.

Louise leaned in, lowering her voice. "Is it about money?" she asked carefully. "Because I'm sure we can find a cheaper space."

Glory shook her head, causing her feathered bangs to shiver. "Money isn't the issue."

"What then?"

"I just think we should wait until after the festival, that's all. We've got enough to plan in the next eight weeks without adding a move to the mix."

Louise sat back, confused. Glory hadn't felt this way just a few days earlier. What had changed her mind so suddenly?

Another possibility flashed.

"You're not worried about Cher backing out, are you?"

Glory's eyes flicked up from her coffee, welling with concern, and Louise felt a flicker of regret.

"Aren't *you*?" Glory plunged her spoon into her cup, swirling it anxiously. "We still don't have confirmation. Nothing's been signed."

"She'll come through, Glory. This is our year." The encouragement earned her a small but hopeful smile. Louise reached across the booth and gave Glory's hand a reassuring squeeze. "And when she does," she added. "We're going to need—"

"A real office." Glory held up her hand to block. "But speaking of expanding, I have been thinking that it's time I—"

"Here you are." Their waitress set down Louise's soup, the sweet smell of the creamy broth rising, and turned to Glory. "Are you sure I can't get you anything to eat?" she asked. One side of her mouth rose mischievously. "You should know I just pulled a beautiful peach pie out of the oven. A little scoop of vanilla on top while it's still warm . . . ?"

Glory's smile was polite but tight. "Thank you, no. Just a bit more coffee."

"Now wait a minute," said Louise. "That was our original vow, remember? That we'd find ourselves a place to eat pie for lunch?"

Glory looked up, her eyes filling briefly with something so close to distress that Louise almost regretted the reminder. Why did everything she said today seem to unsettle her?

The young woman pressed. "Maybe just a sliver to sample?"

"So on top of everything else, you're a pie maker, too?" Louise marveled. "Donny better hurry back or he'll be out of a job."

"Hardly." Their waitress leaned back with a bubbling laugh. "Give me a pile of cold cuts and a loaf of bread, I'm your girl. Even the occasional pot roast doesn't scare me. But baking?" She made her eyes wide and clapped a hand against her cheek. "All that chemistry? Well, you might as well be asking me to split atoms." She smiled between them. "Just let me know if you change your mind about the pie."

Louise watched her snake through the tables back to the kitchen. "Adorable girl, isn't she?"

"Very."

"Now what was this about expanding?" Louise asked, drawing up her spoon.

"I want to hire an assistant," said Glory.

As much as Louise was still stymied by Glory's desire to stall their office move, this announcement was equally thrilling. Their dozens of summer volunteers were reliable and devoted, but there was plenty of work to be done year-round. "Wonderful! I could keep them busy organizing the opening-night party alone, it's grown to be such a beast—"

"Not for the festival," Glory cut in. "For me."

Louise blinked, her spoon suspended.

"Oh please." Glory clapped a hand over Louise's. "As if you need help? You could run this whole thing on your own blindfolded. But if this year really does put us on the map, then I'll need to reconnect with my fan base . . ." She looked down at her coffee, her fingers fluttering thoughtfully over the handle. "I promised when we left Hollywood that they'd remain my number one priority. An assistant could help me build back up those connections. Help me keep on top of fan mail and interview requests."

Louise drew up her spoon and dunked it into the creamy soup. It made sense. Especially if—God forbid—Cher did pull out and Glory needed the immediate ego boost of an assistant's undivided attention to weather the disappointment.

"And now with my treasures safely stored downstairs, the guest room can be put to use again."

Louise swallowed hard, careful not to choke. "You want this person to live with you?" She could understand wanting help during the day, but round-the-clock seemed a bit excessive. "Have you talked to Mitch about this?"

"Of course not." Glory raised her mug then changed her mind, setting it back down in its saucer. "What would be the point? He'll just say no."

Louise digested the idea as she ate, letting possibility swirl as she spooned up generous pieces of portabella mushrooms from the velvety broth. Glory certainly wouldn't have trouble finding someone now that summer was closing in. High season on the Cape always brought an endless supply of college students eager to take thankless service jobs and pack themselves into rental cottages like cigars in a box. Occasionally one would sheepishly appear in Russ's office, needing antibiotics for some venereal disease, or a tetanus shot after trying to climb the pier in bare feet after too many tequila shots.

Louise twisted her spoon absently through her soup, plotting.

"What about Iris? The Ludlows' daughter who worked in Russ's office last summer? Russ always raved about her. Said she was never late, very professional. She's coming home from Tufts in a few weeks—I'm sure she'd jump at the chance to be your assistant. And you wouldn't even have to let her a room—"

But Glory was already shaking her head. "It needs to be someone fresh, someone not from here. And they have to be live-in. That part is nonnegotiable."

Louise didn't see why—especially not to the latter point—but she didn't press. Glory would have her pick of candidates once word spread of the job opening, though there would be one obvious deterrent. It would take someone with a strong disposition to tolerate Mitch's sour moods, particularly if this person was hired solely to bring greater success to the festival . . .

"How was the soup?" Their waitress returned, adding a splash of coffee to Glory's cup.

"Delicious," said Louise.

"Take your time and let me know if you need anything else." The young woman pulled out their check and slid the slip of paper under the condiment basket. "You both have a great day."

"My turn to treat," Louise said, freeing the check before Glory could contest and rising to pay. Only when she'd reached the register did she see the note their waitress had scribbled on the back: *An honor to wait on one of my very favorite actresses! XXOO, Maeve*

She smiled as she waited for the young woman to meet her at the counter.

"Glory will be tickled to know you recognized her," she said, handing over the check.

"*Moonlight Magic* was the first movie I saw in the theater. I was eleven. My best friend Jeannie and I were supposed to be watching *Freaky Friday* but we snuck in."

Louise laughed. "That's a wonderful story. You should have said something at the table."

"I didn't want to disturb you two. I figured she must get sick of being bothered all the time. That she must just wish for one meal in peace."

Louise smiled wryly. "Don't bet on it." She watched the young woman punch in their bill. "Maeve's a very pretty name."

"It was from my father's side," she said, tapping the TOTAL button and sending the drawer sailing open with a loud chime. "They were all from Ireland. Maeve was some kind of warrior queen long ago. Apparently, it means 'she who intoxicates' in Gaelic." She rolled her eyes as she speared the bill onto the stack of receipts. "Ridiculous, right?"

"Not at all," said Louise, handing her a twenty. "I hope Donny pays you double for doing twice the work today."

"I'd be happy if he paid me single," Maeve said low as she dug out a handful of coins and bills, dropping the collection into Louise's opened palm. "I love working here but my roommates aren't too keen on me paying my share of the rent in French onion soup every month."

"I'm sorry to hear that," Louise said, handing her back a five for a tip.

"Thanks," said Maeve, folding the bill into her front pocket. She shoved the cash drawer closed with the heel of her hand and smiled as she reached up to right her teetering knot of hair. "I was hoping to stay on until July but I don't think I can swing it if I don't find a better gig soon."

A better gig . . .

Louise glanced over her shoulder to where Glory sat waiting in the booth, studying the view of the street as she sipped her coffee.

She turned back slowly, feeling the flutter of purpose.

"You know, Maeve . . . I just might know of something."

# 19

Her second morning here, Frankie isn't startled by the veil of mist that floats over the lawn when she draws back the sheers at eight thirty. Nor is she surprised to find the air just damp enough to send gooseflesh trickling down her bare arms. A dull ache presses at the back of her eyes as she moves around the bedroom getting dressed, possibly her body's thanks for chasing those celebratory champagne cocktails with red wine. She finds a pair of Advil in her bag and downs them in the bathroom, knowing coffee will work faster as she heads downstairs.

Stepping into the kitchen, she slows on the threshold, prickles of surprise flaring across her scalp to see Gabe Beckett at the counter, pouring coffee into his paint-splattered to-go mug.

The memory of their exchange last night is still fresh, his hands on her bare skin, trying to free her heel. Had he ever gone home?

Trepidation flickers; maybe it's too soon to be reunited, too early—but he senses her arrival and turns before she can retreat.

"I just came in for a refill," he says.

She sinks into the doorway, realizing this is the second time she's been caught watching him from afar. She only hopes he doesn't let it go to his head.

"Do you actually sleep?" she asks.

"When I get around to it, sure." He holds up the pot questioningly.

She peels herself off the jamb. "God, yes."

"Mugs in there." He motions to the nearest cabinet; she picks a blue speckleware one and he fills it, the crackle of the liquid almost as soothing as its rich, malty smell. "Cream's in the fridge." Capping his mug, he tips his head to the breakfast table, where a stack of photos sits, a Post-it note on the top. "Doc left you those."

She crosses with her coffee, excitement rising when she reads: *Thought you might enjoy seeing your mother when she was here. Russ.* She drops into a chair and sifts hurriedly through the pictures—longing surging when she spots her mother, so young, she's barely recognizable. The other people in the photos certainly aren't—and there are several group shots. She can identify Glory Cartwright and Mitch Beckett, even Louise and Russ. If only Russ were here to help.

A thought sparks. Frankie looks up to see Gabe heading for the slider.

He can always say no, can't he?

"Gabe?"

Halfway through the glass, he slows, blinking at her as if he's genuinely surprised she remembered his name.

She holds up the pile. "I don't suppose you'd be willing to tell me who some of these people are?"

He hesitates, just long enough that she thinks he really might not help her, before he steps back inside and tugs the slider closed.

"Don't expect too much," he says, pulling out the other chair. "My memory's pretty lousy, remember?" He shoots her a look and she smiles.

It's a short table and his legs bump against hers as soon as he settles in, the rough canvas of his workpants firing nerves against her bare calves. She draws her feet under her chair, worried she might find her bare toes under his shoes.

He fans out the photos, taking out one of her mother posing playfully on the deck of a beach house.

"This is your mother, right?"

"Maeve," she says.

Gabe considers the photo for a long moment. "She was beautiful."

"Yes, she was." The past tense sticks briefly in her throat—Frankie is still never sure she'll get it out.

He glances between the photo and her several times. "You look just like her."

Meeting his dark eyes, Frankie feels the tug of longing in her lap. She's been told this her whole life, but somehow the comment from him forces a warm flush to her neck.

Before he can spot her blush, she picks another from the collection, a group on a beach, her gaze fixing immediately on the only kid in the staggered row of adults: a tan, lanky boy with a chunky mop of brown hair, wearing only a pair of checkered board shorts.

She turns the photo to him. "This is you, isn't it?"

He glances over. "Yup."

"You were kind of cute."

He squints at her. "Kind of?"

She smiles as she takes the photo back to scan it more carefully. "Everyone looks so happy . . . and so drunk." Except for Glory, who, blindingly bright in a fuchsia wraparound dress, is the only one in the lineup who doesn't look delighted. "Why does your mother look so upset?"

She turns the photo toward him again, but this time Gabe doesn't bother to look.

"I'm sure it had something to do with the boat or the cold or the smell. Take your pick." He swigs his coffee, swallows hard. "She hated everything about living here. She didn't even pretend."

"She can't have hated everything." Frankie manages to catch his gaze, trying to mine it for an answer, but he shifts his eyes before she can.

"Like I said"—he reaches for another picture—"my memory isn't the greatest."

Then why hadn't Glory gone back to Hollywood? Frankie considers asking the question but holds back. When Gabe identifies friends of his father in the photo, she scans the background, the stretch of beach, and asks instead: "Where was this taken?"

"At our old house."

"Who lives there now?"

"No one," he says. "I think it's on the market again."

While he guides her through a smaller group shot, Frankie steals another glance, seeing a few streaks of white near his crown that could be gray hair or paint, she can't be sure.

And in an instant, the timing of the pictures slams her like a punch. These photos may have been taken when her mother was here, but that also means they were taken in the last year of Glory's life. Asking Gabe to revisit these images, his mother's pained face, suddenly seems deeply cruel. Frankie lost her mother in an accident, but Gabe's mother chose her departure. Glory Cartwright left this world knowing her husband and her young son would remain behind, forever burdened with the weight of unanswered questions and regrets. No wonder he's angry.

Remorse pokes at her, finds its port and anchors. Despite their thorny exchanges, she and Gabe Beckett are both orphans, members of a club no one wants to belong to, and sympathy blooms like a balloon. She's been unfair to him.

He pulls another photo from the pile, a picture of them all on the deck of a sailboat.

She leans in. "Where's that?"

"My dad's boat."

"It's beautiful."

"She," Gabe says. "A boat is always a woman."

His knee falls against hers, heavy and warm. She meets his gaze and lets him hold it.

"*She* must have been beautiful."

"She still is." He shrugs. "Well . . . I'm working hard to get her into shape again."

"You're working on your father's sailboat?"

"I'm living on her."

Frankie leans back and blinks at him.

"Don't look so shocked," he says. "Plenty of people live on their boats."

"That's not the part that shocks me."

"What then?"

She lands her elbows on the table and leans forward. "Last night you complained about your mother's memorabilia collection, and now I find out you've saved something of your father's. A huge something."

"Just because I don't save old costumes doesn't mean I don't care. The only really good memories I have were on that boat." He tosses the photo back onto the pile and shrugs. "That, and I needed a place to live and *Essie* was free."

Frankie studies him. As if someone with his kind of inheritance needed free housing?

She inches her bare foot along the floor, meeting the edge of his sneaker, testing her toes carefully along the prickly rubber.

Gabe looks over at her, his hooded eyes darkening quizzically, as if he's trying to decide whether or not to tell her something. Maybe something about her mother, or maybe that he wants to see Glory's letters after all . . .

He pushes out his chair and stands. "I should get back to work."

She rises, too, her short burst of hope evaporating, and she feels foolish for it. As if the layers of ice he's built up toward his mother might be thawed over a handful of photos.

"Thanks for your help," she says.

But at the slider, he slows, his eyes smoldering again with interest. "So how was the wine?"

Was that the question he wanted to ask her before? Frankie isn't sure, but she's more than happy to answer.

"Delicious," she says.

He rolls his mug against his chest, his mouth shifting into a faint grin. "Bet you're glad you didn't break it over my head then."

She sinks against the counter and smiles. "I might keep the empty bottle, though. Just in case."

He chuckles, a surprisingly rich sound. She thinks it may be the first time she's ever heard him come close to a laugh, and heat charges down her spine.

"Probably a good idea," he says, stepping out and closing the slider behind him.

Frankie's still in the kitchen, the photos tiled across the table so she can take pictures of them for her collection, when Russ returns an hour later. He appears in the doorway with two grocery bags that look far too heavy for one hand and she rushes to rescue him.

"Looks like someone's going to eat well tonight," she says as she helps him unload the contents onto the counter: a wedge of Parmesan cheese, chicken breasts, leafy greens.

"You, hopefully," he says, slowing his unpacking to cut her a curious look. "Unless you already have plans?"

"No, no plans."

"Good." He glances over at the grid of photos. "I see you found them."

"They're wonderful," she says. "Thank you for sharing them."

He crosses to the table, placing his hands on the surface, and leans in to appraise the collection. "I hope it wasn't hard seeing her," he says, his voice soft. "I know it can be difficult. When I lost my father, I couldn't look at his picture for a long time. It physically hurt."

She appreciates his confession. "It's easier with older pictures, I think, because she's so young. She's not someone I recognize, someone I knew. If I've been struggling with anything, it's been the not knowing all these years." She sweeps her hand over the collage. "Looking at these pictures, and seeing how much a part of your world, your families, she was . . . I just can't understand why she never told me about this part of her life."

"Sometimes you just can't tell people things," he says. "Even when you want to."

There's a faintness to his voice that gives his words a cryptic air. Frankie mines his face for an explanation, but he keeps his eyes lowered on the pictures.

"You're probably wondering who some of these people are," he says.

"Gabe went through them with me. He was very sweet about it, actually."

Now Russ looks up. "Gabe? Sweet?"

"Well . . . he was willing." She smiles. "I was grateful."

"I'm surprised. Gabe usually has a hard time with old photos. Unlike you, he doesn't see happy people in these pictures."

"He seemed to lighten up a little for the last few." She rolls her shoulders, her back tight after hunching over to study the pictures. "For a second, I even thought he might finally ask to read the letters."

"Letters?"

Russ scans her face, his brow knotting with confusion, and she feels a pang of remorse; in all the activity of the past two days, she's never told him or Louise about Glory's letters. As she explains, his features shift between surprise and possibly concern, though Frankie can't imagine what about her news might concern him. Unless he's worried for Gabe's reaction?

"And you didn't open them?" Russ asks.

"I couldn't . . ."

She looks up to see the twist of his brow has softened—maybe he already knew that her mother held sealed letters dear? Maybe Maeve had shared that with them while she was here?

"I was just going to leave them with Louise—"

"Don't." As quickly as Russ's brow loosened, it tenses again. "Just hold on to them," he says. "Gabe may want them yet."

Their gazes drift back to the spread of photos.

"I keep looking at them and wondering if one of these men might be . . ." Frankie glances up sheepishly, dreading what she'll find pooling in Russ's eyes, but his gaze is tender.

"It's understandable," he says kindly.

"But is it possible?" She points to the one Gabe told her was taken at Mitch's clambake, her mother and Glory deep in conversation, an assortment of sun-crisped men moving around behind them. "Maybe someone he fished with?"

Russ shakes his head with surprising fervor. "Your mother was too smart to waste her time with those men."

"Maybe not." Frankie shrugs. "Louise said my mother was seeing someone here. Someone older . . ."

His gaze snaps to hers, and Frankie feels a charge of regret, as if she's wounded him somehow, caused him some degree of disappointment. The corners of his eyes tighten briefly with strain before they relax again.

He touches her arm, his smile returning, holding this time.

"Then you'll come for dinner?" he asks.

She nods. "I wouldn't miss it."

# 20

The kitchen is a flurry of rich smells and jazz music when Frankie comes downstairs at six thirty. She settled on her sundress with capped sleeves—deciding if the breeze on the deck grew cool, she could always run upstairs for a sweater. Her hair, however, caused her an infuriating degree of indecisiveness. Up, down, bound tight, spun loose? In the end, she let it hang down her shoulders and clamped a hair clip to her hem, thinking she could always twist it into good behavior if it became unmanageable in the humid sea air.

Russ is working at the counter, sawing through a particularly fat baguette. He looks up at her, his thick white hair spilling over his forehead, giving him a boyish quality. "Well, hello," he says brightly, as if she's a long-lost friend he hasn't seen in years, and maybe wasn't even expecting. "There's wine." He points his knife at the bottle of red behind him. "And a white in the fridge. Oh, and Gabe brought beer if you prefer that."

She scans the space, wondering where he's holed up, telling herself the sudden flutters she feels are hunger pangs, the excitement of eating whatever is responsible for the warm, fragrant air.

"Is Louise here?" she asks.

"She should be home any minute." Russ nods toward the deck door. "Gabe's outside."

So he is. Lounging in a wicker chair on the very same boards he'd been crouched over in near darkness just the night before, although tonight he's traded in his workpants for khakis, and a T-shirt that appears remarkably stain-free, Frankie notices as she steps outside. He wears the same faded old white Chucks, but his hair is damp and shiny from a shower and his jawline scraped smooth of his previous stubble.

The slider whistles when she closes it. He looks up at the sound, watching her approach.

"You can't seem to leave this deck, can you?" she asks.

In front of him, four tidy place settings cover the table, a collection of pedestal candles in the center, their sunken wicks fluttering cheerfully in the breeze. The oily tang of whatever he coated the deck with still hangs in the air, fresh and pleasant. She hears a rustling and glances over to see Garbo skirting the fence of lilac bushes.

"Different dress," he says.

"I have more than one, you know."

She chooses the seat opposite his, feeling a pang of guilt when her wineglass leaves a faint ring on the flawless linen tablecloth. She picks it up, deciding to hold it instead, circling her thumb through the cool layer of condensation at the base of the goblet's bowl.

Looking up again, she catches him watching her, feeling a flutter of victory as he shifts his gaze hastily to his beer. For once, she's not the one caught staring.

The breeze slips under the table, fluttering the gauzy hem of her dress. She slips out of her sandals and crosses her legs.

"Thanks again for going through those photos with me."

He rolls his beer between his palms. "You thought he might be in those pictures, huh?"

She shrugs, but when she meets his exacting gaze, her desire to be cavalier wanes. "Did you ever look for your biological parents?"

He considers the beer's label, working his thumbnail under one corner. "It was a closed adoption. I figured if they wanted me to know who they were, they'd have left that door open." He tips the bottle back for a swig.

"But I can't know for sure that my father didn't want that door open," she says carefully.

"The world we live in now . . ." He shrugs. "It wouldn't be so hard for him to find you if he wanted to."

His words sting, but his expression remains thoughtful, apologetic even, as if he realizes too late that he's said something discouraging.

"And what about what I want?" she asks.

His eyes find hers and hold. "What do you want?"

Her pulse hastens, she knows his question has nothing to do with finding her father, and she can't decide how to answer. A charged silence fires in the space between them like the seconds before a lightning storm, the air sizzling and ready to spark. Then, from the side of the house, the crackle of tires rumbling over the driveway's gravel: Louise's arrival, rescuing her.

Garbo drops a heavy branch on the edge of the deck in offering.

Frankie lifts her wine and takes a long sip.


Louise turns off the engine and looks out at the house, wondering if she doesn't get out of the car how long it will be before someone will notice.

She doesn't know why she should be nervous. This is her home. This is her family.

She takes the brick path as slowly as possible, hoping the butterflies will cease by the time she reaches the front door. They don't. In fact, their batting wings only increase their speed once she hears the clatter of activity from the other end of the hall, and the same strange and unwelcome flash of herself as an interloper in her own home comes over her—though this time she recognizes the source:

Russ, cooking. It's been so very long. And is he playing music? The timing chafes her. That he'll go to this kind of effort for Maeve's daughter. She tamps down the unkind thought. She's vowed to be cheerful tonight.

At the kitchen doorway, she slows to take in the scene of her husband at the counter, dropping a handful of halved cherry tomatoes into a salad bowl. Is that a glass of wine beside him?

"Oh good, you're here," he says, glancing up.

She stares at his wrist. "You're not wearing your brace."

"I didn't want it getting wet. Gabe and Frankie are out on the deck."

"Gabe came?" She slows her pace, experiencing equal parts elation and surprise.

"And—prepare yourself . . ." Russ dips his voice ominously. "He showered and shaved."

She chuckles; he looks over at her, his eyes radiating pleasure.

"I don't kid myself that was for our benefit," he adds, tilting his head pointedly in the direction of the slider. She leans just slightly toward the view of the deck, not wanting to be caught spying, and sees Frankie and Gabe seated across from one another.

"They look like they could be on a first date," she whispers.

"I'm not that optimistic," says Russ. "I'm just relieved to see he still owns a razor."

Louise smiles, continuing to study their exchange. What do men know? A woman sits differently when she's interested in someone, moves herself differently. Legs cross and uncross. Fingers trace throats and earlobes. Fabric, especially if it's loose and naturally fluid, can be adjusted to give glimpses of bare skin. And if there's a breeze? Well . . .

Louise recalls her own subtle cues of attraction over the years, and the thump of envy that sparks behind her chest comes swiftly. How early in it all they are, just on the cusp of possible romance— everything new and unblemished. Nothing confusing yet, no one disappointed. What she wouldn't give for a chance to know that sensation again.

"We're almost ready to eat," Russ says, drawing her back. She turns to find him vigorously slicing up a yellow pepper. She feels suddenly plain, wilted, out of place again.

She needs to help, needs to insert herself into this engine he's built in her absence.

"I can make a dressing," she offers, moving briskly to the fridge.

"Already made." He points his knife at a satiny mustard vinaigrette on the counter.

"Then I'll set the table." She redirects herself to the utensil drawer, then slows, remembering she's just seen the deck. "What about butter for the corn bread?"

"Already put a stick out."

This time, she doesn't seek another task. She simply comes beside him, taking in the scene with gratitude this time, not hurt. "You did all this." There's no lilt at the end of her sentence—it's a statement, not a question.

"I did." His eyes twinkle. He looks so bright to her, so very content. She has never felt so dull.

"I should change," she says.

"What for? You look sensational." He hands her a pepper slice and smiles reflexively. The flood of heat to her cheeks is immediate. She can't remember the last time he complimented her.

"There is one thing you can do," he says, tipping his head toward the counter. "You can pour yourself some wine."

They fill bowls and carry them out to the deck, where the evening breeze is warm and soft, strong enough to soothe but too gentle to do more than rub the lilac branches against the house, Frankie notices when she takes her seat. The pillar candle flames, sunken in their wax pools, flutter in safety.

Russ raises his wine. "To new friends—and surprise guests."

Frankie smiles, adding her glass to the intersection of drinks and tapping gently. "I'm honored."

"I think Doc's referring to me," says Gabe, though there's no edge whatsoever to his voice. His eyes find hers across the table and flash with startling warmth. She looks to Louise, pleased to find her hostess equally lightened by the comment, whatever strain Frankie had seen—or imagined—on her face the day before smoothed away.

Russ passes the basket of corn bread. "So what do you think of the festival so far?"

"It's magical," Frankie says, taking a piece. "I especially love how there's such a focus on the fans, on what it is to be a true movie lover."

"That was always the idea," says Louise. "And you've been able to get into all the screenings?"

"Every one."

"A delighted participant—imagine that," Louise says, arching an accusatory brow in Gabe's direction.

Russ leans in. "Gabe doesn't go to the festival, Frankie."

Gabe looks over at her. "Don't you love when people talk about you in the third person when you're sitting right next to them?"

Frankie chuckles into her wine.

Louise points her fork at him. "I remember that one year—you couldn't have been more than seven—you actually begged Curtis to let you clean out fish lockers for Pete Wilson to get out of attending." She winces. "You smelled like bait for a week."

"It was worth it." Gabe slides Frankie another conspiratorial grin, but she doesn't return this one. What son goes out of his way to hurt his mother's feelings like that? Not that she's surprised. This is, after all, the same son who wanted no part of his mother's final letters.

"Your mother loved it, Frankie," says Louise.

"I'll bet she did." Frankie sinks her spoon into her chili and swirls it thoughtfully. "The irony is that I used to nag her about going and she'd say we didn't need to go across the country to see the same people who walk by our kitchen window. And to think the whole time I pleaded, she'd already been . . ."

The table falls quiet, the mention of Maeve's duplicity causing a momentary bump in the smoothness of the evening.

"Sour cream?" Russ holds up a small bowl, rescuing her.

Frankie takes some with a grateful smile and passes it on.

"It definitely wasn't the grand affair it is now when your mother attended, though," Louise points out, adding a dollop to her chili.

"It used to be much more intimate," says Russ. "Until Glory called in a favor from Cher—and after that, the whole thing just blew up."

Gabe tips his glass in Louise's direction. "All Lou's doing. She made it the success it is today."

Frankie watches Louise's features soften with the compliment, her pale eyes flashing warmly at Gabe. "My cheering section—misguided as he is."

"Stop," says Russ, gently patting Louise's hand where it rests beside her plate. "Don't be so modest. It's true."

Even in the thinning light of dusk, Frankie can see pleased color flood Louise's cheeks before she dips her smile into a sip of wine.

"Those pictures were wonderful this morning. Thank you again."

Russ nods as he wipes his mouth. "I understand Gabe played tour guide for you in my absence," he says, returning his napkin to his lap.

"Really?" Louise blinks at Gabe, then over at Frankie. "How did he do?"

Frankie considers Gabe a moment, long enough to make him frown warily before she answers. "His memory isn't nearly as bad as he claims."

Gabe sets down his utensils and turns up his hands in mock exasperation. "What is it with the third person tonight?"

Laughter rumbles around the table, and Frankie offers him a repentant grin.

Russ turns to Gabe. "It had to be fun seeing those old pictures of *Essie*."

"She's a beautiful boat," Frankie says.

Gabe offers her an appreciative nod—though she's not sure if it's the compliment, or the correct use of the pronoun that pleases him.

Louise plunges a piece of cornbread into her chili. "You should see her now. Gabe's done so much work on her."

When Frankie looks up this time, Gabe's gaze is waiting to find hers, Louise's suggestion hanging in the momentary quiet while Russ offers more wine.

Gabe shrugs. "I wouldn't say so much work . . ."

"Now who's being modest?" asks Louise.

"Do you like to sail, Frankie?" Russ asks.

"I haven't really had much experience." She grins. "Other than seeing *The Poseidon Adventure* more times than I care to admit."

Russ laughs. "No wonder you've avoided the water."

"I remember your mother seemed pretty comfortable on a boat," Louise says.

Yet more startling news; Frankie can't ever recall her mother taking her sailing. She does remember a few times the invitation was made by friends with boats, but her mother always declined, saying she worried that Frankie was too young.

"Glory was always nervous on the water," says Russ. "Probably because she never learned to swim."

"It's not like she didn't have the chance," says Gabe. "My dad was always trying to teach her."

"By throwing her off the side of the boat?" Louise shoots him a chastising glance over her wine.

Looking mildly sheepish, Gabe reaches for the wine, gives himself another splash, then tips the bottle questioningly in Frankie's direction.

"Please," she says, holding out her glass, their eyes meeting as he pours.

"It's been a lot to take in, I bet," Russ says to her.

She lowers her wine. "I still can't believe my mother worked for Glory Cartwright."

"Did you know it was Louise's idea to hire her?"

Frankie looks between them expectantly.

Louise smiles. "She was waiting tables at our favorite café. Glory had just said she wanted an assistant and your mother was looking for other work. It was nothing short of providential. One of those rare moments when you feel certain the universe is listening."

Frankie chuckles. "She always told me she made a terrible waitress."

"Do you have family out in California, Frankie?" Russ asks, and Frankie notices his gaze flicks to Louise.

"I don't really have family anywhere. My mother was my family. I don't mean to sound so tragic—I mean I have friends, neighbors. I suppose they're like family, but . . ." She shrugs. "It's not the same. Not like . . . this," she says, sweeping her glass pointedly around the table.

She catches Gabe watching her again, but this time his eyes remain even with hers.

"No," says Russ. "I suppose it's not."

Garbo tears across the lawn, drawing all of their gazes to her imaginary chase. A new jazz song purrs out from the deck speakers. Frankie finds herself swaying gently with the easy rhythm.

"There's plenty more if anyone wants seconds," Russ says.

Looking around the table, Frankie feels a flutter of peace, a connection, a rolling calm—she's not had nearly enough to drink to credit the wine for the sensation—and then she understands the source: her mother, gone, is somehow here.

# 21

The sun has slipped fully behind the rooftops by the time they all push back from the table. Russ offers seconds, or is it thirds?—Louise has lost track—but everyone agrees it's time for coffee, so she rises to make some.

She's barely at the counter before she turns to find Frankie has followed her into the kitchen, holding a stack of plates.

"You don't have to do that," Louise says, rushing to take the pile from her hands. "I can get the rest."

"You won't let me pay you for my room, or this delicious food. The least I can do is clear a table."

Louise relents, and a moment later, Frankie returns with another stack. Louise pulls out a few leftover strips of chicken from one of the nearly emptied chili bowls and drops them into a plastic container for Garbo.

"Dinner was delicious," says Frankie, still nursing her wine. "You're lucky to be married to a good cook."

Yes, she is, Louise thinks—even if it takes a stranger's arrival to remind her.

Frankie comes beside her at the counter. "What else can I do?"

"There's a little pitcher in that far cabinet. Add some cream to it, would you?"

Frankie moves to the fridge for the carton.

"Do you cook?" Louise asks.

"Some. I'd probably cook more if it wasn't for Saul."

"Is he your boyfriend?"

"My neighbor," says Frankie. "He's a widower, and there are always women bringing him ridiculous amounts of food." She laughs. "It's obscene. I think the only reason he shares with me is to assuage his guilt for taking it all without actually planning to marry any of them."

"There's no one in the running?"

Frankie shakes her head. "He's still crazy about his late wife, Ruth. There aren't enough casseroles in the world to sway his loyal heart."

Louise smiles, touched by the confession. Would Russ have a similar response to being a widower? She doesn't imagine there's a wife who hasn't considered how her husband would live his life without her, who hasn't felt the fist of fear at the possibility that he might, like so many men left alone, crave new companionship and never see the pursuit as betrayal. But Russ . . . She'd like to believe he would be like Frankie's neighbor, devoted until the very end. Did that make her selfish? Unreasonable? Probably.

At times she wondered if Glory considered what Mitch would do without her, if a part of her had dreaded the thought that her husband might replace her—no, not replace her—as if anyone could?—rather just move on with someone else. And what sort of mother that woman would be to Gabe . . .

She slows her measuring to steal a look as Frankie pours cream into the pitcher, deciding Russ is right, her resemblance to Maeve is remarkable, and a flash of longing courses through her.

She tips the beans into the grinder and gives them a quick pulse.

"So it was your idea to hire my mother?"

Louise nods as she shakes the grinds out into the filter. "Glory wasn't entirely sold on her at first."

"But she came around eventually?"

"Eventually, yes."

"So what changed her mind?"

*"Love Story."* Louise glances up to find Frankie staring at her expectantly. She smiles. "It would make sense if I told you the whole story."

Frankie crosses to the breakfast table and slides into a chair. "I'm listening."

# 22

1988

It had been two weeks since Maeve had settled into the slanted-ceilinged guest room on the other side of the beach house. With the festival just a month away, Louise found herself driving over to the beach cottage almost daily with some kind of urgent purpose. Today's visit was her second of the day. Always looking for ways to make the festival more engaging for the attendees, she'd been inspired with an idea halfway through dinner. Russ, God bless him, had indulged her, patient when she'd abandoned the rest of her lasagna, and understanding when she'd split the chocolate cream pie she'd made for their dessert. Pulling into Glory and Mitch's driveway just after seven, she nearly collided on the steps with Gabe, Glory and Mitch's young son in the throes of a savage game of hide-and-seek with friends, twisting in time to keep from spilling her pie. "Sorry, Aunt Lou!" he yelled as he vaulted over the railing into the dunes.

Glory and Maeve were working in the living room when she pulled the slider open. Glory on the sectional and Maeve cross-legged on the carpet, papers spread out around her.

"Why do I suddenly smell chocolate?" Glory asked as Louise walked past them, headed for the kitchen. She pulled three forks from the utensil drawer and joined them in the living room.

"I come bearing gifts," she said, setting the half pie in front of them.

Maeve scooted closer, but Glory just wrinkled her lips reproachfully. "She's trying to fatten me up. She does this compulsively every summer before the festival. I feel like Santa Claus in that Rudolph special. Mrs. Claus buzzing around him constantly—Eat, Papa, *eat!*—worried he won't fill out his damn suit in time for Christmas."

"Oh, stop it," Louise scolded, handing Glory a fork. "Now eat."

Maeve laughed, taking a fork for herself.

"Don't think she doesn't have her eye on you, too, you willowy thing," Glory said.

"I don't need bulking up." Maeve plunged her fork into the dark, silky pool of pudding. "But I'll gladly cave to the pressure."

"I also come bearing ideas," Louise said. "What if, in addition to your collection, we also have a fans-only display of memorabilia this year? Give the fans a chance to have a little celebrity, too? Maybe even have a dealer there to appraise their value, and those who wanted to could leave their treasures—entirely securely, of course—to be displayed among your pieces?"

Glory's gaze narrowed quizzically as she teased a corner of the pie with her fork. "But what sort of items do you imagine they might have?"

"Lobby cards, maybe. Autograph books."

Maeve licked the back of her fork. "I might have something like what you're looking for."

Louise and Glory turned to her at the same time.

"You collect memorabilia?" Louise asked.

"I wouldn't call myself a collector—but I do have something I've saved for years that I consider memorabilia . . ." Maeve smiled. "At least it brings back memories for me." She climbed to her feet, breaking off a flaky chip of crust before she bounded off down the corridor.

Louise watched her disappear, smiling. "Just think, if we'd never gone to Petite's that day . . ." She turned, expecting to find Glory's face radiating agreement, but her eyes were strained, wary.

Glory set her fork on the edge of the pie plate. "Louise, I know you meant well asking her, but I don't know if she's the best fit."

Louise leaned in. "Is it Mitch? Does he not like her?"

"I wouldn't care about that."

"Because Gabe certainly seems smitten with her."

"Are you kidding?" Glory rolled her eyes. "She lets him eat Twinkies for breakfast. She's practically a goddess."

"Then what's the problem?"

Her gaze fixed on the hallway where Maeve had disappeared. "She's so young, Louise. And what I'm asking of her . . ." Glory expelled a hard breath. "It's a lot."

"To mail out fan letters and live in a house on the beach with movie stars?" Louise chuckled as she patted Glory's hand. "I think she can handle it."

Maeve returned with a shoebox, set it down on the coffee table, and lifted the lid to reveal a colorful collection of tickets. "These are nearly all the movies I've ever seen," she said, sitting back down on the carpet, her feet under her rear this time so she could stay close to the box. "They're like my mini time machines. Whenever I'm missing someone or some place, I pull one out and I remember where I was, who I was with, what I was feeling . . ."

Louise peered in. "There must be over fifty ticket stubs in here."

"You can't possibly have memories for all of them," Glory said.

Maeve smiled. "Go ahead," she said confidently. "Pick one."

Louise held out the small box to Glory, and she chose one, hesitating a long moment before she announced, *"Love Story."*

"That can't have been yours," said Louise. "You can't have been more than eight or nine when this came out."

"Seven, actually," said Maeve. "My dad took me."

Louise sat back, wide-eyed. "Your father took you to see *Love Story*?"

Maeve resumed her cross-legged pose. "He and my mother had

this huge fight and she wanted to be alone, so I guess the movies seemed like a good place to take me for a few hours."

"And he took you to *Love Story*?" Louise still couldn't wrap her head around it—such a mature, sad movie for a child.

Glancing over, she could see from the shifting lines in Glory's brow that she struggled to do the same.

Maeve shrugged. "He asked the lady at the window what movie had just started and she sold us tickets. I'm sure she must have thought it was a weird choice for a father-daughter movie—I can only imagine her face. Let alone the guy at the turnstile who tore them." Maeve leaned forward and scooped out another spoonful of pie filling. "I remember being cold because we'd left so quickly I didn't have time to get my heavy jacket so I just kept squeezing the bucket of popcorn, because it was warm."

Louise looked over at Glory, but her gaze was fixed on Maeve, who was staring dreamily out the window, fully lost now. Her voice soft, as far away as her eyes.

"And at some point, I was aware of this jittering. My first thought was that my dad was just tapping his foot—it was this thing he used to do when he got impatient or nervous—and that was what was making my chair shake. But when I looked over, his knee was still and that's when I realized he was crying. And I remember being so confused, so scared. I had never seen my father cry . . ."

Louise and Glory exchanged a quick look.

Maeve reached into the box, absently sweeping her fingers through the tickets. Her eyes brimmed.

"A few weeks later he told me that my mother was sick, and that he'd rushed me out of the house because he didn't want me to see her falling apart." She paused, her tears spilling. "I always wonder if he picked that movie on purpose or if it was just a terrible coincidence." After another long moment, she sat up straight and wiped her eyes. "I found our tickets in his things after he died last year. I couldn't believe he'd kept them all these years."

The room fell quiet, the air heavy with Maeve's confession. Looking around, Louise realized all of them were welling up.

Glory clapped her hands to her cheeks. "Now don't I just feel awful? All those tickets to choose from and I pick the saddest one of all."

"Don't say that." Maeve leaned over and put an absolving hand on Glory's knee. "When I first found them, I remember thinking, why would my father keep something from a moment that was so painful? Until I realized he kept them because she had still been alive when we saw that movie. Because in that theater, she wasn't gone yet." She smiled even as her eyes filled again. "So it's not so sad after all, is it?"

She looked between Louise and Glory, needing confirmation.

They nodded in unison, and the longing in her face softened.

Maeve pushed the box of tickets toward them. "It's not much compared to your incredible treasures, but I'd love to offer it if you think it would be a good fit for what you need."

"This is a perfect fit." Glory reached across the coffee table and gripped Maeve's hand. Her eyes, still misty, pooled with gratitude. "Truly perfect."

# 23

Louise plucks a tissue from her tunic pocket and gives her nose a rough wipe. "After that, your mother's place in that house was sealed. Whatever concerns Glory may have had, she never mentioned them again once she realized the depth of your mother's love for the movies."

Frankie swirls her wine, staring into the glass. "I never knew that about my grandmother," she says quietly. "My mother never told me how she died. I wish she had."

Louise glances over, feeling a sharp pang of sympathy.

Frankie smiles sadly. "I still have the box of ticket stubs, you know. We used to keep them by the register."

"I imagine you and she had added quite a few more to your collection."

"At last count, eighty-nine . . ." Frankie chuckles. "It made me crazy watching people sift through them while we rang up their purchases. I was so worried someone might take one, but my mom always insisted they should be enjoyed. A few dealers offered to buy them but she always turned them down."

Louise dries her hands on a dish towel.

"Seeing her in those pictures this morning . . ." Frankie leans back in her chair. "My mother looked so happy here."

"We certainly thought so."

She's not aware of how her response has come out until she looks over to find Frankie staring at her blankly.

"Russ didn't tell you?"

Frankie shakes her head, and Louise feels a charge of dread.

"Your mother disappeared without saying goodbye."

Frankie frowns at her. "What do you mean, 'disappeared'?"

Louise leans into the counter. Hadn't Russ lectured her on all they had to tell Frankie about her mother, and yet he leaves out the most important part?

In too far now, she might as well finish.

"Glory was on the Outer Banks for her last role," she says. "Your mother was supposed to go down to be with her during the filming, to help her, but she never showed up. No note, no nothing."

"She just took off?"

"Yes."

Frankie blinks down at the table for several seconds, then her gaze lifts, hope clearly sparking. "But surely after the news of Glory's death became public, she reached out to you all?"

Maybe it's the pleading look on her face, but for an instant, Louise is tempted to lie. "No," she says softly. "We never heard from her again."

Frankie looks away. "I don't know what to say . . ." Her voice thins to a whisper. "That you let me stay here anyway, knowing how she left you all. How she hurt you. No wonder you couldn't forgive her."

Louise looks up, regret swirling.

"Gabe's leaving." Russ appears in the doorway, startling them both.

She pulls in a sharp breath, searching the counter for her bearings, and sees Garbo's leftovers. "Here." She reaches for the container, just grateful for something to do with her nervous hands. "It's for Garbo."

Frankie stands and steps forward—darts, really. "Let me," she says.


Frankie finds Gabe in the front yard, trying to cajole Garbo out from the inky blooms of the juniper bushes. She takes the porch stairs to the grass slowly, wobbly with Louise's news. That her mother had run away because she was pregnant and scared was understandable—but going back on her word, abandoning people who'd cared for her like family after such a loss was unforgivable. And not anything like the person Frankie had known her to be. No wonder Louise seemed prickly with her that first morning. She hadn't imagined it.

Emotions collide—contrasting waves of disappointment and confusion—and suddenly her mother feels further away than ever.

She holds out the container, grateful for the anchor of purpose before her conflicted thoughts send her adrift.

"For Garbo."

"Good." Gabe takes the scraps. "Maybe now I can actually get her into the truck."

Frankie squints into the shifting black. "What's she hunting in there?"

"Probably a chipmunk. But between you and me, I think the chipmunk's hunting her. She puts on a big game but Garbo's really all heart."

The breeze picks up, warm and salty, sending Gabe's hair across his forehead. Memories of the evening flash, Gabe's lingering gaze on hers during dinner, and before . . . *What do you want?*

She crosses her arms, chilled.

"Why did you name her Garbo?"

"From the day she showed up on my deck, she kept to herself," he says. "Most Labs love attention, but not her. I always heard that's how Greta Garbo was, that she was a recluse, that she hated the trappings of Hollywood and didn't care who knew it. I always thought that was kind of cool . . ." His mouth slides into a grin. "And they're both, you know, blondes."

"I thought you didn't know anything about movies."

"Yeah, well." He digs at the gravel with the toe of his sneaker. "I tried not to pay attention, but it was almost impossible growing up in our house. My mom was constantly name-dropping, talking about the old legends of Hollywood . . ." He shrugs. "Stand out in the rain long enough, eventually you'll get wet."

She smiles, grateful for the moment of levity, but thoughts of her mother's unfortunate departure resume, and the sound sinks into a sigh.

She looks up to find Gabe studying her, his dark eyes narrowed with concern.

"I'm sorry for before," he says. "About finding your father. I didn't mean to upset you."

Frankie offers him a weak smile, strangely heartened that he thinks her pensive mood is his fault.

Garbo gallops past, a creamy blur.

"Do you want to see her?"

Frankie blinks at him, needing a minute to orient.

"*Essie*," he says.

His boat.

Possibility churns in her stomach. Just the two of them.

"You could come by tomorrow after I get off work. Say, six?" He shifts the container between his hands. The lights of a passing car sweep across the driveway, briefly casting his brown hair gold, and she wonders how it would feel to push her fingers through the thick waves.

"Six is . . ." She hesitates reflexively, as if there's a chance she's busy. "Six is good."

"I'll leave the gate propped open," he says as he walks backward toward the truck and waits while Garbo hops into the passenger seat.

She steps back, butterflies of anticipation still batting against her ribs as he swings the truck out onto the road a few minutes later, Garbo's tan snout pushing out the passenger window, squinting, bracing for the sea air.

# 24

Louise tells herself not to get her hopes up. This was just one night, a special occasion; she's not about to globalize one dinner and believe a single meal can repair months—years—of a dissolving marriage. Just because he said he liked her outfit, just because he touched her hand at the table when he complimented her—an intentional touch, lasting several seconds, too—she knew better than to think they'd turned some kind of corner. But somewhere in the course of the evening, she'd found her earlier wariness shift to something else. Maybe not quite gratitude, but close. What difference did it make why her husband had chosen to cheer up? He had, and that was all that mattered, wasn't it?

And yet, despite reserving all hope, when she's finished cleaning up and eager for a lungful of night air, Russ is still on the deck. Sitting. The way he used to when he'd wait for her to join him before bed. She'd make them tea, maybe plate up a few of Diamond's pecan squares, and they'd take turns sharing the ups and downs of their respective days, or, later on, when Gabe lived with them and they'd have to lower their voice to whispers, debating how best to help him navigate his new universe of loneliness—an orphan, again.

It feels wrong to come out empty-handed, even though she suspects he's as full from dinner as she is.

Russ glances at her over his shoulder. "You look surprised to see me."

"I am." She pulls the slider closed behind her. "I assumed you'd already gone to bed."

"Not with this view."

She glances up at the nearly full moon, a custard yellow. The other Adirondack chair awaits her. She wants to sit, but she wants him to ask her even more, to let the rhythm of interest build for a few measures. The memory of Gabe and Frankie stealing glances at one another during dinner lingers—is it wrong of her to crave a few prickles of romantic interest for herself?

"Join me?" he asks.

And there it is: the invitation. Her whole being wants to rush into the slanted chair, but she forces herself to sink slowly, with restraint, feeling silly for playing games with herself at this age. But where was the harm when they were under the stars together for the first time in months?

Russ rolls his head in her direction, the deck lights wreathing his hair.

"Nice night, wasn't it?" he asks.

"Very." She smooths the pleats of her skirt.

"I can't remember the last time we had dinner with him."

"And when he's been in such a good mood," she adds, thinking she could say the same for her husband.

"They did seem to be getting along, didn't they?"

"Shh . . ." She motions to the second floor. "She'll hear you."

"She won't. She's closed the window. She said she gets cold."

She admires the thickness of his hair, deciding it looks more silver than white tonight. "If you're trying to play matchmaker . . ."

He smiles wistfully at his hands in his lap. "She's so like Maeve, isn't she?"

"I saw it tonight, too," she admits. "Amazing that Gabe sat with her and looked through those photos, wasn't it?"

Russ nods thoughtfully, surely thinking what she did: how rarely Gabe will revisit his past, even in their company. When he moved into their house at thirteen, he never put up any pictures in his new room. She and Russ had inquired, even offered to have photographs of him with Glory and Mitch framed for him, but Gabe had declined. There was no need, he claimed, when they had already covered the hallways and stairwell with so many photographs of his parents that he could visit anytime he wanted. But it wasn't long before Louise began to notice that not only did Gabe never slow in front of their galleries, but he started taking different paths through the house to avoid them. Russ told her it was the normal process of grief, using denial to bury anguish, but Louise lamented, so worried Gabe just wanted to forget. Russ claimed he needed time, that they shouldn't push.

Some days she wonders if they should have pushed more.

Russ moves his hands to the arm rests and spreads out his fingers, drumming them absently. "I'm glad we could share some things about Maeve with her."

Flashes of their talk in the kitchen and guilt flares, the need to confess suddenly urgent.

"Russ, I just assumed . . ."

He twists to look at her, his eyes thinning to questioning slits. "You assumed what?"

"That you'd told her," she says. "That Maeve disappeared on us."

He grips the end of the Adirondack arms. "I didn't see the point. She'd just feel badly. It wasn't her fault." His eyebrows knit. "Did you tell her?"

Her cheeks flare with remorse. "I wasn't trying to be hurtful, Russ."

He scans her eyes intently; whatever fairy dust was sprinkled over their evening is now gone.

"You never told me you knew Maeve was seeing an older man."

She frowns at him, startled at the strange subject, the out-of-the-blue nature of it.

"When did Maeve tell you?" he presses.

"I—I don't remember . . ." Louise sits back, her body, once

relaxed, now tensed again. "Maybe that day Mitch finally took *Essie* out for the first time?" She grows annoyed, feeling like someone on trial. As if she's done something wrong. "What difference does it make?"

"It doesn't," he says, sniffing as he leans back.

And just like that, the air cools—whatever warmth their evening had tendered, suddenly snuffed out.

And when the heavy silence lingers, Louise doesn't try to fill it. She just scans the strings of stars, searching for memories to resurrect it.

# 25

1988
December

Louise tugged her coat collar tighter around her throat and glanced at the top of the passenger window, wondering if a tiny crack was to blame for the car's inability to get warm.

"Why today of all days?" she said as Russ steered them toward the cottage. All around them the swells of dune grass strained against the wind, looking more like the coat of an animal whose fur had been stroked flat. It was far too cold for a sail, but after years of repair and rebuilding, Mitch's beloved boat, *The Great Escape*, or *Essie*, as he preferred to call her, was finally seaworthy—even if the rest of them weren't. "I'm telling you right now—Glory won't want to come, Russ. She won't—and he'll be an absolute bear."

She stared at her husband's profile, waiting to see the wash of agreement strain his features, but he only offered a neutral shrug.

Louise pulled her comb from her purse and gave her bob a quick neatening, letting the subject evaporate as they exited the car and took the steps down to the beach where *Essie* was moored.

"Look at that." Russ whistled low in admiration as they descended the steps to the dock. He'd done a beautiful job with her, Louise would give Mitch that. The sailboat gleamed like a freshly fallen chestnut.

Mitch stood at the stern. "Not bad, huh?" he crowed as they

stepped aboard. Glory and Maeve waved from the cockpit; Glory sat wrapped in a long puffy jacket, her arms and legs crossed against the chill. Maeve stood to offer Louise her seat, but Louise waved her back down. "Sit," she said. "We can squeeze."

"I know, I know—don't even say it," Glory whispered tightly to Louise as they nestled close. "He's out of his mind."

"Which one?" Louise teased back, noting the way her own husband stood with his hands on his hips, puffed up as he surveyed the deck like he'd boarded a great Viking ship.

"Aren't we supposed to break a bottle against something to commemorate this?" he asked.

Glory slid a cool look in Mitch's direction. "The captain's head, wasn't it?"

"Glow's just pissed because I wouldn't change the name for her," Mitch said, pulling Russ close.

"*Glory for All* has a nice ring to it," she defended.

"I told her you can't change a boat's name—it's bad luck."

"As if we need to worry about that," said Glory.

Russ nodded firmly. "He's right, you know."

Even through the wall of down between them, Louise could still feel Glory trembling. She touched her arm. "You're shivering."

Maeve leaned over, looking concerned. "We should get you inside."

"I'm fine, really," insisted Glory. "And anyway, I don't dare move until these waves slow."

The chop was fierce, Louise thought, glancing out at the water. Surely Mitch was rethinking his plan?

Glory's eyes grew huge. "Mitch, why is our son carrying a giant knife?"

Louise turned to see Gabe emerging from the hatch with a smile almost as big as the blade he held proudly in his raised hand. She didn't know whether to be more alarmed by the knife or the fact that the boy was, like his father, barefoot in December.

"Because I let him carve his name next to mine," Mitch said matter-of-factly. "Go take a look."

"Yeah, Mom, come on," Gabe urged. "Look."

"In a minute, baby. I'm still trying to get my sea legs."

"Gabe, your mother's the only person I know who can get seasick on a docked boat."

Maeve climbed to her feet. "I'd love to see it," she said cheerfully, a frosty gust of wind sending her mane of auburn hair whipping against her face as she navigated through the cockpit for the opening.

"Me too." Russ stepped forward, offering Louise an affectionate smile as he followed Gabe and Maeve below. Appreciation swelled behind Louise's ribs.

"Maeve's so good with Gabe," Glory said wistfully, her gaze fixed on the hatch they'd all disappeared through. "I hate that he sees me like this, Louise."

"Seasick?" Louise meant the joke to soften Glory's strained features, but her thin brows only knitted tighter.

"You know what I mean," she said. "He'll look back on these days and he'll remember his dad as this firecracker, this god of all things fun, and I'll be the one who never wanted to do any of it."

"You're not a sailor. There's no shame in that."

Louise had grown accustomed to Glory's constant self-doubt and disparaging remarks, but the defeat in her eyes today alarmed her more than usual. The winter before had proven especially difficult—made more so when Glory decided to get off her medication without telling anyone. Did she have a similar plan this year?

As much as she dreaded asking the question, Louise dreaded the possibility of Glory's answer more. "Glory, you aren't thinking of trying to get off your . . . ?"

She patted Louise's knee. "Don't worry, I'm still taking my meds like a good girl."

Louise pulled in a sharp breath of relief.

"But"—Glory dropped her voice to a whisper, making Louise have to lean close to hear her over the clamor of the rocking boat—"if you want to worry for someone, worry for our poor Maeve. She's been seeing someone."

Louise frowned. "And this is worrisome?"

"She's broken it off."

"Oh?"

"She had to," said Glory. "He's . . . well . . . he's quite a bit older. And apparently, he's not taking it well, begging her to give him another chance."

"Did she tell you his name?"

"No—and I didn't want to press," said Glory, pulling her jacket tighter around herself. "I have theories, of course."

A few usual suspects came to Louise's mind, too—Harpswich men with reputations for engaging young women who came for summer work, only to shed them like old skin when they left after Labor Day.

Gabe bolted from the hatch; Mitch trailed behind him, winded.

"So are we ready to push off, or what?" he said.

Russ climbed through next, offering a hand up to Maeve before he crossed back to Louise. She motioned toward Glory and gave Russ a small but pointed head shake, hoping he might help convince Mitch of the folly of his plan.

"That chop isn't letting up, Mitch. Maybe we should wait for a better day."

"You said the same thing when I convinced Curtis to let us take out that schooner in high school—and we saw that whale and her pup, remember?" Mitch said, wagging a finger at Russ.

Her husband chuckled wistfully. "That was a hell of a sail."

Louise rolled her eyes. So much for that strategy.

Maeve came beside Glory, her hazel eyes flashing with concern. "We need to get you inside—you're turning blue."

"Oh, come on, Glow," Mitch said, climbing over the guard rails. "I'm just talking about one little spin."

"Hey, I have an idea," said Russ, catching Louise's pleading gaze. "Why not make this first sail guys-only? Let the ladies stay here, and you and me and Gabe will christen the old gal. What do you say?"

"Yeah!" Gabe leapt over the deck with an approving hoot.

But Mitch charged into the cockpit and stood over Glory, red faced, his hands fisted. "Dammit, why can't we do one thing as a family?"

Louise froze, her heart hammering, a counterattack bubbling in her throat but refusing to come out. She looked pleadingly at Russ, willing her husband to rescue them all.

Then Maeve bolted to her feet. The fierceness of her posture was nothing compared to the ice in her voice as she pierced Mitch with a hard stare. "Because she's cold and she needs to go in."

Even with the persistent smacks of the chop against the hull, the air seemed to quiet in the wake of her strike.

And in the ensuing seconds, Louise witnessed the most remarkable sequence of emotions flicker across Mitch's furious, sunburned face: shock, outrage, and then, finally, defeat.

Glory gripped her jacket closed and climbed shakily to her feet. "Forgive me, everyone."

Louise rose to help, but Maeve took Glory's elbow to steady her, offering Louise a grateful smile.

"I can stay here with her, Louise," Maeve said. "You enjoy your time on the water with your husband."

Glory pressed her hand into Louise's and gave it a weak squeeze. Her fingers were like icicles. "We'll break open that box of truffles when you come back in, okay?" she whispered.

And as the boat began to drift away from the pier, and she watched Glory and Maeve navigate the snaking stack of stairs back to the house, arm in arm, Louise felt a burst of gratitude—and something else. A flutter of satisfaction. Because when she'd looked across the cash register that day in Petite's, Glory's wish for an assistant sending her thoughts plotting, Louise had never imagined she'd found in Maeve Simon someone who might finally do the hardest job of all, the one task none of them had managed in all their years together: put Mitch Beckett in his place.

# 26

Tuesday

It's not yet six, but as promised, Gabe has propped open the gate to the dock, and Frankie follows the steep incline of the walkway, grateful for the grip of the sandpaper strips on her smooth soles. The stretch of weathered wood planks at the end of the ramp is flanked with boats that are much smaller, and far less decked out (the latter can also be said of the people climbing on and off them), than the ones moored off the main pier. No velvet ropes or mobs with straining selfie sticks here. Frankie nearly collides with a man unloading an enormous cooler off a fishing boat, and he points her to the end of the dock. Even before she spots the curved black-and-gold lettering— *The Great Escape*—she sees Garbo. The dog is cantering across the deck, carefree until she detects Frankie's advance, at which point she hops around and trains her soulful black eyes on Frankie for only a second before she thrusts her snout upward and lets out a series of hard, low barks.

In the next instant, Gabe emerges from the hatch, and the flurry of butterflies that charge up Frankie's throat startles her.

She shifts on her heels. "You must not get a lot of surprise guests."

"Who needs a doorbell," Gabe says, slowing to rub Garbo's head on his way to meet her.

She motions to the edge of the boat. "So do I just . . . ?"

"Here." He holds out his hand and she takes it, grateful for his strong grip as she climbs on and follows him carefully down the three shallow steps into the cabin. The soft light of dusk enters through a row of portholes, washing the cabin's curves in a silvery blue. A single sconce glows above a box of built-in shelves, crammed with what Frankie suspects is mostly junk. Music plays faintly from a speaker buried somewhere in the clutter, something bluesy and slow. Old nautical maps cover the walls, wrinkled and yellowed with age. A crooked sign dangles above the tiny sink: JUST SHUCK IT.

Gabe moves to the wedge of kitchen space, his head brushing the cabin ceiling. "Get you a drink?"

"I'll take some wine if you have any."

She wanders the cabin while he pulls out a bottle of white from a metal bin beside the diminutive stove, fills a plastic tumbler halfway, and hands it to her. On the side of the glass, she sees the ghostly residue of a decal—CHOWDER'S ON THE PIER—and pulls in a ripe whiff of grapefruit just before she sips. The wine swims across her tongue, cold and crisp and tart.

He picks up a beer bottle from the cluttered counter. "Know anything about boats?"

"Not a thing."

"Essie's a '79 Mariner Ketch. My dad got her when he was a teenager. But when I got her, she was a mess." He leans to his right and runs his hand fondly along a panel of cherry-colored wood. "She'd been left on the ground for a year. Rotten thing to do to a boat—literally. Most of this teak I had to replace," he says, sweeping his bottle in an arc. "But she's getting there." His dark eyes drift around the cabin, softening wistfully as he scans the space, his lips curving with unabashed affection, and Frankie doesn't know why she should, but she wonders if Gabe Beckett has ever looked at a lover the way he looks at this boat.

Garbo barks, and they both glance up to see the dog in the opening, her tail swinging expectantly.

Gabe reaches down and flips up a hinged ramp, settling it easily over the treads to create a cleated ramp that the dog miraculously maneuvers her way down.

"Clever," she says.

"You have to be clever on a boat. There's not much storage space." When the dog's safely down, Gabe gives her a congratulatory pat and lowers the ramp back to the floor. "Garbo likes to move around as much as she can in the nicer weather. It gets slippery in the winter months."

"You live on this year-round?"

"It's not as bad as it sounds. I've got a diesel heater, an electric blanket. Shrink-wrapping helps." He offers up a small grin. "So does rum."

She smiles. "I'll bet."

The boat rolls underneath them. Frankie reaches for the rounded edge of the galley counter to steady herself, catching a sugary whiff of overripe bananas. Beside her, the stretch of new, polished boards are interrupted by a foot of weathered wood, two carvings etched deep. She leans in to decipher them: *Captain Mitch Beckett. 1st mait Gabe B.*

Gabe walks over. "My dad carved that top one in there when he first got her. He let me carve the one underneath when I was a kid. As you can see, my spelling still needed some work."

She runs her fingertips over the gouges. "So you didn't replace this board then?"

He shrugs. "Seemed wrong to."

She watches him take a swig of beer. She agrees, of course, but for someone so dismissive of the past, the gesture seems uncharacteristically sentimental.

Gabe catches her studying him before she can look away.

"How do you feel about oysters?" he asks.

"To eat?"

"No, as friends." He grins. "Yes, to eat."

"I've actually never had them."

Gabe grabs at his chest and stumbles back against the counter, like a shot gunslinger in an old western, and she laughs, startled by the playfulness of the gesture. Having come to think of him as reserved—if not even downright gloomy—she would never have imagined him capable of real lightness. She wonders in what other ways Gabe Beckett might surprise her tonight.

"Is that the wrong answer?" she asks.

"Hating oysters is the wrong answer," he says. "Never having had them is good . . ." His dark eyes flash. "It means you can still be turned."

Her skin flushes.

She likes the sound of that.

After she helps him draw up two leaves to create a narrow dining table between the banks of seating, he pulls a plastic grocery bag out of the icebox and unpacks large, gnarled black shells, loud as a pile of bricks when he lowers the oysters into a bucket of ice and carries them to the flip-top table with a small but formidable-looking knife.

"Don't look so nervous," he says, taking a seat beside her on the settee.

"You're wielding a knife. It's a natural reaction."

"For the oysters, sure." He takes one of the shells from the pile, gives it a quick wipe with the towel, then holds it up to her. "Shucking 101." He settles it in his wide palm and bends his fingers around the textured shell. "You want to get a good grip on it. The key is to find the hinge and slide the point of the knife into it."

Frankie shifts closer to get a better view as he works the tip of the blade into the fatter end of the shell and begins to rock it gently, the scent of warm sea water rising, reminding her suddenly and fiercely of an apartment she and her mother stayed in above a Tex-Mex restaurant in Venice Beach—how some nights the smell of fish tacos would drift up from the patio, hot and salty and tinged with lime.

A few twists of the knife point, and the shell gives with a startling pop.

Gabe leans in. "Once you've got it in, you run the blade along the top—gently," he says, "since the oyster is still attached to his shell, and they can hold on hard before they let you in."

Frankie looks up at him, prickles of panic firing across her scalp. "They're still alive?"

He squints. "You'd get pretty sick if you ate the dead ones."

She sits back, blinking dazedly between him and the still sealed—still living—shell in his hand, feeling dim for not realizing this sooner—but feeling queasy even more.

"It's not like they're wriggling around," he says, carefully lifting the top and tipping the shell toward her. "Look." The oyster, silver and cream and so beautifully silky, shimmers peacefully under a glossy film of brine. "See? You can't even tell it's still alive."

The last two words do her in. Tears brim instantly, too fast to blink back.

"Oh shit," he whispers hoarsely.

She swipes roughly at her eyes, her embarrassment only rising when she looks up to find him scanning her face for explanation.

"If this is because I said that about getting sick from the dead ones, I didn't mean . . ."

She shakes her head fiercely. "It's nothing you said. It's me. Losing my mother, and then coming here. Finding out she had all this history that she never told me about . . ." She looks up to find him watching her. "It's a lot."

He nods, the dawning of understanding passes across his face, loosening the knot of his brow.

"Wait here," he says, standing. "I have a better idea."


Gabe emerges through the hatch with a pair of peanut butter and jelly sandwiches a few minutes later, taking a seat across from Frankie in the cockpit where she's come up, needing air.

"The meat and potatoes of the live-aboard," he says, handing her one.

She sinks her teeth into the spongy white bread, the perfect blend of salt and sweet filling her mouth.

"Better?" he asks.

"Better." She appraises him a moment while they eat, enjoying the way the wind blows his hair across his forehead, the way the lowered sun glitters against his jawline.

He swallows. "You should know that most of what I eat isn't alive."

She laughs, grateful for the sound.

Garbo trots over; Gabe tears off a stretch of crust and the dog snatches it up.

"Do you two always eat this well?" she asks. "Or only when company comes?"

He settles back against the hull. "You were expecting a more sophisticated menu, huh?"

"Considering your parents . . ." She holds up what's left of her sandwich. "Let's just say I can't imagine your mother eating one of these."

"My mother rarely ate—period," he says, peeling off another piece for Garbo. "And when she did, it was always some horrible food fad she'd learned about from one of her Hollywood friends. There was this wheat grass phase when I was a kid . . ." He grimaces.

"I happen to love wheat grass juice."

"Of course you do." His squint is condemning, but his smirk is all play. Who knew he was capable of smiling so often? Frankie wonders fleetingly if it's the beer or her reaction to the oysters that's softened his edges before deciding she doesn't care. Her own thoughts are light and breezy like the evening air. "But try being in third grade," he continues, "and opening your lunchbox to find your mother's packed you a bottle—neon green, you could have gone blind—and the next thing you know your friends are calling you Slime Boy."

Laughing, Frankie can't help recalling the photograph of him in Russ's collection, the hard edges of his jaw soft and round, those hooded brown eyes so much bigger on a smaller face, the tanned, weathered brow smooth under a boy's shaggy bangs, and the realization—again—that her mother knew that boy. And that boy knew her mother.

The rumble of a motor nears, drawing their gaze to the distance, where a boat purrs past.

Gabe points to her nearly drained glass. "More wine?"

"Please."

He disappears below, and Frankie hears rattling through the cracked portholes, then the music turned up. She draws her bare feet up onto the bench, pressing her soles over the pebbled surface, and throws her head back to scan the pastel sky. The breeze is still warm but softer now with approaching night. She follows the ribbons of pink and peach clouds, thinking how different the sky looks here than in LA, where they are still hours away from dusk. She imagines Saul shuffling around his patio, Bogart on his heels, before he goes back inside to reheat whatever casserole he's been gifted with today. In a few days, she'll be back there. Back to the store her mother started, which she must now decide whether to keep or close.

Back home.

So why does she already feel a flicker of missing this place?

Gabe returns with the bottle of white and a thick sweater that he hands her. "You looked cold." The wool smells like wet paper but feels wonderfully heavy as she tugs it on.

On the other side of the harbor, the twinkling lights of downtown glow with activity, the hum and pulse of festival after-parties. Garbo rises and begins to circle anxiously; small growls rumbling from behind her bared teeth.

"She hates the fireworks," he explains.

"But the sky's clear."

"She knows they're coming. The air starts to crackle." Gabe pats the bench beside him until Garbo leaps up. "It was like this last night, too. I usually take her for a ride in the truck to calm her down." After a few spins, the dog curls up against Gabe's thigh, but her eyes still dart nervously toward the sky.

"So why not leave town for the week if she hates it so much?"

"I usually do," he says. "But this year, I didn't feel right leaving. Not with Lou being so busy, and Doc still so down—although he's seemed in much better spirits since you got here."

She's not sure if Gabe means the comment as compliment or suspicion until she sees his smile.

In the distance, another cruiser glides past, this one nearly silent.

He draws up one knee and leans back against the boat. "Anyone waiting for you back in LA?"

She studies her wine, considering her answer in the pool of soft gold. "Not anymore."

"Any chance you might work it out?"

When she shakes her head, he searches her tilted face, his brow bent in playful contemplation. "He was seeing someone else?"

"Worse. He raised the rent on the store."

"You dated your landlord?"

"I wouldn't recommend it." She takes a quick sip. The chop of the passing boat finally reaches them, rocking them gently and filling the inky silence with the even, lazy rhythm of the waves smacking the hull.

"Can you afford to stay open?" he asks.

"I don't know." She swirls her wine, surprised by his question, doubtful he could really care. But when she meets his probing gaze and finds genuine interest flashing, a rush of pleasure fills her. "I suppose coming here was a way to avoid having to make that decision."

Garbo shifts suddenly in her sleep, kicking her back legs hard against Gabe's knee, as if to force the subject aside. He gives Garbo a comforting stroke along the dog's jittery flank, the gesture remarkably tender.

"She's just dreaming," he says. "Probably chasing something through the marsh."

Frankie smiles. "Do you think she has all four paws in her dreams?"

"I hope so." He runs his hand fondly over the animal's head. "Seems pointless to have dreams if you don't get what you want in them."

His eyes rise to meet hers, and Frankie feels her skin warm.

She brushes loose tendrils behind her ears. "I'm sorry I fell apart like that." The prickle of tears threatens to return, but she sniffs them back, shifting her gaze to the water. "I never used to think about death before I lost her. Now I see it everywhere."

"Because it is," Gabe says. "We just have to pretend it isn't or we'd never get out of bed."

He finds her gaze again, and Frankie lets him hold it, her stomach plummeting when his eyes sink to her mouth, appraising it as if he's trying to decide which lip to taste first, and heat floods her face.

"Come on." He scoops up the bottle. "There's somewhere I want you to see."

## 27

Garbo takes the passenger seat, trampling across her legs as Frankie slides into the middle of the bench, and she's more than happy with the arrangement. Her upper half is toasty under the blanket of Gabe's thick wool sweater now, but her bare legs are riddled with gooseflesh and his thigh against hers is hard and warm. Tufts of dog fur whirl over the top of the dashboard like tiny tumbleweeds as Gabe pulls them out of the lot. The road, clogged with traffic in the other direction, curves uninterrupted. When the truck hits a rutted patch of road, her leg knocks against his knee, and she's suddenly aware of the other places their bodies nearly touch—his right hand on the seat—her shoulder, his arm.

After a few miles, a FOR SALE sign—yellow and blue, the only splashes of color against the landscape of pale greens and browns—appears, and Gabe steers them toward a modest-looking two-story house covered in the same weathered-gray shingles as so many other homes Frankie's seen on the Cape. The simplicity of the structure surprises her—this is where Glory Cartwright re-created her Hollywood home? She expected something grander, flashier. Over the surrounding bluffs, she makes out the silhouettes of several other good-sized but equally unremarkable-looking homes—their distances near enough that you could travel over for some sugar if you were desperate, but not so close that you would worry about making love with the windows open.

She follows Gabe up a stretch of sand-dusted stairs to a generous deck that overlooks the water, and a wall of glass windows. Cupping her hands around her face, she peeks in, trying to envision her young mother moving around the dim space, sweeping past Glory Cartwright and Mitch Beckett and eight-year-old Gabe. Was there music playing in the background, maybe a TV? Had Glory's perfume masked the smell of the sea? Or maybe something simmering on the stove? Frankie squints, shifts—but there's not enough light to see clearly.

Gabe stands at the railing, staring out at the water, and she joins him. The beach below is empty, the sand smooth and unblemished by footprints, the only depressions those made by shells, cast out by the surf's foam, and her thoughts flow with every retreat.

How many nights had her mother looked out onto this view? Had the crash of the curling waves helped her sleep or kept her awake? A crooked ribbon of steps winds its way down to the shore. There must be over fifty of them, all weathered the color of thunderheads. How many times had her mother followed them up and down in the year she lived here?

The sun has nearly slipped below the horizon, brushing the sand a milky blue. Frankie studies Gabe's hands where they hang over the plank of splintered wood, the streaks of leftover paint across his knuckles she'd observed during their first real exchange gone now. She wonders what it would feel like to touch the chapped ridges, to slide her fingers inside of his and let them stay there. Despite the chill of the breeze, his body radiates heat. She longs to slide closer to him, to absorb his warmth, but her feet remain planted.

"It must have been wonderful growing up by the water," she says. "I always wanted to live in a house like this. A proper house . . ." She can feel his gaze turned to her now. "But my mom always said it was easier to move out of someone else's house than get them to leave yours, so we never had our own place. Instead we were always moving into other people's houses. Men who fell in love with her wanted to take care of her. Which always pissed me off, because *I* took care of her. We took care of each other . . ." The confession spills out, unexpected and sharp. She blames the growing dark for her candor, the bite of the wind on her cheeks. Gabe shifts his feet beside her—has she startled him with her admission?

Let him be startled, she decides, raising her face to the sea air. If she's allowed a tear in the seam of her heart, so what? Why should he be the only one revealing surprises tonight?

"If it makes you feel any better, I never really thought of this place as ours either." He twists to face the house and leans back against the railing, studying the dark panels of glass. "But that's because my mom was always pretending she didn't really live here." He toes the frayed end of a loose board, testing it absently. "She treated it like a rental. Like it was someone else's home and she was just visiting."

"It must have been hard living here after you lost her," she says gently.

"You can't lose someone who was never here to start with."

Frankie considers his profile, the hard set of his jaw, the corners of his eyes tight. Maybe she's not the only one here unbuttoning their heart.

"Are you sorry you brought me here?" she says.

"Are you sorry you came?"

She pierces him with a narrowed gaze. "I asked you first."

He leans in. "Want to get closer?"

And it takes her a second to realize he's talking about the beach.


Gabe warns her of splinters and raised nail heads when they reach the top of the stairs, but Frankie toes off her sandals anyway, wanting to feel the weathered, gritty boards the same way her mother would have. The sand is cold as they walk silently toward a pier several hundred yards down the beach. When the frothy fingers of the surf crawl her way, she scoots back to safety, but Gabe lets the water soak his Chucks. They reach the pilings and step under the long roof of the pier. She finds one clean of barnacles and leans against it, savoring the corridor of breeze and the cold prickle of rough wood against the back of her thighs.

"What did you mean back there—that she was never here to start with?"

"Just what I said." Gabe reaches down to pry a clam shell from the sand, rubbing it clean with his thumb. "My mom always wanted to get back to Hollywood. She was here in body only."

"But she stayed."

"Because she had to. The business left them behind. The roles dried up." He chucks the shell into the surf.

Frankie holds herself, chilled again. "That doesn't mean she didn't want to be with you and your dad. You have to know she loved you."

He stares out at the water. "You want to know what I remember?" he says. "I remember my mother never getting out of bed for days. I remember my dad begging her to eat . . ." His voice deepens. "I remember some days trying everything I could to get her to smile or laugh, just once, and then some stranger would show up and ask her to sign her autograph on a napkin and she'd light up like a goddamn bonfire . . ." He plunges his hands into his pockets and turns to her. "I know she loved that fucking napkin, Frankie. *That's* what I know."

She searches his gaze, longing and affection swirling. She lowers her crossed arms and runs her hands along the cool column, the surface slick with damp, letting his painful confession hang in the air.

"Do you ever think about moving away?" she asks.

He shrugs. "I like people knowing who I am. Certain people . . ." He considers her a long moment. "Isn't that why you stay in LA? Because it's home?"

Was it? People know her there, people who care, sure. But home?

Home was where you had friends over for dinner, where you hung pictures of people you loved.

Where you stayed somewhere long enough to unpack, to fill a drawer.

A pair of shorebirds lands a few feet away, regarding them curiously until Garbo dashes past, sending the birds skittering down to the surf.

Gabe appears around the other side of her piling and leans in, a woodsy smell coming with him. His eyes search hers, still waiting for her answer.

"I stay because that's where my mother was," she says. "And in a way, she's still there."

He rolls closer, and she shifts on her bare feet to find balance, the sand suddenly too damp to hold her. The moisture of the piling has soaked through the seat of her shorts. His fingers find hers, teasing her hand into his.

Frankie looks up at him as he leans in. "But my mother was here, too," she whispers. And when his mouth covers hers, she exhales into him, a small but urgent sound, something between a sigh of relief and craving that deepens the kiss so quickly she grabs him, pulls fistfuls of his T-shirt into her fingers like she's sinking, because she might as well be. The sand is soft. The breeze is soft. Every part of her is so soft. And he must know it, she thinks, because his hands rake through her hair and grab, too, twisting her already-loose knot free. She arches against the piling, reaching up for his shoulders and linking her arms around his neck. His hands travel down her back, scaling her spine over her sweater, then dropping to her waist so they can slide underneath the thick wool, his fingers searching—

A snap, a pop.

Gabe releases her and steps back as a second rattle of fireworks shudders, drawing their attention to the house, where the top edge of a bloom of white and red needles pierces the darkening sky. They stare dazedly at one another, as winded as if it had been them, not Garbo, chasing shorebirds down the beach. As cold as she is, she doesn't want to leave.

Garbo arrives and stays close, whining faintly with distress.

Frankie swallows, but still her breath is labored. "We have to go, don't we?" she asks, as if there's a chance they could stretch out this moment, as if they could will the fireworks to rain down in silence.

Gabe offers the dog a calming pat, but Frankie can see his eyes darken with remorse when they find hers again.

"Have to," he says. "Not want to."

Only a first-floor window is lit when Gabe turns them into the driveway, pulling alongside the Subaru and shoving the truck into park. The recessed porch lights are on, bathing the weathered shingles in silver. The air that drifts through the truck's open windows is damp but cool, the sizzle of night insects rising above the idling engine, moths and beetles batting their wings against the glow of the bulbs.

Frankie shifts on the warm seat. The memory of their kiss floats through the cab, still radiating from their bodies like dried salt water after a swim.

Gabe lets his hand fall from the wheel to his thigh. Frankie studies his fingers in the streaks of the house light, remembering how he'd driven them into her hair, the startling heat of his tongue when she'd let him into her mouth, and her abdomen tightens.

A light flickers to life in the kitchen window.

She jerks reflexively and chuckles.

"It's like we're back in high school, isn't it?" he says.

"How long before one of them comes out?" she asks.

Gabe glances up at the house. "Oh, they won't come out. They'll probably just keep turning the lights on, one at a time. It's much more effective."

She laughs, then claps a hand guiltily over her mouth, fearful of discovery.

His hand slides across the bench to find hers, the rough tips of his fingers brushing hers.

"Have dinner with me tomorrow night?" When she looks over to find his face in the speckled light, he adds, "I promise nothing living."

She searches his gaze, wondering if they dare try again for a good-bye kiss, but Garbo climbs over them, trying to decide which open window offers the better smells, and forcing them apart.

She reaches for the door, then slows. "You'll think I'm crazy for asking this but . . . Can you put them back?"

Confusion pinches the corners of his eyes.

"The oysters," she says. "If they're still alive, can you return them to the sea?"

Gabe rubs his jaw thoughtfully, one side then the other. "It would depend. Even if they came from the bay, not all habitats are the same and . . ."

She must wear such a desperate look of hope that his reasoning trails off.

"Sure," he says. "I can put them back."

Louise has just closed the tin of tea bags when headlights swing across the kitchen window, startling her until she sees it's Gabe's truck and then—is that Frankie climbing out? She steps back from the window, afraid of being spotted, indecision mounting as she listens to Frankie's footsteps approach the porch. A part of her wants to flee unnoticed, to avoid causing Frankie any embarrassment—but another part is curious to know what she and Gabe did tonight.

When the door opens in the next instant, she is still at the counter. Frankie slows in the doorway—is that Gabe's sweater she's wearing?

"Just fixing myself some tea," Louise says, raising her mug. She thinks she sees a flicker of interest in Frankie's smile, but suspects she's too polite to ask outright. "The water's still hot if you'd care for a cup?"

"I'd love one," Frankie says, stepping around the table to join her at the counter.

The truck's retreating beams swing back through the kitchen like a parting wave. Louise thinks she sees Frankie's skin flush pink.

She takes down the tin again and hands Frankie a mug. "Nice night?"

"Very." Frankie glances up, her color deepening as she picks out a packet of peppermint. "*Essie* is a beautiful boat."

"He's done a great deal of work on her."

"Clearly." Frankie tips the teapot over her mug, the scent of peppermint quickly rising. "I do find it curious that he pretends he can't afford to live somewhere else, though."

Louise looks over at Frankie. Gabe hadn't told her?

She wonders if she shouldn't divulge this, in case there's a reason Gabe doesn't want Frankie knowing—her guilt over her telling Frankie of Maeve's departure still lingers—but this confession would be different. This one might impress, not wound. And even though she doesn't know why she should put effort into Gabe's possible love life—as if he ever let her?—Louise feels a swell of relief to think that he's found someone to share his time with. Even if it's only for a few days.

"Because he can't afford much," she says. "He gave up his inheritance. Gave it all away to charity."

Frankie blinks at her. "He didn't want any of it?"

Louise shakes her head.

Frankie lobs her tea bag thoughtfully for several moments. "Did she really hate it here?"

She means Glory. *Interesting,* Louise thinks. While Gabe may not have told Frankie about relinquishing his inheritance, he clearly shared other things.

But Louise isn't sure how to answer, or if she even should.

"It's . . . complicated."

"Of course." Frankie's smile is thoughtful, almost sad. "It's always complicated."

The room settles in the hush, the reminder of Frankie's loss drifting in the silence, and Louise feels another burst of remorse for her initial coolness, her reserve. Maeve's betrayal was her own—Louise was unfair to place the burden of explanation and absolution on her daughter. Especially when all Frankie can be blamed for is lightening the heavy moods of the two most important men in Louise's life since she showed up.

And anyway, despite Maeve's hurtful departure, the times before that were rife with joyful moments—when she and Maeve and Glory were a united front, the three musketeers even.

"Thank you again for the flowers." She points to the arrangement on the table Frankie surprised them with that afternoon. "You really didn't have to do that."

"I was at the farmers market and smelled them three booths away."

"Dianthus do have such a lovely smell," Louise says, leaning in for a whiff of the vanilla-like fragrance. "I miss fresh flowers." She scans the grouping fondly, running her fingertips over the flowers' fringed pale-pink petals.

"Russ told me you were quite the gardener when he gave me a tour. He said you made beautiful arrangements, too."

Pride swells behind Louise's ribs. She smiles helplessly. "I used to fantasize about opening my own place like the Vickerys have done."

"You still could."

Louise glances over at Frankie, and a memory flashes: she and Glory in their backyard, Glory's similar encouragement.

Her phone lights up with a new message, so bright on the other end of the counter, it can't help but draw their attention to it.

Louise knows she's languished long enough. "I'm glad you had a nice night," she says, reaching for her phone. "Just turn off the kitchen light when you come up."

"Of course," says Frankie. "Good night."

Only when Louise moves to the stairs does she feel a flush of shame. Frankie knows where Russ sleeps—surely she questions why Louise isn't joining him?

Or maybe not, Louise tells herself as she continues up the steps. She doesn't know why she should be so certain—but she is—that Frankie hasn't come here to cause pain, or shed fresh light on their problems.

And anyway, hadn't they just agreed? Life was always complicated.

# 28

1989
January

"I knew I'd find you two down here."

Louise stopped at the bottom of the basement stairs just as Maeve was helping Glory to free a bright-red bolero jacket from its hanger, the glass door of the display case yawning open. It was Maeve's birthday, and the day had been a gorgeous one. Sunny and nearly fifty degrees. Unseasonably warm for the middle of winter. Best of all, Mitch had gone sailing, leaving them to celebrate in peace.

Louise crossed to meet them, careful not to spill any of her champagne on the plum carpet—her second glass from a bottle they'd opened to toast Maeve after Mitch had left.

"You do realize the whole point of installing these cabinets was to keep the collection *behind* the glass, right?" Louise teased.

"I know, I know." Glory sighed, her lips pursing unrepentantly at Maeve. "But I hate to think of them trapped under there. Unable to breathe."

Louise and Maeve exchanged knowing smiles. They'd all grown accustomed to Glory's tendency to refer to her collection of movie memorabilia as living creatures.

"It still fits like a glove," Louise marveled as Glory slid her slender arms into the jacket's buttery velvet sleeves and gave a little spin. But winter was, after all, the season of Glory's annual fasting, when even spandex hung on her.

"Remind me again which movie that's from?" Louise asked. She could never keep the collection straight.

Maeve, however, possessed an uncanny knowledge. "*The Last Mirage*, right?"

Glory gave an approving nod. "It was my third movie for MGM but my first screen credit, tiny as it was."

"And wasn't that the one where Robert Redford gave you your first on-screen kiss?"

"In this very jacket," Glory said, her green eyes flashing. She bit her lip coquettishly. "I like to think I taught him everything he knows."

They laughed.

"I loved him in *The Way We Were*," Maeve admitted, then added quickly, "I know you're not supposed to. I know Hubbell turns out to be such a huge disappointment, such a coward, but he's just so . . ."

"Gorgeous," Louise finished, tipping her blushing smile into her flute for a long sip.

Glory raised her glass. "I'll toast to that."

"And that part at the end"—Maeve darted forward—"when Katie brushes back his hair?"

Louise held her flute against her heart and glanced between them, waiting a beat so they could all recite in unison: "Your girl is lovely, Hubbell."

Glory pointed to the bottle in the chiller. "Who needs a refill?"

Maeve did the honors, giving them each another generous splash. "I bet he smelled great, too."

"See for yourself." Glory held out a sleeve, and Maeve leaned in for a deep whiff, her face blooming as she drew back.

"That's incredible! I can still smell his aftershave."

"Paid to be kissed by Robert Redford," Louise marveled, rolling her eyes.

"Eight times," Glory said. "I kept count."

"Mitch must hate that story."

Glory slid them each a mischievous grin. "I told him we got it on the first take."

Louise laughed. "Wise."

The muffled but distinct trill of a ringing phone quieted them.

Maeve rose. "I'll get that."

"No answering phones on your birthday," Glory said, touching her arm to slow her. "Let the machine pick it up."

But Maeve's gaze remained fixed on the ceiling, as if she was trying to discern something in the silence that followed the final ring. Louise heard it, too. Footsteps. Too heavy to be Gabe's. When had Mitch returned?

Glory looked to Maeve, and Louise watched a strange flicker of something too close to panic cross both women's faces.

In the next instant, a pounding of footfalls turned them all to the basement door as it swung open and Mitch appeared. If he'd come off the boat, he'd done so recently. His face was still flushed with sun, and his dark hair bore the stylings of the sea air, making him look especially wild.

He charged down the stairs, his eyes sweeping the room.

"I didn't hear you come back," Glory said.

"I guess you didn't hear the phone either." Mitch's jaw clenched. A tremor of dread circled Louise's scalp. "Don't you want to know who called, Glow?" Using her nickname did nothing to warm the frost in his voice.

Glory's voice was soft, pleading. "Mitch, can't you see we're—"

"Joyce. From Outer Banks Rentals."

Glory's eyes shot up. In the strained silence, Louise searched their faces, trying to understand what could possibly be so concerning in the message.

"She wanted to confirm the location of the house the studio rented for you for the movie shoot."

Movie shoot? Louise looked at Maeve, confident she wore a

similar look of confusion, but her even expression remained vigilant. Surely Maeve hadn't known if the rest of them didn't?

"We were done, Glow. Dammit, we agreed."

Glory stiffened, thrusting up her chin as if someone had laid a cold hand on her spine. "We never agreed, Mitch. You *decided*."

"You wanted a festival, so you got a festival," he said, stabbing a finger in her direction. "You want an assistant to help you pretend you're still some big movie star who doesn't really live here—hell, I agree to that, too. I even let you and Lou turn our basement into a goddamn memorabilia mausoleum—"

Louise's face flamed.

"—so you tell me, Glow? When is it enough, huh? When?"

The ice in the chiller shifted suddenly, the crackle of the sinking champagne bottle they'd nearly emptied shattering the choking silence.

Glory shrugged, her sinking shoulders a heartbreaking mix of resignation and defeat. "When I'm gone, I suppose."

A bolt of pain shot across Mitch's features, as if he'd been stung.

"Then go," he said low. "Jesus, just go already."

And as Mitch climbed the stairs, his steps fell hard with the weight of surrender. Even the door, thrown open like a lion's roaring mouth on his arrival, uttered only the sigh of a weak click after his exit.

The room hushed.

Maeve touched Glory's hand, her eyes strained with affection. "He doesn't mean it."

Glory smiled, her misted eyes still trained on the door he'd disappeared through. "I know he doesn't." After another beat, she rolled back her shoulders and looked between them, her face so full of emotion that Louise felt gooseflesh skitter up her arms. "Now someone please tell me that bottle's not drained."

Later, when Maeve was upstairs with Gabe, and Mitch was still sulking in the den, Louise and Glory made tea in the kitchen.

"Were you going to tell me?" Louise asked quietly. But they both knew what Louise really meant with her question.

Glory's eyes welled with apology. "I never meant to tell her first, Louise. But she found the script and, well . . ."

Louise lowered her gaze, feeling suddenly childish, selfish. Her wounded pride was hardly the most pressing part of this. After ten years away, Glory was finally getting her wish to return to the screen. No wonder she'd seemed to be wasting away—she was dieting for her big comeback. That, at least, was good news.

"When do you go?" Louise asked.

"Filming starts the middle of May."

Alarm pinged behind her chest. "But you'll miss the festival."

"I know." Glory offered a pleading smile. "Please don't be angry with me."

Louise reached across the island and took Glory's hands, startled to feel her knuckles so close to the skin. Just how skinny did she have to get for this role?

"I'm so happy for you, sweetie."

"I knew you would be." Glory took a beat. "I want you to know I've asked Maeve to join me on location. The studio has offered me an assistant, but Maeve knows my life so well, it just seemed . . ." Louise wasn't even aware that her disappointment had strained her features all over again until Glory added urgently, "You know I would have asked you, Louise, but I need you here to keep the festival running smoothly. There's no one who can manage it the way you can. I couldn't trust it to anyone else."

"Of course," she said, trying to hide an unwelcomed flutter of hurt behind an agreeable smile. "You know I'll take care of everything here."

"I know you will." Glory's grip tightened. "Everything, and everyone."

Louise searched her face for explanation, but Glory's eyes were unyielding.

A burst of noise erupted from the den—an exciting play from whatever game Mitch was watching.

Glory's gaze drifted longingly in the direction of the hall.

"He'll get over it, Glory."

She sighed. "Which one?"

"Both of them."

Still Glory's eyes brimmed with tears. "All I want is peace," she said, so softly that Louise wasn't sure she even meant her to hear. "Just peace."

# 29

Wednesday

Garbo greets them with a chorus of enthusiastic barks that Frankie doesn't take for a compliment; she's carrying half of the succulent-smelling take-out dishes Gabe bought them at the market when she follows him onto the boat and down into the cabin. He's also picked them up a bottle of red. Frankie frees it from its brown paper wrapping and admires the label before she hands it to Gabe to open. The neighboring boat is hosting a large and loud party, so Gabe suggests they eat in the cabin; Frankie's more than happy for the privacy.

While he disappears down the narrow corridor to change, she searches the cluttered shelves above the dinette, casually snooping. Marine catalogs and bills, a tin of business cards. She thumbs through the collection and sets it back.

"So what big premiere party are you missing tonight to slum it with me?"

She grins, flipping through a pocket guide to marine knots. "Louise mentioned something about Steven Spielberg and an infinity pool . . ."

When Gabe returns, he's traded his work pants for shorts and a collared polo. Not a paint stain in sight. Pleasure swells from a deep place; she smiles with it.

"Finding anything good?" he asks.

"No, unfortunately," she says as she tucks the guide back into the shelf. "No room on boats for skeletons, apparently."

"I can store a few in the bilge but it tends to flood."

They slide into opposite sides of the narrow dinette booth, the heavy fragrance of garlic and ginger from the opened containers already filling the cabin. The evening light has shifted, coating everything with the glittery peach of dusk. While he slices the seal off the neck of the wine bottle, Frankie admires the way the glow rides along his jaw. All day, in expectation of their date—because this is, unquestionably, a date—she felt the prickles of uncertainty, the possibility that their kiss under the pier, the way his heavy gaze tears through her like a fever, was all because of wine or sea air. But here with him again, there's no convincing herself that what she feels isn't craving—the tremors of attraction.

Even the way he drives the corkscrew into the wine turns her on.

She smiles. "So how long's the waiting list for this seat?"

"In inches or centimeters?" He eyes her as he tugs out the cork. "Turns out most women prefer to eat on land." He fills two glasses and hands her one, tapping it in a toast with his.

"I think eating on a boat is romantic." She swirls her glass. "But then I have a strong stomach."

He squints playfully at her. "Is that a reference to the boat, or the captain?"

She smiles into a sip of wine and sits back, grateful for the cool wood against her bare arms. "I thought women loved men with boats."

"You must be thinking of men with motorcycles and guitars."

"Boats aren't loud enough, I guess."

"Luckily I don't mind the quiet." Gabe moves his hand toward his wineglass, absently sliding the stem between his index and middle finger.

She tears her eyes away, quivers of want firing in her stomach.

"You live on a boat with a dog," she says. "I would think that's a prerequisite."

He grins. "It's not as hard a life as it seems."

"I don't think it seems hard at all," she says. "Never having to really put down roots, having things your way all the time? Seems incredibly easy to me."

Gabe's lips rise higher then slow, as if he's not sure whether to be amused or insulted. He empties a pair of chopsticks from their sleeve, snaps them apart, and plunges them into the nest of noodles.

"You're not attached either," he says, serving her a large tangle, then another for himself.

"Only because I haven't found the right person, not because I prefer to be alone."

"And what makes you think I do?"

"Like I said . . ." She clamps her chopsticks around a shrimp. "You live on a boat."

He reaches down for the wine and raises the bottle questioningly. Frankie nods, savoring the rising pool of deep plum as he pours.

There's a faint tinkling of metal. Garbo has arrived, tail spinning.

Frankie reaches down to pat her, pleased when the animal leans into her hand.

Gabe returns the bottle to the floor. "She likes you."

"I think we're getting used to each other," she says, seeing the flash of suggestion when she meets Gabe's dark eyes, sure he's caught her double meaning and maybe even agrees. His knee leans against hers, the weight of him insistent and suggestive.

"So have you decided what to do about your store?"

She bristles reflexively at the pronoun. "Not yet." Van Morrison's "Into the Mystic" rises in the quiet. "I have to admit I've enjoyed this break."

"It can't be easy work."

She smiles. "It's not work at all. For the right customer, I don't have to convince them. Their connection to that movie—that memory of seeing it—is so strong, they can't not have that piece of memorabilia. They touch that costume or that prop and every joy and hope that movie let them feel all those years ago comes back to them." She points her chopsticks behind him to the wall. "You obviously feel deeply enough for the memory of that carving to not replace it."

"That's because it's a real memory," he says. "Movies aren't real."

"No. But they can still be part of our memories." She watches him sink his chopsticks into his noodles, his lips slanted in a skeptical smile. "There must be one movie you remember losing yourself in."

"Can't think of one," he says, too quickly to have possibly tried.

She sets down her chopsticks and leans close. "You're telling me you can't think of one movie you saw that you remember fondly?"

He twists another knot of noodles and shoves them into his mouth, chewing vigorously for several moments while he thinks.

"Okay," he says. "Maybe there was one."

She picks up her wine and sits back.

He sets down his chopsticks and picks up his glass. "One night my dad says we're going out, the three of us, but he doesn't say where. We pile into the car. My mom's decked out, because she thinks we must be going out to some fancy dinner . . ." He swirls his wine absently. "He pulls into this dumpy drive-in. SUPERMAN, ONE NIGHT ONLY, on the marquee. You should have seen her face. It's not even dark and we're the only car in the lot. He gets out, says he'll be right back. I'm in the backseat, and I'm sure she's going to start crying, or they're going to start fighting . . ." A small, wistful smile begins to tease one side of his mouth. "Then my dad comes back with a huge bucket of popcorn, and this little bottle of champagne." His gaze, still soft with the memory, drops to his wine. "I got between them in the front seat and we watched that movie and ate all that stale popcorn . . ." He rolls the stem between his fingers, studying his glass in the silence before he lifts his gaze to find hers. "That was a pretty good night." The pressure of his thigh against hers intensifies. "But this one might just top it."

Frankie raises her bare foot and rides her toes up his leg. He reaches under the table, taking her foot in both of his hands and rubbing his thumbs into her arch, sending her sinking against the bench with the pleasure of it. She closes her eyes and tips her head back, even as doubt flickers. *It's been four days. This isn't some movie. People don't connect this quickly in real life . . .*

Opening her eyes, she considers him as he continues to work, her breath quickening.

"This is crazy, isn't it?" she whispers. "It's too fast."

He grins suggestively. "I can go slower."

She tilts her head in playful admonishment and smiles. "You know what I mean."

"Maybe. Maybe not." He shrugs easily, but his eyes are heavy. His massage deepens. "Still hungry?"

She slips her foot free from his hands and rests it on his chair, easing her big toe forward until she finds the ridge of his zipper, and the hard heat of him underneath.

Her gaze sinks to his mouth. "Starving."


Sometime after midnight the sound of Garbo shuffling around the darkened cabin wakes her. Slipping from bed for a glass of water, Frankie pads into the galley and sees her purse dangling from the row of hooks beside the hatch. Thinking she should check her phone, she reaches inside and her fingers graze a sheet of plastic. Pulling out the letters, she appraises them fondly in the faint blue glow from the marina lights, her heart thundering. *It's not an easy decision,* she thinks as she scans the small space; every surface—and there are few to begin with—is littered. Even the dinette, where they'd paused their feast to make love then returned even more ravenous an hour later, was quickly reinstated as a makeshift desk as soon as they'd cleared their dishes. So when her eyes fall on the softly swinging tier of mesh baskets beside the galley, she doesn't hesitate. A trio of apples makes a perfect stand when she props the envelopes up, considering them a moment before turning back to the berth, her gaze drawn to the same view of the bed corner as her first time below, only now Gabe's bare leg juts out from the tangled sheet.

Passing Garbo on the settee, she rubs the dog's head, careful not to wake her, or Gabe, when she slides back under the salt-dampened sheet and burrows deep, folding herself inside the warm curve of his chest, letting the heat of his skin and the lapping of the water against the hull pull her under to sleep again.

# Part Three

Love means never having to say you're sorry.

*Love Story*

# 30

## Thursday

I never knew it could be like this . . . nobody ever kissed me
the way you do.

*From Here to Eternity*

Louise blows across the top of her coffee and takes several deep sips, letting the nutty flavor soothe her tangled thoughts. The last day of the festival, and the building is buzzing with others who, like her, have gotten an early start on the day's lineup and last-minute preparations for the evening screening of Glory's final picture, *A Season of Us,* on the town green.

*The last day.* Louise feels a shudder of dread at the realization—but not just because it means the end of so much hard work. Knowing she would need all her focus on making sure the festival ran smoothly, she decided to put away the subject of her crumbling marriage until the festival was completed, and now that deadline is in sight.

So why doesn't she feel the same urgency as she did just days before?

*Frankie.*

Louise sits back, letting the realization sink in.

There's no question the young woman's arrival has changed things. Who else to credit for that breezy dinner on the deck? Or for Russ abandoning his brace to cook up a storm? For bringing them together in a way she had feared was all but lost? And Gabe. *Flirting.* Talk about something in danger of extinction.

When Frankie first arrived, all Louise could focus on was her resentment of Maeve's disappearance, but in the past few days, she's found the hard edges of her bitterness softened. And the truth is, despite how Maeve left them all, she was—until the end, at least—self-possessed and fiercely loyal to Glory. To all of them.

Louise would give anything to have those kinds of emotional reserves.

Maybe it wasn't too late to borrow them?

Like her mother had, Frankie clearly follows her own path, too. Louise recalls Frankie's words in the kitchen: "You still could." How easy she made it sound, and how, for an instant, Louise imagined it could be. She can't keep up this festival pace forever—and a home-based business would certainly allow her more time to be with Russ. Assuming they can get on the other side of this emotional canyon they've found themselves on the edge of.

A burst of fierceness blooms—why does she have to make this plan suit Russ's needs?

All the years she'd judged Glory harshly for not fighting to get back to Hollywood because Mitch wanted to stay in Harpswich—and here she is, doing the same: making her goals fit her life as a wife. It's not as if Russ is so concerned with her needs; otherwise, he would take the seat on the ethics board—she's certainly made it known how much she wants him to, how good it would be for him, let alone their marriage, for him to have purpose again.

"Good morning."

Louise looks up to see Lana in the doorway. "You're here early."

Lana sets down a stack of mailers. "George is thinking of recommending me for the Cannes internship, so I figured I'd use the last few days to make a good impression before it's too late."

"How big of you," Louise says dryly, picking up the flash drive Lana has placed on top of the pile. "What's this?"

"Those ferry images for the video retrospective you asked for."

"Weeks ago," Louise reminds her.

Lana shrugs. "You did say you wanted them no matter what."

So she had.

"Apparently there's even one with your husband in it," Lana says as she turns to go. "At least Anna said she thinks it's him and she's been here forever, so she'd obviously know."

Louise won't point out that Anna has been here fifteen years less than she has—forever, indeed.

But the tease of an old picture of Russ holds great appeal, so she inserts the flash drive and scrolls through the thumbnails, clicking on one that looks promising of passengers waiting in line at the ferry's ticket booth. The photo is from May of '89, and Louise is tickled to find Anna is right—the man standing just at the edge of the line is definitely Russ. She could spot her husband's favorite navy-blue windbreaker anywhere.

But what about the bag at his feet? She leans in, squinting harder. They didn't own a floral suitcase. Their luggage was always a canvas duffel.

Tiny sparks of worry start to flicker deep in her stomach.

*Whose bag was he watching?*

Scanning the photo for another familiar face, her gaze snags and holds on the woman nearly at the front of the line. And even before her thumb and forefinger land on the screen to broaden the image of the auburn-haired woman in a faded peach sundress, Louise's heart has already started thumping with dread.

No wonder she'd felt prickles of recognition. That suitcase had belonged to Glory.

It's Maeve.

With Russ.

She scrolls back, and in the seconds it takes to locate the date stamp of the photo from the file, she allows herself—forces herself—the grace of possibility that she's made a mistake, that there's simply no way her husband was helping Maeve onto a ferry in the same month she disappeared from Harpswich. Before Glory's frantic call arrived from the Outer Banks: *Have you heard from Maeve? She was supposed to arrive yesterday* . . .

Heat soaks her cheeks.

She sinks back, her gaze growing blurry on the grainy section of the image, her pulse throbbing in her ears as memories collide and seams of reason are joined—Glory's words ringing: *He's quite a bit older . . . Apparently, he's not taking it well* . . .

Louise claps a hand over her forehead, sure her skin is on fire, but it's as clammy and cold as winter sand.

Is this why Russ was so enthusiastic to host Frankie? Why he's defended Maeve all these years?

Her cell chimes on the desk; Louise clicks it silent and buries it in her drawer as if it's an unpinned grenade.

She had suspicions before, but she always talked herself through them, out of them. How could she have been such a fool?

She looks dazedly out at the lobby, filled with envy for all these people rushing around, purposeful and confident and blissfully unaware, while she's sure her heart will push its way out of her chest. But there's simply no pretending otherwise; it all makes absolute and crushing sense.

Russ is Frankie's father.

# 31

1989
April

Louise gripped the handle of the picnic basket with both hands and closed the passenger door with her hip, careful to keep the contents level; one tilt and the container of soup could easily topple, despite the wreath of dish towels she'd nested it in. The day, overcast and raw, crept its damp up her skin as she carried her husband's surprise lunch down the sidewalk to the entrance of his practice.

Through the door, she was relieved to find the waiting room empty. Her husband's receptionist, Lily, recently graduated from community college, slid the window open and waved her over. "Hi, Mrs. Chandler. What smells so good?"

"Potato and leek soup—and a decidedly unhealthy serving of apple crisp," Louise said, settling the basket on the narrow counter. She tipped her head toward the corridor. "Is he with a patient?"

"Actually, you just missed them."

Mitch. It wasn't the first time her husband's old friend had thwarted her surprise plans with an impromptu lunch invitation. Why did she never learn?

She exhaled a defeated sigh. "And I assume they went to Mr. Beckett's usual haunt?"

"Actually, it was Dr. Chandler and Miss Simon."

Louise blinked, a strange prickle of something near to dread, but not quite, crackling across her scalp.

"He didn't say where but they can't have gone far. He has an appointment in twenty minutes." Lily looked mournfully at the basket. "Are you sure you don't want to wait?"

Afraid that her expression betrayed her rattled thoughts, Louise offered a cheerful smile.

"Have you had lunch?"

"No, but . . ." Lily sat back, putting up her hands to demure. "I couldn't possibly take Dr. Chandler's food."

"Well, I'm not having it go to waste, and I don't relish carrying it back to the car," Louise said, already unpacking. When the container of apple crisp emerged, Lily's eyes bloomed. "And don't tell him I was here—he'll only feel badly."

"Are you sure?"

"Absolutely."

But of course she was suddenly far from sure about anything. Walking back to the car, she scanned the sidewalks, her heart hammering foolishly, even as she reminded herself, this was a tiny village, filled with people who knew Russ and Louise—and Maeve, too, by now. Her husband wouldn't have done anything to suggest impropriety in the company of their neighbors—his patients, their friends.

And this was, after all, Maeve. The girl she had brought into their lives to help Glory. The girl who Glory—who all of them—had come to cherish.

Still, tremors of suspicion flickered the whole way home, sparking like a pilot light, just waiting to flame.

At the beach house for dinner the following night, Louise tried to put the suspicion from her mind, especially since Glory was still recovering from a stomach bug. The last thing Louise wanted to do was add to her worries, knowing how dependent Glory had become on Maeve, how devastated Glory would be to think Maeve had betrayed them, never mind Russ's betrayal. But as the night drew on, proof seemed to be everywhere. Had Russ and Maeve always laughed so much together? Had Maeve always stared at Russ with such unabashed affection when he talked?

After dinner, desperate for distraction, Louise offered to take up Glory's tea.

"Your color is definitely better," she announced as she set down the mug.

"How is everyone down there?" Glory asked. "It's been so quiet."

Louise met Glory's weary eyes, doing a quick translation. She was, of course, referring to Mitch. "He's actually subdued tonight." Louise grinned. "Did you finally put something in his drink?"

Glory managed a tired chuckle. "He's been that way these past few weeks." Ever since the news of Glory's impending film shoot was revealed; Louise did the math. "Maybe he thinks if he doesn't make any more waves, I'll change my mind and stay—I won't, of course," Glory added before Louise could ask.

"Are you sure I can't bring you up some of the chowder? Just a little bowl?"

"I don't dare." Glory pressed her fingers to her lips, but her gaze was exacting. "Are you all right?"

As if she could hide her feelings from a seasoned actress?

Louise pressed her hands into her lap. "Remember when you said Maeve was seeing an older man?"

Glory nodded. "She broke it off."

"You're sure?"

"I think so. Why?"

Louise pushed out a wary sigh. "Yesterday . . . I went to surprise Russ with lunch and Lily told me he and Maeve had already left for lunch together."

"So they had lunch. They're hardly strangers."

"But when I asked him how his lunch was, he said he'd just ordered in a club from Chowder's. Now why would he lie?"

"Maybe it wasn't a lie. Maybe he really did order in a sandwich."

"Then why not tell me he was out with Maeve? Why hide that?"

Glory shrugged. "Maybe it was something medical. Something private he didn't feel he could share." But when Louise didn't offer a reply, Glory leaned closer. "You don't think Russ and Maeve are . . . ?"

Louise tipped her head to avoid Glory's mining gaze, but she was captured by it anyway.

"My God, you do," Glory said incredulously.

"It's not just that." Louise chewed her lip. "I saw her staring at him tonight. In the living room. And then again at the table."

"Staring?"

"Fondly. Almost dreamily."

"Louise." Glory withdrew her hand from under the blanket and pressed on Louise's, her palms soft and warm. "Your husband is the most devoted—let alone honest—man I've ever met. And never mind that Maeve wouldn't jeopardize her life here with all of us. We're all far too close. If she's staring, it's only with admiration."

Just hearing the argument laid out made Louise's racing pulse slow.

"You're right." She smiled, gently clapping her hand over Glory's, regret bubbling from somewhere deep. "Of course you are."

# 32

Gabe is on deck when Frankie wakes. She can hear him knocking around as she wedges herself into the closet of the bathroom—the head, was it?—and still when she pulls on her T-shirt and pads into the galley to seek out food. Had they polished off all the noodles, or did a few scraps remain? She hopes to find coffee already made, but the French press on the stove is empty. The galley's sole cabinet offers a tin of already-ground; prying off the lid and taking a deep whiff is nearly as good as a sip. She finds an empty—sort of clean?—pot, then turns her hunt to some water. As she searches, memories of their night together swim through her thoughts, dueling moments of tenderness and patience, then feverish hunger. Laughter when he bumped his head trying to peel off her jeans. More when she slipped off the narrow berth.

But did it mean something that he'd risen first, that he was atop still? Alarm and doubt wiggle in again, just as they did last night. She pressed him to agree that this whirlwind they found themselves caught up in was the stuff of movies, that it was too fast to be real. So was his head throbbing with regret now, and was he just hoping she'd grow so tired of waiting for him to come below that she'd just dress and leave?

She has always hated these morning-after mysteries. It's why she avoids one-night stands.

And yet here she is, waking up with a man she's known only a few days.

But a man with whom she shares a common past—and it is that remarkable link joining their two chains that made her want to throw out all her rules last night, that makes her want to keep casting them out this morning.

And despite all of her doubt, she can think of more reasons to stay than she can to leave. Maybe she can even convince him to join her for tonight's screening of Glory's final film on the green. She's feeling so flush with possibility, she might just ask . . .

Footsteps thump down the cabin steps, and before she can turn to see, Gabe is behind her, his mouth in her hair. He reaches around her body, landing his hands on either side of her, fencing her in as he drops a hot kiss against her neck and leans the weight of his body into her spine.

"Good morning."

Frankie feels her limbs sink with relief: mystery solved.

She tips her head back against his chest, closing her eyes and drawing in a deep whiff of the sea's morning damp he's let soak his T-shirt. "Good morning," she says back, her eyes still closed. "I wanted to surprise you with coffee but I couldn't find anything that looked like a—"

She feels his body stiffen and opens her eyes, looking down in time to see his hands drop from the counter.

Turning to face him, she sees where his gaze sits. The basket. The letters.

Her stomach plummets.

"What are those doing here?" His voice is raspy with emotion—bewilderment or frustration—Frankie can't decide which, and alarm charges up her spine.

"I thought, after yesterday . . . After we talked . . ." When she moves toward him, Gabe steps back.

"We've been over this. I thought you got it."

She stares at him, whatever measure of remorse she may have felt for leaving the letters fading, shifting quickly to exasperation. "Well,

I don't, okay?" she says hotly, throwing out her hands. "I don't understand why you can't just open them?"

"Because she doesn't get to have the last word." Gabe moves for the galley. "She doesn't get to make all of us feel like consolation prizes for years and then try and fix it in one goddamn letter." He trains a hard look on her, as if waiting for her consent, but Frankie just feels the swell of fresh understanding, and her voice softens with it. Why hadn't she seen it before?

She shakes her head slowly. "I don't think that's it at all."

"You don't, huh?" His tone is sharp, defensive, and his posture follows. "Then please," he says bitterly, throwing out his hand to direct her to continue. "Enlighten me."

In too deep now, she holds his cool glare and answers evenly. "I think you're afraid."

His eyes flash with apprehension, but his gaze doesn't leave hers. "And what exactly am I afraid of?"

She reaches back for the rounded edge of the galley counter, suddenly unsteady. Her heart hammers. "I think you're afraid that if you read those letters, you'll find something inside that will have to change this narrative you've become so desperately attached to—and that you'll have to stop moping around this old boat, wounded and unwanted, and actually figure out how to be your own person—instead of just Glory Cartwright's black sheep son."

He makes a throaty sound, part snicker, part growl. "You're one to psychoanalyze me about paving my own way. Do you even know what you want?"

She blinks at him, goose bumps of dread erupting along her arms. "What is that supposed to mean?"

He comes toward her. "You're running your mother's store because that's what she wanted. Now you're here with those goddamn letters because you think she wanted that, too—and you're lecturing *me* about being my own person?"

"It's not the same thing."

"Isn't it?"

"I make choices in my life out of love," Frankie says. "You make them out of anger."

She's sure the accusation will send him bolting up the hatch, but Gabe remains in place, just searching her face.

"At least I'm honest about who my mother was."

She squints at him. "Meaning what?"

"You talk about how unselfish your mother was, how everything she did was for you—"

"Because it was." She pierces him with a hard look, dread mounting behind her ribs.

"Like moving you in and out of other people's houses instead of finding your own place? Or not telling you about your father?" His eyes narrow condemningly. "Sounds pretty selfish to me."

Her cheeks flame. "Go to hell."

She jettisons off the counter, using the wall to keep her balance as she marches to the berth, not sure if it's rage or the rolling boat that has stolen her balance. She stabs her legs into her jeans, frantically trying to locate her sandals in the tower of clothes and towels that cover the floor. Finding them, she charges back out, sure Gabe will have disappeared up top again, but he's waiting for her at the steps.

She grabs her purse off the hook and rummages for her phone.

"What are you doing?" he asks as she taps in a search for a car service. When she continues to ignore him, he tells her, "If you're looking for a lift, you'll be waiting for hours."

"Then I'll walk," she says, dumping her phone back into her purse and searching madly for a hair tie.

"Don't do that." Gabe's shoulders, rigid before with consternation, fall now with surrender. "Just give me a minute to walk Garbo and I'll give you a ride."

"No thanks. I think you've taken me on enough of those."

He stares at her, clearly trying to mine her fierce gaze for meaning in the quip, but Frankie can't offer him any—she's not even sure what she meant by the comment, only that it came from anger and hurt and it felt damn good to say it.

"Have it your way." He snatches Garbo's leash off its hook. "But make sure to take those goddamn letters with you," he says, already climbing the steps. "Otherwise I'm tossing them."

*Then do it,* she thinks sourly as she watches him disappear out the hatch, then waits while he pounds across the deck, the clip-clop of Garbo's gait trailing him and growing faint. *Throw them out unopened,* she wants to yell as she swings her bag over her shoulder and climbs out into the punishing glare of morning. Tear them into a thousand pieces. She's done trying to show Gabe Beckett the way to his heart.

# 33

"You're Frankie's father, aren't you?"

Despite Louise's every intention on the drive over to deliver her terrible theory in a calm and measured way, the instant Russ meets her in the doorway, she lets the question bolt from her throat like a spit lemon seed.

For several interminable seconds, his expression is frozen in bewilderment, the shock of her words needing several moments to sink in fully, and when they have, his eyes squeeze so tightly Louise can barely see the pale-blue pools.

His voice comes out more as a breath than a whisper: "What?"

"That's why you've been acting this way, isn't it? Why you insisted she stay with us, why you've been trying to impress her?" She rolls her lips together, her heart pounding. "Is that why you refused to blame Maeve for leaving like she did?"

He glances around, scanning the porches on either side of them for prying eyes, but no one is out. "Let's not do this outside, all right?" He reaches for her elbow, as if she's a woozy post-op patient coming out of anesthesia and needing help back to bed, but Louise yanks her arm out of reach, panicked at his choice of words as he steers them into the house. He hasn't denied her claim, he's only said he doesn't want to do *this* outside. What is *this*? His confession?

Russ points her to the couch, but she doesn't dare sit for fear she won't be able to stand up again. "Now what the hell is this about?"

"I saw you with her, Russ. At the ferry. There was a picture in the archives." Louise punches every syllable like typewriter keys as she watches his face, waiting for her accusations to break the hard cover of confusion he continues to wear.

"What picture?" He blinks at her. "Saw me with who?"

"Maeve!"

His face falls.

"Around the time she disappeared—you took her to the ferry."

"Lou." He rubs his forehead. "Just sit down, okay?"

"I don't want to sit down!" She's getting shrill. "I want you to tell me why you were helping Maeve leave with Glory's suitcase when the rest of us believed she took off without anyone knowing. But you were there."

Russ grabs the sides of his head, pressing at his temples. "And you think because I was with Maeve at the ferry that I'm Frankie's father?"

"You haven't denied it."

"Because it's lunacy!" The volume of his voice startles both of them into a sharp silence. Relief sparks behind Louise's ribs, small still, but enough that she can sit down finally, even if her descent feels more like a collapse.

Russ comes beside her. His voice is calmer now but no less firm. "I gave Maeve a ride to the ferry that night and I waited there with her. It's true." He pushes out a hard breath. "She needed my help."

"And you never thought to tell us? All those months we wondered? And you knew? The whole time—you knew?"

Russ claps his hands on his thighs and pushes off the couch. "You make it sound like I was trying to hurt you."

"Of course I'm hurt—God, Russ, I've been nothing but hurt since you moved into the downstairs bedroom and proceeded to shut me out of everything. And now this?"

He comes back toward her, his eyes pleading. "Lou, I swear to you there was nothing between Maeve and me."

He scans her face, and she can see he's desperate for some proof of her confidence, but her mind has already spun in another direction, circling back to his earlier words.

She stands. "What do you mean, she needed your help? Did something happen?" Louise mines his fraught gaze, prickles of understanding crawling up her spine.

*He's protecting someone.*

"Was it Mitch?" she says, nearly breathless with her theory. "Did Mitch say something to Maeve that night? Did he do something?"

"It wasn't Mitch," Russ says, his voice even and tempered, the tone of truth. And as Louise watches her husband pace toward the window and back again, she takes stock of things in the choking silence. So he's not Frankie's father. All right. But the wildfire of this possibility now doused does little to bring her comfort—for a moment she finally had a reason for why Russ has pulled away from her. Now she's back to having none. And the hole seems larger than before.

Tired of waiting, she's determined to fill it—his secret meeting with Maeve suddenly brushed from her thoughts like table crumbs after a meal. "Then are you angry with me because I didn't bow out of the festival when you had to close the practice?"

"Of course not."

"Is that why you refuse to take the seat on the ethics board? Because you think if you actually find something to occupy you, I won't *ever* quit?"

"What? No!" Russ says, harder now.

"What then?" Louise can feel the tears bubbling up, can hear them in her voice. She swallows to force them down. "Why didn't you ever say anything?" she whispers. "If you knew where Maeve had gone, why did you let us all wonder?"

The question out, Louise stares at him, expecting more silence, but his voice shatters the strained hush, rough and weary.

"Because I promised her."

She scans his fraught features. "Maeve?"

"No." He sighs. "I promised Glory."

She stares at him expectantly, craving explanation even as her heart thumps with dread.

And again he pleads: "You should really sit, Lou."

Something in his gaze chills her. Russ takes her hand and turns her back to the couch, where she sits again. And what should have been the startling sensation of his touch, the dread of possibility is so shocking it overwhelms the simple fact that it is the first time he has held her—any part of her—in months.

"Wait." He looks toward the window, where a taxi has just pulled into the driveway, Frankie stepping out. "I want her to hear this, too."

# 34

1989
March

Looking back—and Russ has in thirty years, many times—he was already unsettled to see Maeve and Glory waiting for him when he'd come back from lunch. It hadn't been seeing them together—by that point, Glory and Maeve were as inseparable as the teeth of a closed zipper—nor was it that he could have counted on one hand the times in ten years Glory had visited him at his office. The reason for his discomfort had been something in Glory's expression when she saw him step through the door. A strange flash of disappointment, as if she'd hoped he might not show, despite her obvious intent to see him. It could have simply been the weather, Russ had thought, too, as he led the two women back to the privacy of his office and closed them all inside—a heavy, gray day, one of those especially bleak ones after the tease of sun.

"Is everything all right?" he asked as they took seats. "Is Gabe okay?"

"Gabe's fine," Glory said, carefully peeling off her leather gloves, the same shade of coral as the silk scarf that swirled around her neck like the foamy head of a tropical drink.

Russ scanned her lowered face, dissecting her answer. *Gabe* was all right.

He laced his fingers together and sat forward. For nearly a decade of winters now, they'd all watched Glory bear the swells of seasonal depression, some more successfully than others, and even though Russ wasn't her doctor, he'd observed the toll of the affliction on her like one. It wasn't uncommon for her to lose weight, or some days simply not get out of bed. During one particularly grueling February a few years back, Russ had even suggested to Mitch that he take Glory to LA for a visit; Mitch had joked that he didn't dare because he didn't think he'd be able to get her to come back. Russ never believed he was kidding.

But they were nearing the end of the siege. This wasn't the time to be despondent. Especially not when Glory was greeting this spring with victory, finally returning to a film set after so many years away. Her dream in her grasp—what could possibly be troubling her?

Glory's gaze drifted absently to his collection of framed pictures on the bookshelf, holding there briefly, before she flashed Russ one of her *Action!* smiles—his nickname for the megawatt beam that appeared so quickly and convincingly, it could have been cued by the snap of a director's clapboard.

"Did Louise tell you Paul and Joanne might swing through for the festival this summer?" Glory's voice was as bright as her smile. "They're doing summer stock in Williamstown again and they think they can make the scheduling work."

"Lou mentioned that, yes." He glanced at Maeve. She smiled at him.

"It's wonderful, isn't it?"

"Wonderful," he said. "Very."

"And you heard that Michelle Pfeiffer wants to premiere her new film with us this year?"

Russ nodded patiently and shifted another quizzical look in Maeve's direction, finding the young woman's expression even and patient. They were stalling. But why?

"Glory . . . ?" He could hear the whistle of concern in his own voice. "What's going on?"

Maeve's folded hands pushed deeper into her lap, causing the shiny plastic of her windbreaker to crackle.

Glory's face was a split screen—her smile was high but her eyes flickered with alarm.

"I'm not well, Russ."

"If this is about your medication . . . I told you we can look into—"

"I'm not talking about depression."

He stared at her, waiting for the rest, for more, even as his stomach sank with dread.

"It's ovarian cancer. Stage four."

Russ glanced at Maeve, expecting to see her previously calm features now tangled with strain, but Maeve's expression didn't shift.

"Maeve knows, Russ. She's known this whole time. That's why I needed an assistant, someone to live with us. I knew radiation would leave me weak, and I needed someone to help me keep up with things when I couldn't, someone to keep people from asking questions, from worrying more than they already do . . ."

Russ scanned the top of his desk as she talked, tearing through his memory to assign a timeline to this impossible news. Glory had hired Maeve last May, which meant Glory had been living with her condition, her death sentence, for almost a year.

Guilt twisted, making fists of his hands where they fell in his lap. As a doctor, he should have seen the signs. Her lack of appetite, her constant need for rest. They'd all assumed it was depression, but he was a doctor. He was trained to look closer, to see clues where others couldn't.

The shame of his failure sickened him.

Especially remembering that he'd just seen Mitch the day before, his old friend stopping by with a bucket of crabs. They'd snapped the tabs off a pair of beers and laughed over a memory of the two of them getting drunk the night before their high school graduation when they'd tried to catch lobsters with their bare hands. Laughed! How had his oldest friend managed to appear so carefree when he knew his wife was dying? No one was that good an actor—

Russ's breath caught, panic sizzling across his scalp.

He fixed his gaze on Glory, but her resistance to meet it was answer enough: she hadn't told Mitch.

Maeve reached across for Glory's hand and squeezed it. "I'll just be outside, okay?"

It was a thin excuse, but Russ was inexplicably grateful for it; he offered Maeve a small smile in thanks as she crossed to the door and closed it behind her.

"I don't know what I would have done without her, Russ," Glory said quietly. "I've asked so much of her. Made her the keeper of so many secrets."

"Glory . . ." Just the two of them now, he pulled in a ragged breath and let it out slowly, determined to keep his voice even and calm, as if she were a feral cat he'd finally lured close enough to catch. "You have to tell Mitch and Gabe. They have to know."

"Why? So they can worry and feel nothing but dread and fear and pity? And don't tell me they won't, Russ, because I know." She climbed carefully from the chair and crossed to the window that looked out onto the street, her gaze trained on the view. Her chin rose, as if to keep her voice from falling. "As you know, I'll be filming on the Outer Banks—"

"You're not still going?"

"I have to."

He pushed out his chair and stood. "Don't be ridiculous. You're ill. There are clauses in contracts—"

"No, I mean I have to do this, Russ."

It was her emphasis of the word—*this*—combined with the steely point of her gaze that sent his heart racing with dread. After nearly a year of being oblivious, he was suddenly reading the compass of her features with devastating clarity.

"I didn't only come here to tell you I'm sick, Russ. I came because I need your help as a doctor. As a friend. We both do."

We? Russ squinted at her, as if she were something tiny on the horizon.

"It just seemed the perfect time," she said. "I don't have to worry that Mitch or Louise or, God forbid, Gabe will find me."

He swallowed, needing moisture. Surely she wasn't suggesting . . . ?

Jettisoned by fear, he came around the desk.

"Glory, there are other treatments." Despite the confidence of his words, his voice still trembled. "Just the other day, I was reading about a trial at MD Anderson . . ."

But when she turned to face him, the remainder of his plea sank in his throat. Her eyes pooled with resolve.

He reached for her hands and she let him have them.

"This isn't some movie, Glory. You don't get to write the ending."

"Don't I?" She gave his fingers a reassuring squeeze, then pulled free, sliding her gaze back to the window. "I watched my mother fade away, knowing she just wanted peace—not just for herself, but for everyone who stood by helplessly watching her suffer. I won't go through that, Russ. I won't put the people I love through that."

And in the anguished hush that followed, he knew she didn't just mean Gabe and Mitch, or even Louise and Maeve. She meant her fans.

"Glory, I'm begging you to think about this."

Her laugh was thin and sad, and not even a little bitter as it should rightly have been after a statement so absurdly, shamefully stupid. Did he honestly think she'd thought of anything else in the past year?

This time, it was she who took his hands. Russ looked down at their joined fingers, feeling a swell of affection. Ten years knowing her, his oldest friend's wife—had they ever shared this kind of exchange?

If his voice was as brittle as blown glass, hers was hard as stone.

"You'll need to explain everything to Maeve. She's smart, Russ.

And she won't panic. The timing is, of course, crucial. We'll need to create an excuse so she can't travel south with me as we planned. She'll have to disappear, at least a week before I do. I'll, of course, pretend to be shocked. I'll call Louise and ask her if she's seen Maeve, I'll say that she's disappeared. You'll have to make sure she has what she needs when she goes."

Instinct took over. "I want to be there," he said. "I have to be there."

"No." Again, her gaze flashed stubbornly. "Maeve has already agreed. I know what's involved, Russ. It's not so complicated."

"But it can be, Glory. Things can go wrong . . ."

She shook her head; he wasn't sure if it was to argue his point or simply a refusal to believe anything might.

"I can't ask that of you, Russ."

"But you can ask her?"

Glory's eyes welled. "She's strong enough."

"No one's that strong, Glory. Believe me—I know." He clenched his teeth. "I'll be there. Or I won't do it."

He hadn't meant the last part to sound threatening, but her features flickered. He meant it. He'd find an excuse—a conference, somewhere near enough to the Outer Banks that he could get there by car, but not so near to cause suspicion. But even as he plotted, his head spun with the sudden weight of what he was agreeing to—all the people who would grieve, the years ahead he'd have to see the confusion and heartbreak on the faces of those he loved most, and never be able to give them solace—but he forced his thoughts to still. He was a doctor, he'd taken an oath. And if he'd learned anything about Glory Cartwright, it was that once she made her mind up, there was no changing it. Clearly she'd found someone in Maeve who was the very same. All Russ could do now was help. And to help, he had to listen.

So he did.

And when Glory was done, he looked her full in the face. "You trust her?"

"I trust her. I trust you both with my life." Despite the sudden veil of tears, she smiled at the irony of her statement: it was the end of it she was entrusting to them. "There's another thing," she said. "I want Louise to have the festival—it's always been hers more than mine, as devoted as she is to it. And I want Maeve to have my collection. I've set aside a few things I want to stay with the festival—mostly the pieces that we already display—but the rest I want her to have. I know it won't be easy—you'll have to orchestrate the packing and the shipping when the time comes. Mitch can't know, not that I kid myself he wouldn't be thrilled to see it all disappear when I'm . . ."

Her voice caught on the last word.

"Glory. Please." Russ gripped her hands again, tipping his face to catch her gaze. She let him hold it, even as her eyes brimmed with tears.

"Don't you dare make me say it, Doctor."

He whispered, "What?"

"As if you don't know?" And there it was, shining back at him: the smile that had won so many hearts, for the moment, blinding. "The show must go on."

# 35

Louise stares out the wall of glass and lets her gaze wander aimlessly over the staff members milling around the lobby. Two hours after Russ's admission and she still feels as if she's walking through wet sand. When her cell chimed, the festival calling with an emergency, she was shamefully but immeasurably grateful for the excuse to flee the impossible silence that was choking their living room. But now, escaped, she feels twinges of worry and regret. Her gaze slides reflexively back to her quiet phone screen. Russ has gone to find Gabe, to confess his secret to Glory's son, and as much as Louise wanted to be there to soften the blow of the truth, she knows Russ has to bear that burden alone.

Now she waits for news of his painful delivery. And even though she still has a million things she must do before tonight's screening of Glory's final film, she can't seem to do anything but pace with her thoughts.

"Louise?"

Lana appears in the doorway to stir her from her trance, and she climbs quickly to her feet, seeing Russ behind her assistant, who steps back to allow him to enter. Her mind races with certainty: Gabe took the news badly—not that she imagines Glory's son could take this sort of news any other way—but what else could it mean that Russ has come to give his report in person? That he looks especially drawn, that even the soft recessed lights of her office can't soften the deep crevices of his brow? Nothing like the cheerful way he'd blown in just days earlier with news of Frankie's surprise arrival. From a tempest to a breeze. And for years, she has to remind herself, in the seconds while he takes the seat across from her desk, hiding the truth of the storm that brewed inside his heart.

She holds herself. "What did he say?"

Russ turns up his hands. "He's gone."

"What do you mean?"

"The slip's empty. He obviously took the boat out."

"Did you try calling?" she asks weakly.

"Three times." He glances up at her. "Maybe if you tried?"

Louise doesn't kid herself that a call from her would grant an answer either. In the foggy moments after Russ's confession, while they'd all lingered in the kitchen with cups of barely touched coffee, Frankie shared the news of her strained parting with Gabe, that he was angry with her for leaving the letters. They all glanced at one another, thinking what those letters might have contained, knowing that Gabe had surely torn them up without reading them.

Louise lets her hands drop to her sides, her shoulders falling with them, all of her surrendering. Even her eyes well with defeated tears. In the fraught moments after Russ confessed his secret, shock had numbed her. Now, seeing him again freshly, the hurt teems and bubbles over, questions spilling out with it.

"How could you keep this from me all this time?" she whispers.

But even as she searches her husband's eyes across the desk, she knows the real question she should be asking: *How could I not have seen it on your face?* Her thoughts whirl, the last thirty years spinning, and she reaches madly into the swirl of them, trying desperately to find one instant she might have missed, one second of proof of her husband's terrible burden. How she could have lived with him for all these years, lain in the dark with him, shared that impossible quiet of night where confessions can't hide, and not sensed his terrible pain? The failure feels wholly hers, and it takes her breath away.

But it's not the only one. That Glory, who trusted Louise to manage so many things, who Louise considered a close friend, hadn't let her help her face this nightmare, hadn't even given her the chance to try. She mines her memory, recalling the last time she'd seen Glory, the morning before she'd left for the Outer Banks—how hard her friend hugged her, how long. And how Louise teased her that it wasn't as if they might never see each other again.

Longing pinches her heart.

She closes her eyes as the tears prickle behind her lids. "Why didn't she tell me, Russ? Why didn't she ask me to help her? I was her closest friend."

"Which is exactly why she could never have asked that of you." Russ stands and comes around the desk. "She wanted to spare you, Lou. She wanted to spare all of the people she loved," he says without hesitation, because this question is an easier one for him, Louise suspects. "And maybe because she knew you'd all want her to keep trying, that you'd be hurt or angry if she wanted to stop treatment."

Dizzy with regret, Louise combs her memories again. The night Glory had confessed that Maeve couldn't handle all she was asking of her . . .

Louise feels her face flame with remorse for her glib reply, thinking Glory was talking about filling envelopes and scheduling phone interviews.

Anger flares again behind her ribs. An utterly useless, helpless fury. The kind she'd felt when they'd first lost Glory.

And here she was. Losing her all over again.

"But she asked you."

"Yes," says Russ. "Yes, she did." His eyes rise to find hers. "And I failed her. I failed them both, Lou. I left that poor girl all alone to do the impossible. I told her I would be there. I promised. She was waiting for me and I couldn't . . ." He stops, fixing his lips into a hard line. "Don't you see? Maeve wasn't the one who never showed up. I was."

She steps back, trying to digest it all. How much she thought she understood. All of it wrong. Even the note they found beside

Glory's bed—*I'm so tired. I just want peace*—words with entirely different meaning now.

"And you never considered telling Mitch?" She's careful to keep her voice soft, not wanting the question to sound like an accusation.

"Only a million times," says Russ. "When they wanted to do an autopsy, I was sure I would have to tell him, but he went ahead and refused one, thank God."

Her gaze drifts around the room, desperate for some anchor, then settles on a tangle of lanyards on her desk.

She looks over at Russ, panic flaring suddenly. "Where's Frankie?"

"She was at the house when I left."

"You can't let her leave."

He stares at her. "Why would she?"

Louise recalls the abrupt way she'd left the house without saying goodbye, how easily Frankie could misconstrue Louise's shock as an unspoken dismissal, and urgency rises.

They can't let her go. Not like this. Not now.

"You were right, Russ. We have so much to tell her." Louise feels the burn of tears again.

*Starting with I'm sorry.*

# 36

Frankie picks up her T-shirt and presses it to her nose, drawing in a deep breath of damp sea air, immeasurably grateful to find the scent lingers. The previous hours sift through her thoughts, carrying with them the weight of fresh truths, more weight on an already heavy day. And the question of *what now* hung in the strained silence that followed Russ's revelation, floating over everything like the Cape's now-familiar morning mist. But unlike the mist, refusing to evaporate.

After Russ and Louise left the house, each looking as dazed as Frankie herself felt—no, surely more so—Frankie took a few moments to tour the empty house, wanting to draw the space into her memory just like she pulled the scent of Gabe's boat into her lungs from her shirt.

And somewhere in the quiet, she found room for another kind of reflection. Gabe's words that morning, so biting, certainly left teeth marks on her heart, but in the hours after the swelling of the blow had diminished, she peeled back a few more revelations of her own. As hurtful as their fight had been, and especially on the heels of their beautiful night together, Gabe was right: her compass in life, then and now, right or wrong, had always been her mother. And even without her, she was still following Maeve's true north.

At some point, Frankie would have to make a map of her own.

"What are you doing?"

She looks up to find Russ in the doorway, his features strained with confusion. He can't honestly be surprised to find her packing?

She folds up the shirt and stuffs it into her bag. "Now that I know what happened, I can't possibly stay."

"It seems to me you can't possibly go." He comes into the room, stopping at the dresser, newly cleaned of her things. He sweeps his hand absently over the empty surface. "Lou was afraid you'd want to leave."

Frankie couldn't imagine Louise wanted her to stay?

"Did you find Gabe?" she asks.

Russ shakes his head. "I went down to the marina but he's taken the boat somewhere. When I tried calling he didn't answer. And, well . . ." He shrugs and offers a weak smile. "It's not the sort of thing you leave on a voice mail."

She considers her bag, nearly packed, tremors of disappointment fluttering. She hoped, like her, Gabe might have let the morning's battle soften as the hours passed, that they might have come back to one another to repair, maybe even to resume.

Would he return in time to say goodbye? Did he even want to?

As if reading her thoughts—or perhaps just the mournful set of her lips—Russ offers hope. "I'm sure he hasn't gone far."

She smiles, grateful, though they both know when—if—Gabe does return, Russ's news will prove another bump for them to find their way over.

But for now, Frankie thinks, there are other considerations that drift between them in the hush.

She moves to the edge of the bed and sits. "I always thought my mother just didn't like their films and that that was why we never carried any memorabilia of theirs in the store. And the whole time . . ." She smiles. "Glory's things were everywhere."

Crossing to the far window, Russ draws back the sheers and scans the view of the backyard, his eyes wistful. "Your mother worried people would think she'd stolen it all. I don't think she ever felt right about taking it—but she knew it was Glory's wish. And she knew she had to protect her legacy."

Frankie presses her hands into her lap. Another memory flashes, her mother teary after an early sale. *I promised I would never sell it . . .*

Russ's eyes swim with feeling. "When I learned how your grandmother died, how young your mother was, how she'd watched her suffer . . ." His gaze shifts again to the view, the thoughtful softness in his voice hardening with certainty. "I always believed there had to be a reason your mother would take such a risk. That she felt remorse, or maybe even duty after what she'd witnessed."

Frankie smiles down at her laced fingers, feeling a fresh prickle of tears. "Or maybe the reason was just love," she whispers. Because Glory wasn't a stranger. She was a friend. Maybe even family. "My mother was supposed to deliver those letters after Glory died, wasn't she?"

In the hush that follows as Russ considers his answer, guilt swells, but his gaze is warm and absolving.

"I have to believe she was afraid to—and who could blame her? I know she was pregnant when she left and I'm sure she was terrified that if Mitch knew someone had helped Glory end her life, there might have been an investigation. They'd learn that I had supplied her with the cocktail . . ." His hands dig in his pockets, the faint tinkling of change rising. "I suppose she worried for both of us."

Frankie nods slowly.

"Or maybe," says Russ, "she hoped one day you might deliver them for her. That you might come here and meet all of us and finally know the truth."

Several more beats of silence pulse through the room, broken only by the brief cackle of passing gulls, and Frankie smiles, understanding dawning: now she knows the real reason her mother felt so strongly about never opening sealed letters.

Russ tilts his head at her. "Louise says you're planning to go to the screening tonight."

"I am, yes." She stops, reconsidering. "At least, I was."

"Please stay." He smiles. "I'd like to tell you more about your remarkable mother."

# 37

Frankie stops at the edge of the town green and scans the landscape. A pop-up screen stands at the far end of the lawn, still a good half hour from flaring with color, she decides, glancing at her phone, telling herself she's just checking the time and not whether or not Gabe has tried to reach her. Patches of people settle in across the grass, spreading out blankets and unfolding camp chairs. It's a decent crowd but not nearly what she would have expected. Louise warned her the crowds for Glory's last movie had been thinning noticeably over the years, many attendees drawn elsewhere, festival endorsers and film companies offering their own closing night parties around town. One part of Frankie feels sad for the dimming interest in Glory's final work, but another part, a selfish part, is grateful for the smaller turnout. She won't have a problem finding the perfect seat. And when she cries, which she will, there will be fewer people to stare.

Food trucks line the other side of the lawn, the source of the rich smells of onions and fried seafood she's been catching whiffs of—sandwich boards offer lobster mac and cheese and cranberry cobbler—but her gaze slows on the outdoor bar that has been set up in a billowy white tent, a banner announcing Stardust Margaritas stretched across the opening, and she smiles. The line isn't long. She's more than tempted, and not just for the taste. She enjoyed one on her way here, and now she can enjoy one the night before she has to leave. There's a certain symmetry in it, she thinks as she takes her place in the queue.

"Buy you a drink?"

The familiar voice comes from behind and she spins, her breath catching to see Gabe. The silvery light of dusk washes across his face, deepening the shadows beneath his brows. He looks tired. Weary. As if the day, wherever he spent it, has taken him to rough and unexpected places. Worry trembles behind her ribs. Surely he's talked to Louise and Russ by now, surely he knows.

And yet he still manages a small smile. "Buy you dinner, too, if you'll let me."

Hope swells. The need to touch him is urgent, instinctive. She glances at his hands, sunk in his pockets, and all she can think about is how she'd watched those hands travel her body the night before, how she'd crossed her arms over his to keep them there.

Then the memory of how they'd been thrust apart this morning dims the sparkle of her gratitude at seeing him. They can't pretend things weren't said. The flickering of apprehension in his dark eyes makes her think he doesn't want to.

"Did Louise tell you I'd be here?" she asks.

He shakes his head. "I haven't talked to them. I just got back and figured you'd be here."

Fresh pulses of worry spark. If he hasn't yet talked to Louise or Russ, then he doesn't know about—

"I wanted to see you." His hands remain in his pockets while hers cling to the strap of her pack, clenched.

The line shuffles forward, forcing them briefly apart.

"I wanted to see you, too," she says. "I was worried when—"

Another shifting of feet, forcing the rest of her sentence to wait. But before she can start again, they are waved over to the counter by a bartender. Frankie advances, but Gabe touches her elbow to stop her.

"Not him," he says, gesturing toward the far end of the bar. "We want Mike."

Nearly there, recognition flares when she sees the bald man with the gray beard. Now this really is symmetry.

"Gabe!" The man's weathered face lights up as they approach. He thrusts out his hand, his sleeve of tattoos nearly purple under the tent lights, and Gabe takes it for a rough shake. "Man, talk about the last person I ever expect to see here."

"Mike, this is Frankie." Gabe steps back to allow her room to reach the bar.

The bartender squints thoughtfully as he takes her hand. "You look familiar—and I never forget a face."

She smiles. "You served me on the ferry a few days ago."

"Ah." He grins. "Your very first Stardust Margarita, right?"

She wants to tell him it wasn't her first—not even close—but he's already pulling a plastic cup from the tower of them behind the bar, one of the collectible glasses she'd eschewed on her way in, fearful of the extra weight. She'll find room in her bag for this memory now. It's important.

"What are you drinking, Gabe?"

"IPA. Whatever you have on draft." Gabe tugs out his wallet and threads out a twenty, setting it down on the bar. "Mike makes the best Stardust Margaritas around. Hell, he invented them."

"Almost," the bartender says, shoving a cup under the spout and letting the amber liquid rise. "I can take credit for everything except the peppers. For the first few years, it was always topped with strawberries." He sets down Gabe's beer and tilts his head to the left as he starts to mix her drink. "Did you see Donny's here with the truck?" Mike winks at Frankie. "Best clam strips in Harpswich."

"After my dad's, that is," says Gabe.

Mike gives the capped tumbler a few hard shakes and leans in to Frankie. "If this guy wanted to impress you, he'd make sure to get you an order before they run out."

Gabe rears back in playful indignation. "Are you getting a commission, or what?" But his teasing frown softens when he looks over at her. "Want some?"

Frankie smiles. She wants some, all right. Right now she wants all of it.

"Be right back." Gabe takes his beer and touches her arm before he goes—the gentlest brush but intentional enough to send a charge of pleasure through her.

She turns back to Mike just as he's pierced a pair of serranos with a bamboo skewer.

"So when did it change to peppers?" she asks.

"Must have been . . ." He considers the roof of the tent. "Almost thirty years ago now, I guess. There was this woman who came into the bar I was working at. Knocked my socks off. Pile of red hair on her head, kept bobbing back and forth when she talked like a damn buoy . . ." He chuckles. "I tried to give her a Stardust on the house, but she told me she didn't like them, said they were too sweet. Told me she thought I should balance it out with something spicy because—and I always remember this part—life, she said, was both."

Frankie feels the flush of fever soak her face. And as Mike continues to explain, his words become so sharp and clear in the din of the bar. All other sounds evaporate.

"I took her back to my house and we tried it out with some peppers I had. And damn if she wasn't right? Never used another strawberry after that." He snaps the top off the shaker and tips the contents into the plastic cup. "We dated off-and-on. She broke my heart, if you want to know the truth." His gaze is still wistful as he sets down her finished drink, foamy and frothy and fragrant. "But yeah," he says. "She was the one."

It takes Frankie a long moment to reach for the glass, not sure her hand will slow its shaking. She can hear her heartbeat in her ears.

She stares at him as he sweeps his towel across the bar, then slaps it over his shoulder.

"Was her name Maeve?" Her question comes out in a whisper, or maybe just a breath, but it's too soft for him to hear.

He cups his ear and leans over. "What was that?"

A new customer arrives beside her—forcing Frankie to shift down the bar. And as easy as it would be to ask again, louder this time, she knows she doesn't need to. Eventually, maybe, but not tonight.

Because right now Gabe is at the other end of the green, buying them clam strips, still crackling and hot in their greasy paper baskets, and in a few minutes, the great white screen at the end of the lawn is about to light up with Glory Cartwright's final film.

So before Mike's wide smile—maybe somehow her smile, too—is shining on someone new, she says instead, "That's a really great story."

She and Gabe choose a section of grass in the shade of an oak and lay down the blanket Russ has lent her. The breeze that sails across the green is still warm but tinged with the crispness of dusk.

Frankie slips out of her sandals and presses her bare feet into the cool grass. While Gabe peels open the plastic tub of tartar sauce, she already feels the tears building behind her eyes. It doesn't occur to her to try to stem them, even though she has only brought a few tissues and the film is close to two hours long. She'll use the napkins that Gabe picked up with their clam strips, and when they run out, she'll use a corner of the blanket.

She suspects the greatest rush of tears will come as soon as Glory Cartwright appears on the screen. Or maybe it will be when she sees Glory on the beach, a beach not so unlike the one Glory lived above with her husband and her son, and then, for a season, with her mother. Before her mother slipped from their lives on a ferry, breaking the hearts of people who loved her, including a man named Mike.

Gabe holds out the basket of clam strips, and she takes one, savoring the crackle and crunch of the fry, then letting the velvety meat underneath melt in her mouth.

"I'm sorry for what I said this morning." He searches her eyes, his gaze growing heavy with longing. His voice deepens with it. "I was scared. I was wrong."

"No." She puts her hand over his, the gesture reflexive, the feel of him familiar to her now. "You were right. I've been living her life, thinking it's the only way I can keep her close, but it's not. I need to find my own way, I know that now. I'm just not sure what that is yet." She smiles, even as she feels tears prickle. "And I'm scared, too."

He tilts his hand to cup hers, weaving her fingers inside his, sending heat firing up to her scalp. In the silence, she traces the heavy lines of his palm with her fingertips, the fence of calluses, compelled to confess.

"Gabe . . . there's something you should know . . ."

He looks up and holds her gaze, his eyes resolute. "I read the letters, Frankie."

She sinks, breathless with hurt for him. "I'm so sorry."

His brow tightens with strain. "Me too."

And in the silence while his eyes drift tenderly over her face, she reaches up to brush back his hair off his forehead, thinking fleetingly of Katie and Hubbell, of Carol from Cleveland and Barbra Streisand's gloves, of hellos and goodbyes and all the moments in between a person can never hold on to long enough.

Above them, light flickers on the empty screen, and a wave of excited murmurs rumbles across the lawn.

She looks around, as if for the first time.

"I've been thinking my mother left me those letters so I could find my father, but now I think she left them so I could find this place," she says. "Besides me, you all were the closest thing to family she ever had. The closest she ever got to having a home . . ." Gabe's hand climbs her face, settling at her cheek, tracing it with his thumb. "And I think she wanted you and me to meet. I think she knew we could be friends."

He leans in, his eyes falling to her mouth, holding there briefly before they rise again. "Or maybe she knew we could be more."

*Dearest Gabe,*

*This letter is hard for many reasons, which is surely why I've waited so long to write it. This past year I've kept a terrible secret from you and your father, from everyone, and I don't expect to be forgiven for that. But I'm sick, Gabe. And I won't be getting better.*

*Do you know how well I remember the day I was going to meet you for the first time? I was so nervous I actually poured orange juice in my coffee instead of cream. Maybe I've told you that story? I remember being panicked at the thought of holding you, because I worried I wouldn't know how, and thinking I should. So I pored over magazines and watched every movie I could with mothers and babies. That's how afraid I was of not doing it right, Gabe. And sure enough, I fear I did it so wrong. I thought you needed me to play the part perfectly. Now I understand that you just needed me to be me. That maybe that would have been enough.*

*You'd love it here on the Outer Banks. The surf is so loud you can barely think, but the beaches are so quiet, you can't do anything but. Last week I met a man fishing from the shore and he showed me how to tie a sheet bend. He told me it's more secure than a square knot, which he says can often come loose. I've been practicing and I think I can finally make one that's good and tight. Better late than never, right? You might just be proud of your mother after all, and that would make me so happy.*

*Promise me you'll take care of your father, Gabe. Make sure to take care of each other. Men when they get older need to fix things, and he won't be able to fix this and it will be terrifically hard for him. He's so lucky to have a son with such a strong spirit, who knows who he is and can be true to himself no matter what. To be nine years old and filled with such self-confidence. How remarkable you are.*

*Gabe, I know you think I'm silly to save so many things, but maybe you'll save this letter, and maybe sometimes, when you're not being as kind to yourself as you should be, you'll read it again, and you'll be reminded that you came from love, and that you deserve to live with love always.*

*And that I loved you.*

# 38

Friday

I really hope you've found happiness, and if you're ever in need of anything, like someone to love you, don't hesitate to call me.

*An Affair to Remember*

There's a knot in the strip of teak paneling beside where Frankie's head rests, a perfect silver-dollar-sized whirl. She reaches up to trace it, marveling at its symmetry, how rough it feels against the rest of the satiny board. Underneath her fingertips, she can feel the smooth wood shudder with the lapping of the water on the other side of the hull, the rhythm of the sea so close she might as well be a jellyfish floating below its surface.

"You can't believe how long it took me to seal that spot."

Gabe's hand lands just above hers, his chapped fingers roaming the wood, slowing at the seam where two boards meet. His voice is still rough with sleep, crackling in the hush of the cabin. Frankie strokes the firmness of his forearm, feeling the ropey muscles under the net of copper hair. He lifts her hand up with his, turning it in the path of silver light, their fingers laced. It had been easy to escape in the darkness hours earlier, to let the night, and the shelter of his cabin, hide them. But now it's morning, or nearly so, and dawn spills through the portholes, fuzzy shafts of light that crawl slowly up the blanket like timid fingers, tapping them awake.

She's not ready.

Shifting on the narrow mattress, she turns to find Gabe's face in the watery blue, determined to mine his features for evidence of his heart's fresh weight, and this time she finds proof. The lines between his brows are deep; his hooded eyes flinch, as if he's trying to look directly into the sun.

The cabin is so quiet—only the tinkling of Garbo's collar tags rings out in the hush—and Frankie knows there's nothing she can say to fill the silence, or to shrink the balloon of regret that swells in the wake of loss. She and Gabe will have to live with these fresh truths, and the questions they yield, forever waiting for an answer. One more in the stack of them that death leaves behind.

Gabe reaches up to capture the loose tendrils that have slipped from her braid and slides them behind her ear. She leans into his hand.

"You asked me what I want . . ." She smiles. "I want to fill a drawer."

He scans her face, frowning quizzically for several seconds before understanding smooths his furrowed brow, then his hand slides under the sheet, the heat of his palm closing over her breast and moving lower.

The bellow of an arriving ferry seeps through the cracked portholes. As if she needs the cruel reminder that her time here is running out.

His voice is gritty, the scrape of sandpaper. "I lied."

She rises up on her elbows, scanning his face expectantly.

"When I told you I didn't remember anything about your mother." He tilts his head, catching a thread of light across his brow. "I do."

# 39

1989
March

As soon as he heard the knock, Gabe knew it had to be Maeve. When his bedroom door was closed, his mother never asked to come in, and his father always just stormed in without knocking. He'd already figured one of them would come up; they'd be worried, but they didn't need to be. He had his Game Boy and a new Batman comic. Heck, he was fine.

"Yeah?"

The door creaked open, and Maeve poked her head in. "Hey, buddy . . ." She smiled. "I put out some chips, if you're hungry?"

"No thanks." He turned back to his screen.

"Can I come in?"

He sank lower against his headboard, bringing his knees to his chest. "If you want."

Maeve stepped over the maze of his dirty clothes and junk-filled shoeboxes and sat down on the other end of his bed, close enough that he could catch a whiff of her warm coconut smell. He always liked the way she smelled—like the beach, even when it was cold out. His mother always smelled like some faraway place, somewhere fussy and fake, like one of those sprays they put in bathrooms to try to convince you you're washing your hands on some tropical island.

But Maeve smelled familiar. She smelled like home.

He kept playing, pumping his thumbs over the buttons, waiting for her to say why she'd come.

"You okay?" She dipped her head, clearly trying to get him to look at her, but he kept his eyes on the screen.

"I'm fine."

"You don't seem fine."

He lowered the Game Boy and rolled his head toward the window. "My dad says she's leaving us."

"She's going down to North Carolina to make a film."

"You say that like it's not the same thing."

"Because it's not." Maeve's voice was soft now, like she was telling him a bedtime story. "Going away isn't always leaving, Gabe."

He squinted at her. Typical grown-up answer, always trying to make it seem like something was way more complicated than it was, something a kid couldn't possibly understand.

But he knew better. "My dad says if she loved us enough, she wouldn't go."

He didn't look up to see Maeve's reaction, but he could feel her sit a little straighter, like someone had just touched her back with a cold hand.

"He's wrong," she said, her voice not soft anymore. "Your mother loves you with her whole heart."

Her eyes were warm and kind. Even though she was obviously lying.

"If she was happy here," Gabe said, "she wouldn't want to go."

"Her being sad has nothing to do with you."

He'd been sure Maeve would lie again, would tell him his mother *was* happy here, but she hadn't. And he felt a swell of gratitude to her for that, even if the truth made the knot in his stomach tighten.

"It's not your job to make her happy, Gabe. And she doesn't ever want you to think it is."

"How do you know that?"

"Because she told me." She put her hand on his raised knee. "Want to know what else she told me?"

He punched the console, starting a new game.

"She told me that she worries you don't know how much she loves you."

He lowered the device and turned toward the window.

Maeve scooted closer. "Gabe, you have to understand . . . Your mom had a whole world before you came along." He looked up, feeling a flash of anger. So this was his fault? "Sometimes it can be hard in a family to want something for yourself and not feel guilty for that. It's especially hard for moms."

How would she know? Was she a mom? It was possible. She was old enough. And it wasn't like she ever talked about her family.

He shifted, curious now. "Where is your family?"

"I'm not really sure . . ." She smiled. "For all I know, they may be right here."

Gabe frowned at her—what kind of answer was that? Everyone knew where their family was.

She reached down into one of his opened shoeboxes and pulled out the stake his mother had given him a while back, turning it in her hand. "What's this?"

He shrugged. "Just some dumb block of wood that's supposed to be an ice crystal from the Fortress of Solitude," he said, reaching out to take it back. "You probably don't even know what that is."

"Excuse me?" She yanked the piece out of reach and fixed him with a withering stare. "Do I look like someone who doesn't know anything about Superman?"

He gave her an appreciative grin, but he couldn't keep it high for long. "It's dumb."

"Well, if it's so dumb, maybe you should just get rid of—"

"No!" He lunged forward and snatched it from her hands, feeling silly for his reaction when he saw her face break into a smile. She never had any intention of throwing it out.

She patted his foot and rose. "If you do get hungry, snacks are downstairs."

He watched her cross back to the door, feeling a curious swell of relief.

"Maeve?"

Her hand on the knob, she stopped and turned back to him.

"Thanks for saying that stuff," he said. "And I think I know what you mean about finding your family."

She smiled. "I thought you might."

# 40

The marina is waking. Frankie watches the slow dawning of Gabe's water neighborhood from *Essie*'s deck, warm thanks to the mug of coffee between her palms and Gabe's wool sweater that she's been living in for several days now. Staring out into the screen of mist, she can see only spectral outlines of boats and slips, and it's an oddly peaceful sight.

*Peace.*

She recalls Glory's inscription on the back of the photo, once mysterious, now so clear.

Russ and Louise ripple through her thoughts. How are they facing this morning?

Like Gabe, their world has been toppled. Russ. All the years he's had to look upon the faces of people who loved Glory, who felt cheated of answers, of a goodbye, and he's had to keep her secret. Russ, and her mother, too—passengers on the same doomed ship. And she feels a swell of culpability, because her part in this revelation is unescapable. Gabe told her he didn't want the letters—so what if she'd never come to Harpswich? The possibility that he could blame her fills her with a bloom of dread. She can hear him below, clattering around the galley.

When he finally emerges from the hatch, he's barefoot with a mug of his own, wearing long pants and a T-shirt. He joins her in the cockpit. Frankie catches a whiff of his skin, hot and salty, and just like that, she's back in his bed, his body wound around hers, his sheet twisted around their linked legs, binding them like one of those marine knots she saw in his book.

Leaving his bed was hard. Leaving Harpswich will be harder.

Garbo arrives with a half-eaten chew, circling several times before she drops down to the deck to finish it off. The lights of the ferry cut through the fog, then the horn.

Gabe studies the harbor. "What time's your flight?"

"Four."

"I could take you."

She falls against him and smiles. "All the way back to LA?"

And for a moment, his eyes darken with possibility. He reaches for her hand, threading his fingers through hers, and they keep their eyes there, sparing them both from having to pretend that things might be simple. His thoughts are surely crowded now, as tangled as the coils of rigging at their feet. He'll need time to unravel them—and she doesn't dare to look for a timetable.

And anyhow, she has occupations of her own to return to, decisions to make. The store and all its contents. Her mother's past and her future. What will she keep? What will she let go?

Still, she and Gabe remain linked. Not just by their parents, and the bond they shared, but by the knowledge that people you loved, people you believed you knew, could still show you something of themselves, something beautiful, even after they've left you.

And it's a remarkable thing to have in common.

Maybe even enough of a thing to bring two people back together again someday.

Gabe pulls her into his arms, and she sinks into him. "I don't want to go."

"So stay," he whispers into her hair.

"I can't stay."

He shifts his jaw and smiles against her temple. "So come back."

She eases out of his embrace and sits back, searching his eyes for truth in his offer and finding it. "Then I'll come back."

"How's tomorrow?"

She presses her hand over his heart and grins. "What's your hurry, Beckett? Afraid you'll forget me?"

His eyes flick over her face. "I'm more afraid I won't."

Garbo scrambles to her feet and releases a shrill bark. Their hands still clasped, they twist to find the source of the alert, and Frankie feels Gabe's fingers tighten around hers.

Russ and Louise, coming down the slip.

Louise has told Russ not to be surprised if Gabe should disappear belowdecks when he sees them, or if he simply tells them to go away—she's braced herself for the possibility. Which is why relief floods her when Gabe remains in the cockpit as they draw near, his arm around Frankie. And there are flutters for that sight, too—that he's not been alone, that they've had each other to share the weight of this impossible news.

Frankie slips from Gabe's arms and rises. "I'll let you all talk privately."

"No," Louise says. "Stay. Please."

On board, she takes stock of their surroundings, curious if they will have an audience, but the adjacent boats are quiet, their decks empty, their captains and passengers still sleeping off another night of bacchanalia.

There's more than enough room for them to all sit in the cockpit, but Gabe stands to offer Louise his seat, a gesture she imagines is equal parts kindness and self-serving retreat. Even as a teenager, he had never been able to sit still during an argument. Already he's pacing the edge of the deck.

Garbo's worried gaze flicks around at them all; if she were closer, Louise would offer the dog a soothing pat. God knows they could all use one just now.

Russ grabs his knees and rubs them harshly.

"You'd think in thirty years I'd have thought of something to say."

Gabe scans the water, his voice rough with hurt. "You should have told me, Doc. You should have told both of us."

"I wanted to," Russ says, his voice crackling like paper in a fire. "You have no idea how much I wanted to."

"Then why didn't you?"

When Russ hesitates, Louise lays her hand over his. She rubs his tight fingers, trying to relax his grip on his knee.

"Because I made a promise, Gabe. And because after a while . . ." He stops to glance at her, the flash of desperation in his watery blue eyes causing her ribs to constrict. "It just seemed too much time had gone by."

"It doesn't matter." Gabe drags his hand around his neck and jams it into his pocket. "The point is, she didn't tell us."

"Because she wanted to protect you."

"From what? Did she honestly think I couldn't handle seeing her sick?"

"It wasn't just that." Louise climbs to her feet. It's her turn now. "There were other things she protected you from, Gabe. Things about your father . . ."

His eyes darken with strain, thinning to slits. "What things?"

She glances over at Russ, seeing the flash of approval in his eyes, giving her permission to continue. Frankie's eyes are fixed on her, yearning.

She starts slowly, carefully. "He wasn't honest with your mother when they came here. He let her think it would only be a year, that they would go back to their life in Hollywood."

Gabe shifts on his heels. Louise glances over at Frankie and finds her gaze is now trained on Gabe, the breeze casting back her loose auburn hair to reveal a deeply creased brow.

"It wasn't like my dad moved them into a shack and made her gut fish for him. She had the festival. It wasn't like she didn't still get to be a star here."

"The festival helped some," she says. "For a while. But it was never going to be enough."

When he turns back to her, his dark eyes are blazing, but his voice cools with a heartbreaking mix of anger and longing. "You mean, *we* were never going to be enough."

Louise's skin prickles—his words sparking a memory of Mitch's tirade in the basement all those years ago.

*So you tell me, Glow? When is it enough . . . ?*

She looks down, suddenly breathless with remorse. "That isn't what I meant."

"But that doesn't make it not true." Gabe studies the harbor. "Finding out what really happened that one day on the Outer Banks doesn't change all the ones that came before it," he says. "My mother didn't live her life—she performed it. You know I'm right, Lou. You both do." He casts a questioning look at Russ, seeking his agreement.

Russ sighs. "It's not that simple, Gabe . . ."

Gabe shakes his head roughly. "My dad may have been hard to live with, but at least I knew who he was. I knew there was a real person in there. Being a wife and a mother was always just a role to her."

"Maybe so." Louise steps across the cockpit, needing to be closer to him. "But I know she never worked harder at a role in her whole life, Gabe. And she did that because she loved you."

Gabe's eyes finally shift to find hers. "He shouldn't have let her go."

"Would you believe"—Louise reaches for his hand, her heart filling when he lets her have it—"he said the same thing?"

# 41

1989
May

Louise wasn't surprised to find the beach house quiet when she entered through the slider with the still-warm chicken—any more than she was surprised to find it unlocked. Russ had told her that Mitch was planning to take Gabe out for a sail that afternoon. It was the only reason she'd agreed to come by herself, knowing she wouldn't have to see Mitch's dour face (even though she would have loved to have seen Gabe's) when she came to make her delivery.

The smell struck her even before she saw the pile of dirty dishes in the sink. Barely a week since Glory had left, and already the house reeked of fry oil. Equally unsurprising, the interior of the fridge was mostly empty—which was good only because she didn't have to move contents to find a place for her large pan. Turning to go, she debated whether or not to tidy up, then recalled her vow to Russ not to meddle—that it was enough to bring the occasional dinner, but maid service was above and beyond. Still, she felt compelled to at least check expiration dates on milk and eggs, fearful of Gabe ingesting something rotten.

Back outside, she was nearly across the deck when she caught sight of a lone figure sitting on the beach, facing the water, his telltale black hair dancing in the breeze—Mitch—and debate raged again:

whether to pretend she hadn't seen him or follow the sandy steps to say hello. Once again her concern for Gabe made the decision for her.

"Mitch?"

He swung his head around, his eyes glassy and red from the sun. Stubble crept along his jaw, more than a day's worth. He gripped a can of beer.

"Russ said you were taking *Essie* out."

He shook his head. "Too much chop."

She scanned the beach, seeing only a couple walking hand in hand. "Where's Gabe?"

"Clamming with Billy." Mitch looked past her. "Russ up at the house?"

"He's with a patient." She gestured to the cottage. "I just came to drop off a baked chicken. I promised Glory I wouldn't let you two starve."

He patted the rise of his ample stomach. "No chance of that." He gave her one of his trademark crooked smiles, but it couldn't seem to hold its shape. He looked wretched, frankly. Worn out. And it occurred to her what emotion she'd first read on his sunbaked face: shock.

He really didn't think Glory would go.

The redness of his eyes wasn't from too much sun. He'd been crying.

"I never should have let her go." He sniffed and swallowed hard. "What if she doesn't come back?"

Louise had never heard his voice so thin, and the swell of empathy she felt startled her. So close, she could have laid her hand on his shoulder, an impulse she had never felt in over twenty years of knowing him.

"Of course she'll come back."

A flock of gulls descended nearby. Mitch watched them circle a clump of seaweed.

"You want to know the real reason I brought her here?" His voice was slow, his words slurred.

"She told me John Cassavetes wanted you both to star in his movie and you didn't want to."

"That's what she said?" He snickered, then shook his head. "He didn't want us—he just wanted her. He told me I didn't have the chops for the part . . ." He swung his beer to his lips and swigged, wiping the back of his hand roughly over his mouth as he swallowed.

Louise pulled the edges of her cardigan tighter across her chest, the news rattling. Had Glory known the truth and simply wanted to protect him? Or had Mitch merely been protecting himself?

"The first time I ever saw her on set, that terrible picture with Nicholson, I knew how good she was. How far she could go . . ." His voice crackled, thin with emotion. "And I knew it was only a matter of time before she woke up and realized what a hack I was. That I didn't deserve her. That I was just holding her back . . ."

He shifted his gaze to meet hers, but Louise felt the even line of her lips tighten, whatever sympathy she may have had for him a few moments ago vanished. If he hoped for forgiveness or understanding after that sort of confession, he'd find none.

They continued to regard one another in the chilly quiet, the breeze growing stronger off the water. Perhaps as he finally sensed that no amount of staring would pressure her to soften, whatever plea pooled in Mitch's eyes faded, his blue eyes hardening to gray.

The earlier edge returned to his voice. "You never liked me, did you?"

The baldness of his question startled her like a slap.

"I remember when Russ first introduced you to me," he said, swirling his beer before raising it for a long pull. Louise scanned his profile while he swallowed. "I remember he brought you over to the crab shack and you barely touched the clam strips my dad made for you. I even told all those jokes to get you to laugh but you wouldn't."

"Because they weren't funny," she said.

He turned to her, a look of startled hurt—practically childlike—washing his weathered features. "That's no reason not to like a person."

She closed her cardigan tighter, folding her arms over the seam, not sure if it was the wind or the subject that had her suddenly chilled. A part of her, the kind part, knew he was in pain and wanted to soothe him, wanted to forget all the years she'd resented how selfish he was, watched him derail Glory's passion through neglect. And now, having been witness to his ultimate admission: that he'd brought her here to protect his own pride . . .

The realization sent ice water through her veins. Forget grace or forgiveness. This was her chance for truth. How many times had she admired Maeve for standing up to Mitch, for being brave enough to say the things that Louise could only think?

She rolled her lips together.

"I think you're a deeply selfish and spoiled person."

He reared back, blinking at her as if she'd thrown a drink in his face. And for a moment, while the lines between his brows grew deep and twisted, she wondered if he might lunge at her, purge his grief and fury.

Suddenly uncertain, she stepped back, but he remained seated, his strained gaze shifting to the surf. He stared vacantly for several seconds before he released a deep sigh, then he reached down to screw his beer can into the sand and climbed slowly out of the chair, his hands on his hips as he scanned the horizon.

"You don't think I love her, do you?" he asked low.

When he didn't turn to look at her, Louise wondered if he meant for her to answer, or if he'd already decided for himself.

She pulled in a deep breath. "I think you're afraid of losing her. I'm not sure they're the same thing."

The air filled with the crash of the surf, rougher now with the rising winds.

If she couldn't lie, maybe she could at least offer something hopeful.

"But it's not too late, Mitch."

He swung his gaze to meet hers, his features softening with resignation as he scanned her face, nodding slowly. "You know, I was thinking . . . when she comes home . . . I'm going to take the three of us back to LA for a few weeks. Show Gabe our double stars, drive him by Shadowlands, take him to the studio. Show him our old life back there. Like she always wanted . . ." Hope flashed in his pale eyes. "What do you think?"

Above them, a gull cawed.

She smiled. "I think that would be wonderful."

# 42

Louise goes below to find Frankie, wanting to give Russ and Gabe some time alone, and hopefully grant herself a few moments without tearing up. She's spent so much of this day crying; her tunic pockets are swollen with the tissues she's collected.

Frankie's in the berth, trying to assemble some order to the tangle of sheets and blankets, and emerges with a thoughtful smile. "Not exactly smooth sailing out there, is it?" she says, glancing warily at the hatch.

"Waters could be a little choppy for a while, I think." Louise considers her. "Did you enjoy the movie last night?"

"It was a wonderful role for her."

"It was supposed to be her big return to Hollywood . . ." Louise pulls in a steeling breath, feeling the prickle of longing. So much for thinking she'd gotten a grip on her tears.

Frankie's gaze is warm and open. "I like to think it was," she says.

Louise smiles, gratitude swelling. She comes around the dinette and takes a seat. "I can't tell you how many times I watched that movie, always seeking some kind of clue in her expressions, in her voice. I know it was a role, of course, and that she was only acting, but I couldn't help thinking she never looked sad to me in that movie. If anything, she just seemed so full of longing."

"Maybe she longed for more time."

Didn't they all? But Glory's clock was so much shorter than any of them realized.

Absently scanning the cluttered table, Louise catches sight of an oddly familiar shape. She leans forward and picks the short wooden stake off a pile of catalogs.

"I found that in the cabinet when I was looking for a piece of scrap paper," says Frankie. "I was going to ask Gabe about it."

Louise turns it fondly in her hand, recalling the day Glory had given it to her son, and her lips stretch with astonishment. After everything, Gabe had kept it.

"Glory said it was used as a template for those crystals that made up Superman's ice palace in the movie."

"You mean the memory crystals."

Louise looks up. "Memory crystals?"

Frankie nods. "In the movie, whenever Superman wants to know something about where he came from, he would pull one out of the ice and get a little story about his world and his parents . . ." She stops, seeing Louise's admiring stare, and smiles sheepishly. "What can I say? I watch a lot of movies."

Louise studies it anew. A memory crystal. Remarkable. Had Glory known its significance when she'd given it to Gabe?

"Louise . . ." Frankie's eyes flick anxiously over hers, flashing with remorse. "I'm so sorry."

Louise blinks at her. "Sorry for what?"

"I only came here to look for my father. I never thought I would turn everything upside down. I keep thinking, if only I'd opened the letters first, like everyone wanted me to . . ."

"Then what? You'd never have known this part of your mother's history. We'd never have met one another. You'd never have met Gabe . . ." She dips her head, trying to catch Frankie's roving gaze, seeing the incriminating flush growing on her cheeks. Frankie glances up and smiles appreciatively. Even though Russ is well out of earshot, Louise's voice quiets. "And because of you, my husband can finally be free of something that has kept him in knots, and kept him at arm's length from me, for so many years." Their eyes meet again and hold. Louise reaches for Frankie's hands. "I'm the one who's sorry. I never should have doubted your mother, Frankie. And I'm sorry she had to face that alone."

They consider their clasped hands as the boat lilts in the quiet. Then the thumps of Garbo moving across the deck draw their gazes upward.

"If it's not too much trouble," Frankie says, "could I catch a ride with you and Russ back to the house to get my things?"

"You're leaving so soon?" It's a curious comment, Louise realizes with chagrin, considering she had initially contested Maeve's daughter being there at all—now she felt pangs of longing to think of her going away. She smiles. "I'm sure you must be anxious to get back."

Frankie looks wistfully in the direction of the hatch. "Honestly, I've never wanted to not leave a place more in my life."

"Then don't."

The words come out so quickly—Louise isn't sure who is more surprised at them, she or Frankie.

"I've been thinking . . . What if you stayed?"

"Another night?" Frankie asks.

"For good."

She blinks at Louise, urging her to continue.

"You said you don't think you can afford to keep your store open—so why not move your collection here? We could exhibit it in the old office building in town. We've been trying to figure out something to do with the space for years."

"That's a lovely offer but I'm not sure I can afford to—"

"It would be a paid position, of course. Director of memorabilia." Like the offer, the proposed title also flies out without consideration. "I'm offering you a job, Frankie."

"Can you do that?"

Louise shrugs. Why couldn't she?

"And maybe, down the road—if you're interested, that is—maybe something bigger even. In case I might . . . I don't know . . . look to take a step back?" She takes Frankie's hands again. "We could call it the Maeve Simon Collection."

Frankie's eyes rise to meet hers, pooling with wonder—or is it something else? Louise feels a bolt of regret for her impetuousness, that it's too much, too soon; that she's made assumptions based on her own affections, that Frankie may not feel the closeness as acutely—or maybe not at all.

Desperate to retract her frantic offer, she leans forward.

"Please don't feel pressure. I know it's a big decision and you need time—"

"Yes."

Frankie's eyes flash, like someone who's just been given her first taste of champagne.

"Yes," she says again, slower, as if it's a magic spell that won't come true if she doesn't repeat the word enough times.

And Louise exhales, not even aware she's been holding her breath in anticipation.

# 43

They are quiet as they walk through the parking lot and climb wordlessly into the car. When Russ turns on the radio to a classical station as soon as the engine roars to life, Louise doesn't contest. If anything, she's grateful for the slow swell of the violins to fill the silence, grateful for the few minutes of contemplation before they are returned home. Not so unlike an airlock on a ship meant to minimize a change in pressures between two spaces, granting them a few moments of peace as they move from one emotional room to another.

Only after they are out of the car and up on the porch, do she and Russ finally turn to one another—slowly, like nervous dance partners, reunited after too long, sure they've forgotten steps.

Louise catches her husband's gaze, amazed and grateful when he lets her hold it.

"This is why, isn't it?" Her voice breaks but she continues. "Why you pulled away?"

Russ draws in a ragged breath and lets it out slowly. "I don't think I realized how hard it would be when I stopped working." He glances up, scanning the pale blue of the porch ceiling. "I don't mean the lack of practicing medicine—I mean the forgetting. Whenever the guilt crept back in, I could box it up. I could still justify what I'd done, that every doctor has regrets, patients that haunt him; it was just something a doctor had to live with. But when I retired . . ." He crosses to the railing and scans the sky, searching. "I just didn't expect it to hit me so hard, Lou. I didn't expect it to change me. All those years I carried the guilt, it didn't change me."

"But you didn't carry it, Russ. You buried it—and I understand you had to, I do. Or at least, I'm trying to," she says, "but there's a world of difference."

"I tried to apologize to Maeve for being such a coward when I sent her Glory's collection."

Just the sound of the word—"coward"—pierces her heart. She wants to contest it vigorously, but she knows his regret is the toxin that has sickened their marriage—his confession will finally draw the poison out.

"I pleaded with Maeve to contact me," he continues. "To let me know she was okay, to let me help her get on her feet . . ."

He runs his hands along the top of the railing, the whisper of his palms over the weathered wood reminding her of brush strokes, and she tries to remember how many times they've painted this porch over the years, how many coats sit beneath this newest one, just five years old. How they stood at the paint counter a good ten minutes debating between Linen and Heavy Cream until Russ had pulled out a coin, tossed it up, and asked the clerk to call heads or tails. Looking closer now, she can see spots of wear, chipping along the spine of the columns and the balusters. Because regardless of the promises on the can, no single layer of paint can weather life forever. Sun burns, rain drowns, and wind beats. Everything needs a fresh coat eventually.

She takes a step closer. "That's why you didn't take the seat on the ethics board, isn't it?"

He lowers his hands into his pockets; his fingers dig, the jingle of change chimes. "How could I possibly?"

And yet, knowing what he's endured, who better to take it?

She inhales deeply, this next question requiring extra fortitude. "If Frankie never came here . . . would you have ever told me?"

The quickness of his reply startles her. "I don't know, Lou."

Her breath catches at the honesty of his answer, but a flutter of relief returns it to her lungs. At last, the truth.

He comes closer, his hand emerges from his pocket and brushes her closed fist, seeking entrance. Slowly she unfurls, and his fingers lace through hers, her eyes filling again at the familiar heat of his palm.

"I've never regretted the choices we made, Lou. I've mourned, I've been disappointed . . . but I've never regretted a minute. Not one minute."

She twists to him, finding his gaze already there. "Can we ever get back?"

"We're still here." The squeeze of his hand around hers—a heart pumping again. "We never left."

Gabe is inspecting something near the bottom of the mast when Frankie climbs through the hatch to find him. The air feels warmer than it did this morning, softer. The wind off the water, relentless earlier, has quieted. Even the thick smell of diesel and tidal mud has a touch of sweetness.

She waits before emerging fully, wanting to steal a few moments to watch him as he moves around the deck, checking things, tightening, testing.

*He's puttering,* she thinks with a smile. He's a putterer.

So what else is he?

Possibility swells, desire with it. The universe of a lover's life, so small in the beginning of a romance, expands quickly. She's tired of questioning the speed of their connection—now all she wants is to explore the galaxy of everyday with him. She only hopes he'll let her.

In the wake of Louise and Russ's departure, she's wanted to give him time alone, though she's not sure there's enough time in the world to fully absorb all he's learned in the last twenty-four hours.

All she knows is that when he looks up and sees her, he smiles, and whatever threads of worry have laced themselves through her heart snap free.

"Wait much longer and you're going to need a rocket ship to get you to the airport on time."

"It's okay," she says, crossing to meet him where the deck is highest. "I called the airline and told them I'd need a later flight."

"How much later?" He scans her face, his dark eyes smoldering with possibility—maybe he's already guessed?

"Quite a bit, actually . . ." Nervous butterflies take flight. *Just tell him.* She pulls in a deep breath. "Louise offered me a job."

"I heard."

The first part out, she might as well see it through.

"I told her I'd take it."

"I heard that, too."

The news free, she searches his gaze madly, worried for a second that she'll see regret flashing back at her, but there's only the heat of anticipation, the flaring of desire.

He wraps his arms around her, drives his hands deep into her back pockets and draws her close. She studies the curve of his eyebrows, a fine stitch of blue paint just below his temple.

"You'll need a place to live," he says. "A few drawers."

"Or maybe even a whole dresser."

She lays her hands on his chest, splaying out her fingers, trying to connect the constellations of white paint splotches that blaze across his navy shirt, and she smiles.

Everywhere, stars.

"Lucky for you, I know a guy with a boat . . . ," he whispers as he tips his head to find her mouth, kissing her deeply.

When he retreats, she clenches handfuls of his T-shirt and tugs him back for another. Parting for air, she tilts her head toward the bow where Garbo continues to tear at what's left of her chew. "He better ask his first mate," she says. "I wouldn't want to cause a mutiny."

Gabe searches her eyes. "No chance."

She rears up, hungry for him again.

"I hope you didn't bother making the bed," he whispers against her mouth.

The ferry horn bellows. And as Gabe threads her hand inside of his and leads her below, Frankie feels the swells of desire and longing spinning. There's so much she still needs to tell him, wants to tell him. But she has time now. Not forever, and certainly not close to enough, because there's never enough time when you want someone to know how much they mean to you. But there is something in the middle, she decides as she follows Gabe into the berth and lifts her arms so he can peel his sweater off her again. Where memory and love can be collected for always. Something lasting, something real. And more perfect than any movie.

## Acknowledgments

The only bigger gift than the generosity of others is the opportunity to tell them how grateful you are for them.

To my agent, Rebecca Gradinger, whose wisdom and support has always made all the difference—thank you doesn't even scratch the surface. I have been the lucky recipient of your guidance on this journey since the beginning and with each step we take together, I am reminded how fortunate I am for your kinship and your counsel. My deep gratitude as well to Christy Fletcher and Veronica Goldstein.

Every writer hopes to find a perfect home for their stories and St. Martin's Press is a writer's dream home—no wonder I have pinched myself repeatedly at the enormous support and love I've been showered with there. To my editor, Alexandra Sehulster, the first time we talked on the phone, I swore I heard an audible "clicking" of our kindred spirits and I was right. Thank you for your passion for this book, and for always knowing just what to say to help me dig deeper. I can't wait to build more stories together. Huge praise must also go to the rest of the amazing team at St. Martin's Press who I've been privileged to work with, they are true magic-makers, especially to Marissa Sangiacomo, Naureen Nashid, Sarah Schoof, Mara Delgado-Sanchez, Brittany Dowdle, and Elizabeth Curione, and also to Danielle Christopher, for the gift of such a beautiful cover. Thank you all for giving so much to this book, and for helping to bring this story to the place I always wished it would be: in the hands of readers.

While this novel draws its inspiration from the fantasy of movies, nothing on the silver screen could ever come close to the beautiful reality of my family. To Ian, Evie, and Murray, whose love and light are quite simply, everything. You are my heart, my soul, my whole world.

1. How does Frankie's connection to her mother through The Memory Shop inform the decision she makes to find out more about her mother's past? If they didn't own the store together, do you think she would have made the same decision to go to Cape Cod?

2. What do you think Russ's top responsibilities are as the town doctor? Do you think he upholds them throughout the book?

*Discussion Questions*

3. Explore the theme of finding your home in the novel. Glory tried to make Cape Cod feel like home, but never could. Maeve had a home there, but left it. Frankie grew up without a drawer to fill, and found her place by the end of the novel. Do you think home is a place, or people? Have you ever felt at home in a place that isn't where you live? Have you ever felt out of place where you consider your home to be?

4. Louise has the most objective take on everyone's personalities in the novel. Would you have disliked Mitch from the start? Befriended Glory? Held a grudge against Maeve?

5. Put yourself in Glory's shoes. Would you have given up your career to go back to your husband's hometown? Would you have ever tried to go back to Hollywood?

6. Fast-forward five years from now. What does Gabe and Frankie's relationship look like? Louise and Russ's? Has the festival changed in any way?

ST. MARTIN'S GRIFFIN

7. Louise wants children and can't have them, whereas Glory adopts Gabe but struggles with the pressure of motherhood. How are they able to be there for each other, despite coming from two very different places in life? Do you think Louise and Russ being childless made it easier to adopt Gabe, or harder?

8. Do you think Maeve betrayed her found family in Cape Cod? Did she make the right decision to leave? What would you have done?

9. The past events in this novel very much affect the present. Has anything happened in the past that has had a big effect on your life? Why do you think the ripple effect of events is so strong in this book?

10. At the start of the novel, where did you think it was going? Did that expectation or prediction change when Frankie arrived in Cape Cod? When Louise and Glory met? When Maeve is hired?

11. Feeling at peace is important to Glory. In her final moments, do you think she was able to feel this?